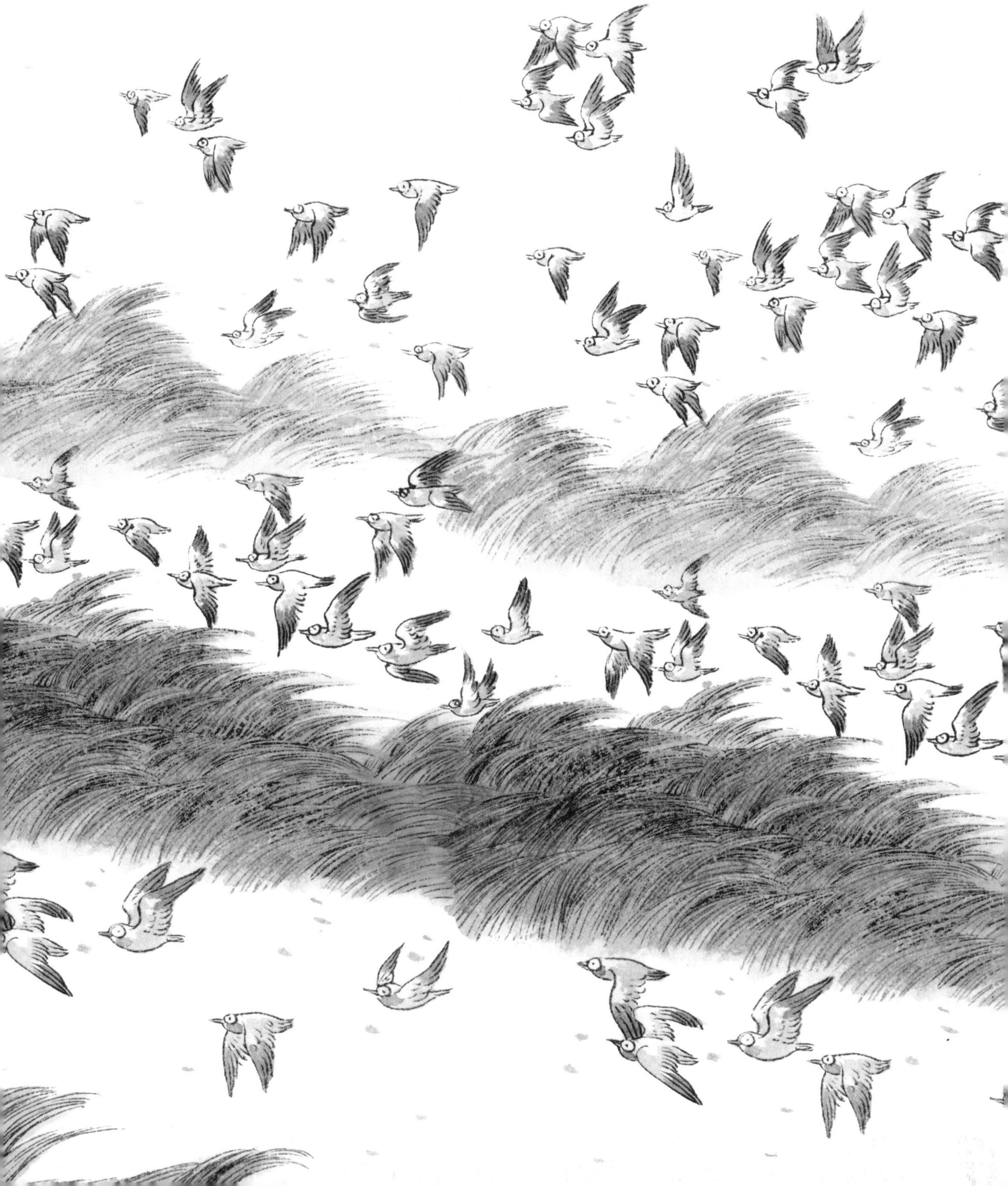

ZAO DAO

Cuisine Chinoise
Tales of Food and Life

Translated by **Brandon Kander** & **Diana Schutz**
Letters by **Adam Pruett**

Dark Horse Books®

President and Publisher
MIKE RICHARDSON

Collection Designer
LIN HUANG

Editor
BRETT ISRAEL

Digital Art Technician
ADAM PRUETT

Special Thanks to **Kari Torson** at Dark Horse Comics

NEIL HANKERSON Executive Vice President | TOM WEDDLE Chief Financial Officer | RANDY STRADLEY Vice President of Publishing | NICK McWHORTER Chief Business Development Officer | DALE LaFOUNTAIN Chief Information Officer | MATT PARKINSON Vice President of Marketing | VANESSA TODD-HOLMES Vice President of Production and Scheduling | MARK BERNARDI Vice President of Book Trade and Digital Sales | KEN LIZZI General Counsel | DAVE MARSHALL Editor in Chief | DAVEY ESTRADA Editorial Director | CHRIS WARNER Senior Books Editor | CARY GRAZZINI Director of Specialty Projects | LIA RIBACCHI Art Director | MATT DRYER Director of Digital Art and Prepress | MICHAEL GOMBOS Senior Director of Licensed Publications | KARI YADRO Director of Custom Programs | KARI TORSON Director of International Licensing | SEAN BRICE Director of Trade Sales

Published by Dark Horse Books
A division of Dark Horse Comics LLC
10956 SE Main Street
Milwaukie, OR 97222

First edition: June 2020
ISBN 978-1-50671-776-0
Digital ISBN 978-1-50671-777-7

1 3 5 7 9 10 8 6 4 2
Printed in Korea

Comic Shop Locator Service: comicshoplocator.com

I've heard all the popular fables and funny folktales, but have always maintained a definite respect, tinged with trepidation, for Heaven and Earth. I'm reminded of a story I drafted some years ago: in one of the panels I drew an old man eating a centipede. Not long afterwards, I was bitten by a small centipede myself! Ouch! This proved to me that everything has a soul in Mother Nature, and the spirits that hover within her can latch onto even a slightly wicked thought that may run across your mind.

For this reason, it seems to me, we must respect our Mother Nature, keeping a positive attitude towards her at all times!

— ZAO DAO

INSECT SPIRITS

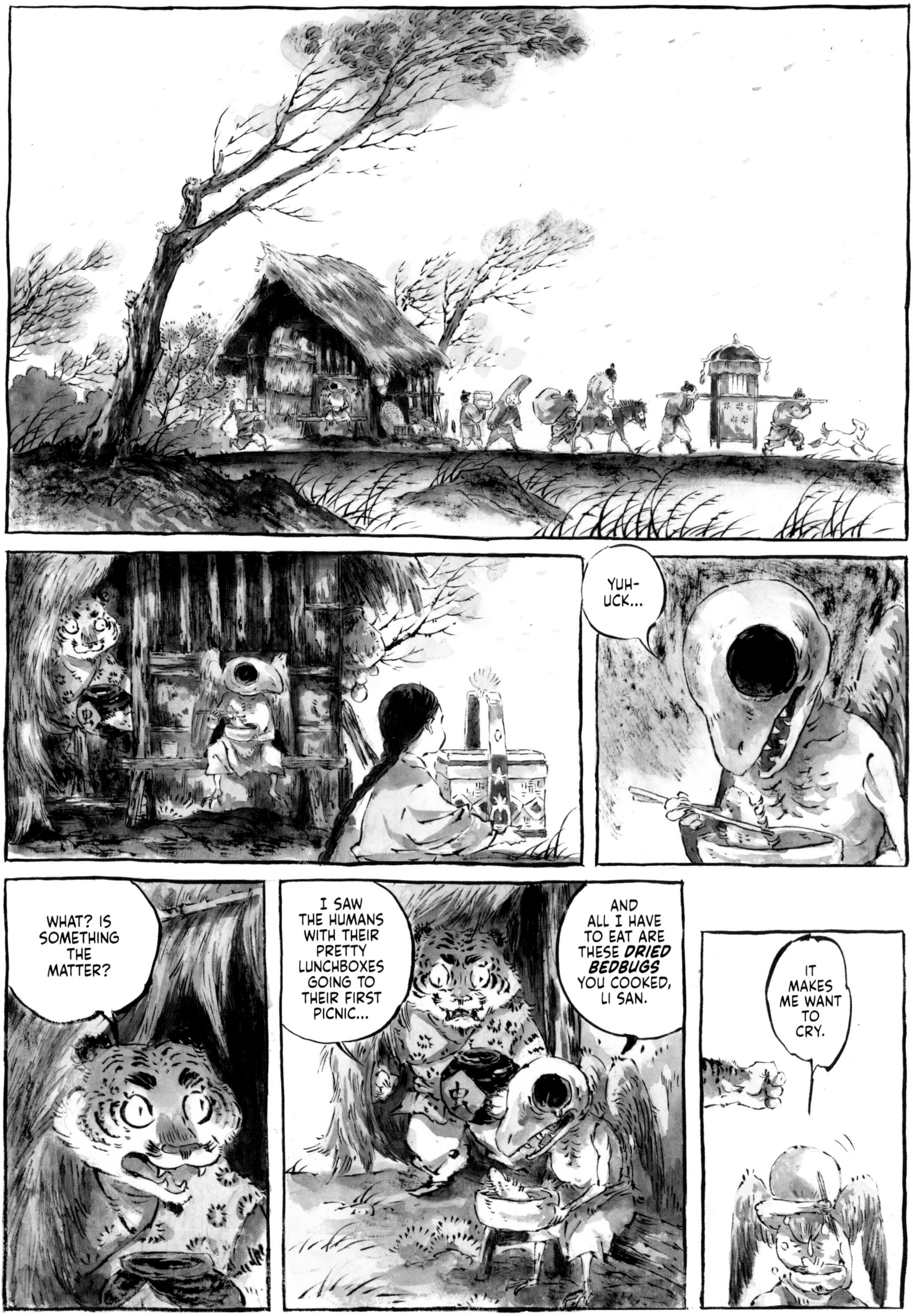
YUH-UCK...
WHAT? IS SOMETHING THE MATTER?
I SAW THE HUMANS WITH THEIR PRETTY LUNCHBOXES GOING TO THEIR FIRST PICNIC...
AND ALL I HAVE TO EAT ARE THESE ***DRIED BEDBUGS*** YOU COOKED, LI SAN.
IT MAKES ME WANT TO CRY.

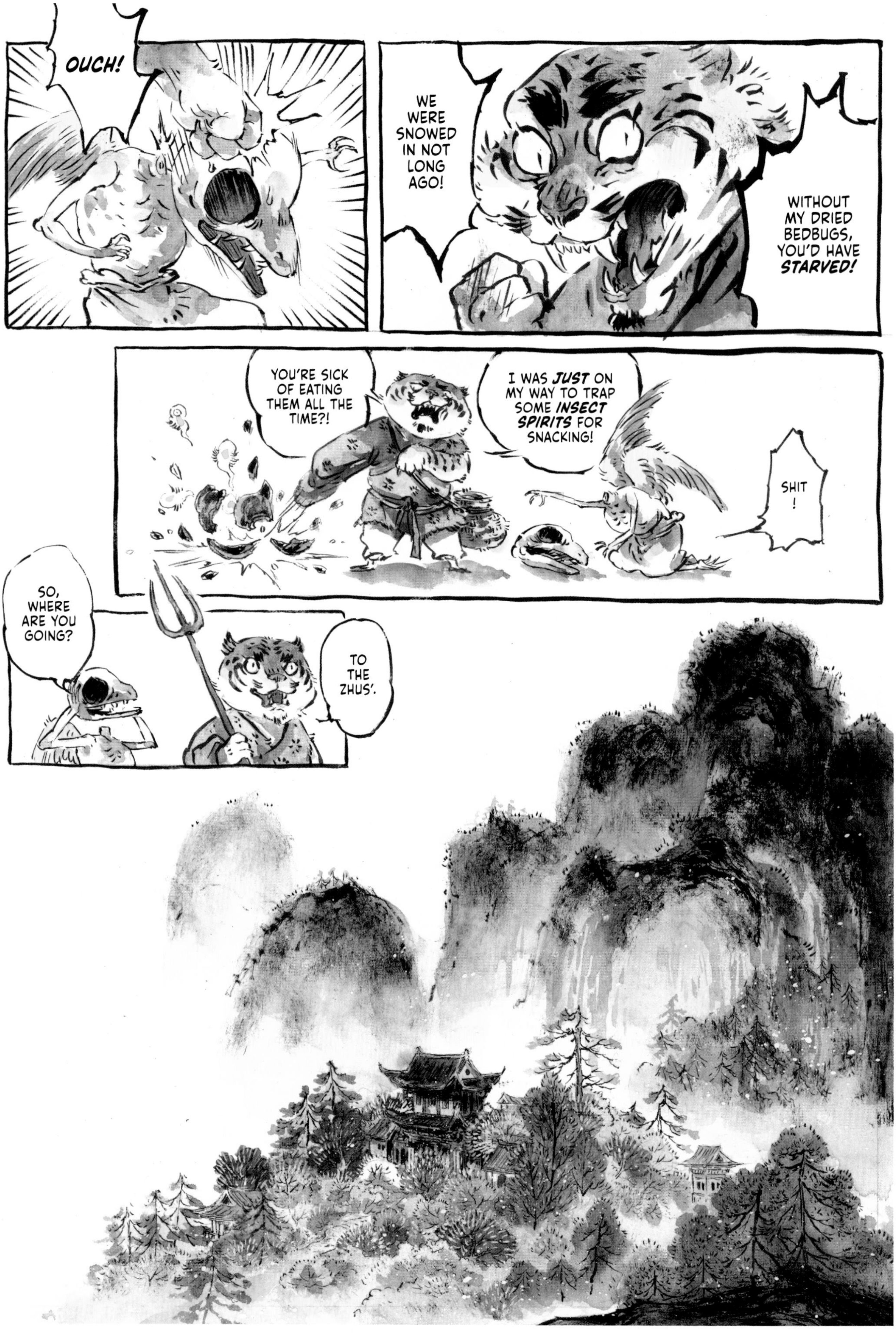
OUCH!
WE WERE SNOWED IN NOT LONG AGO!
WITHOUT MY DRIED BEDBUGS, YOU'D HAVE STARVED!
YOU'RE SICK OF EATING THEM ALL THE TIME?!
I WAS JUST ON MY WAY TO TRAP SOME INSECT SPIRITS FOR SNACKING!
SHIT!
SO, WHERE ARE YOU GOING?
TO THE ZHUS'.

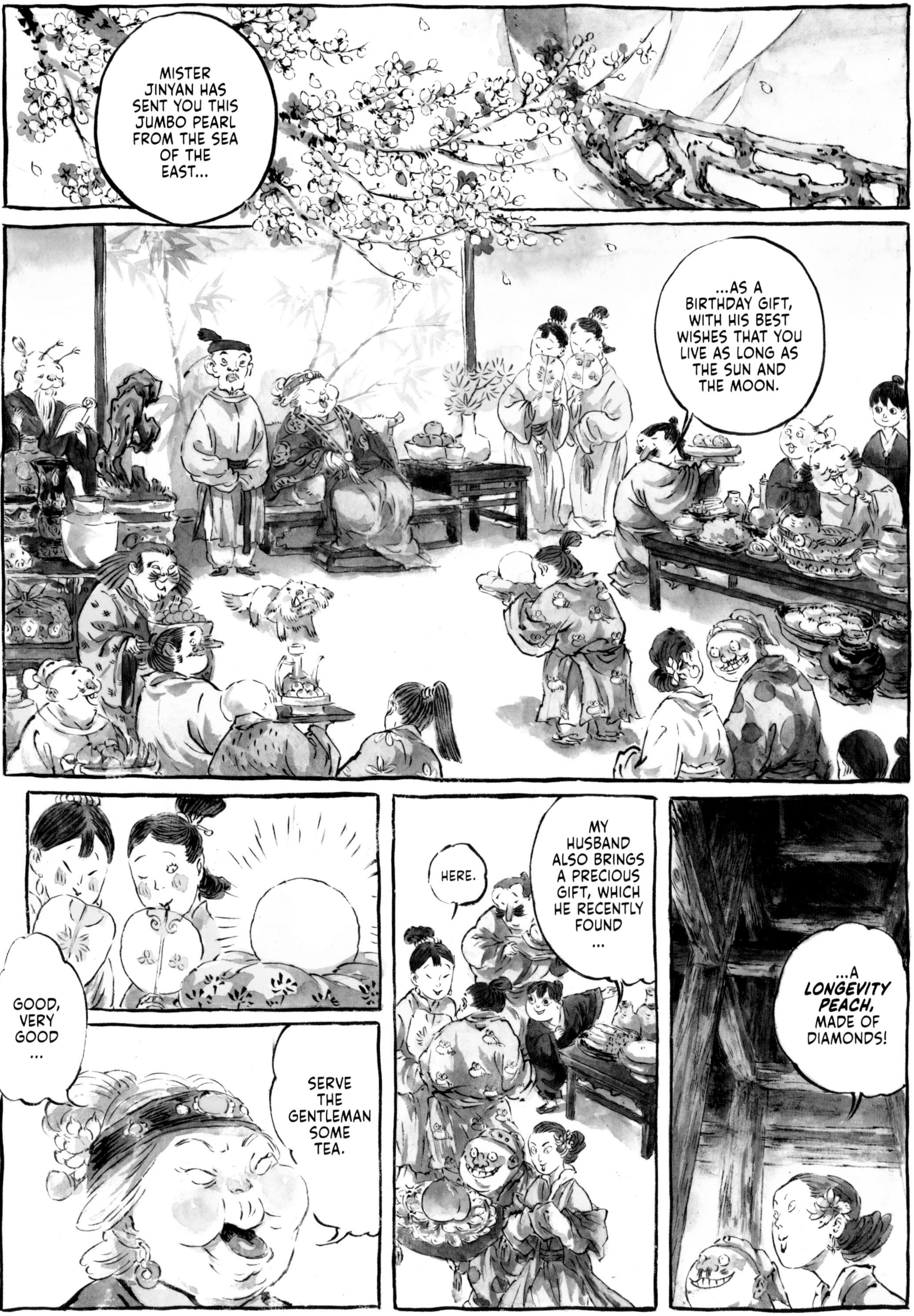
MISTER JINYAN HAS SENT YOU THIS JUMBO PEARL FROM THE SEA OF THE EAST...
...AS A BIRTHDAY GIFT, WITH HIS BEST WISHES THAT YOU LIVE AS LONG AS THE SUN AND THE MOON.
GOOD, VERY GOOD ...
SERVE THE GENTLEMAN SOME TEA.
HERE.
MY HUSBAND ALSO BRINGS A PRECIOUS GIFT, WHICH HE RECENTLY FOUND ...
...A ***LONGEVITY PEACH,*** MADE OF DIAMONDS!

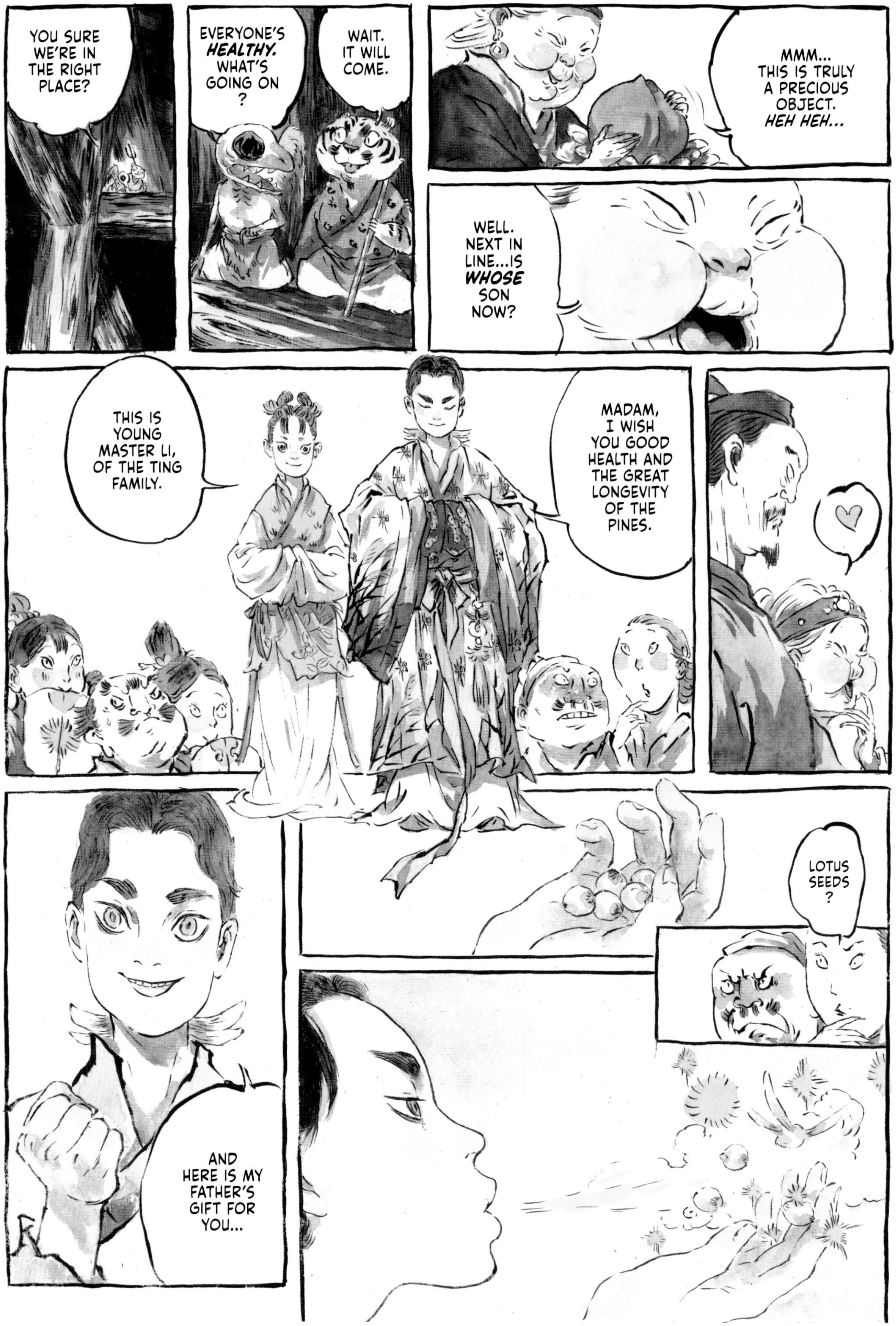
YOU SURE WE'RE IN THE RIGHT PLACE?
EVERYONE'S *HEALTHY.* WHAT'S GOING ON ?
WAIT. IT WILL COME.
MMM... THIS IS TRULY A PRECIOUS OBJECT. *HEH HEH...*
WELL. NEXT IN LINE...IS *WHOSE* SON NOW?
THIS IS YOUNG MASTER LI, OF THE TING FAMILY.
MADAM, I WISH YOU GOOD HEALTH AND THE GREAT LONGEVITY OF THE PINES.
AND HERE IS MY FATHER'S GIFT FOR YOU...
LOTUS SEEDS ?

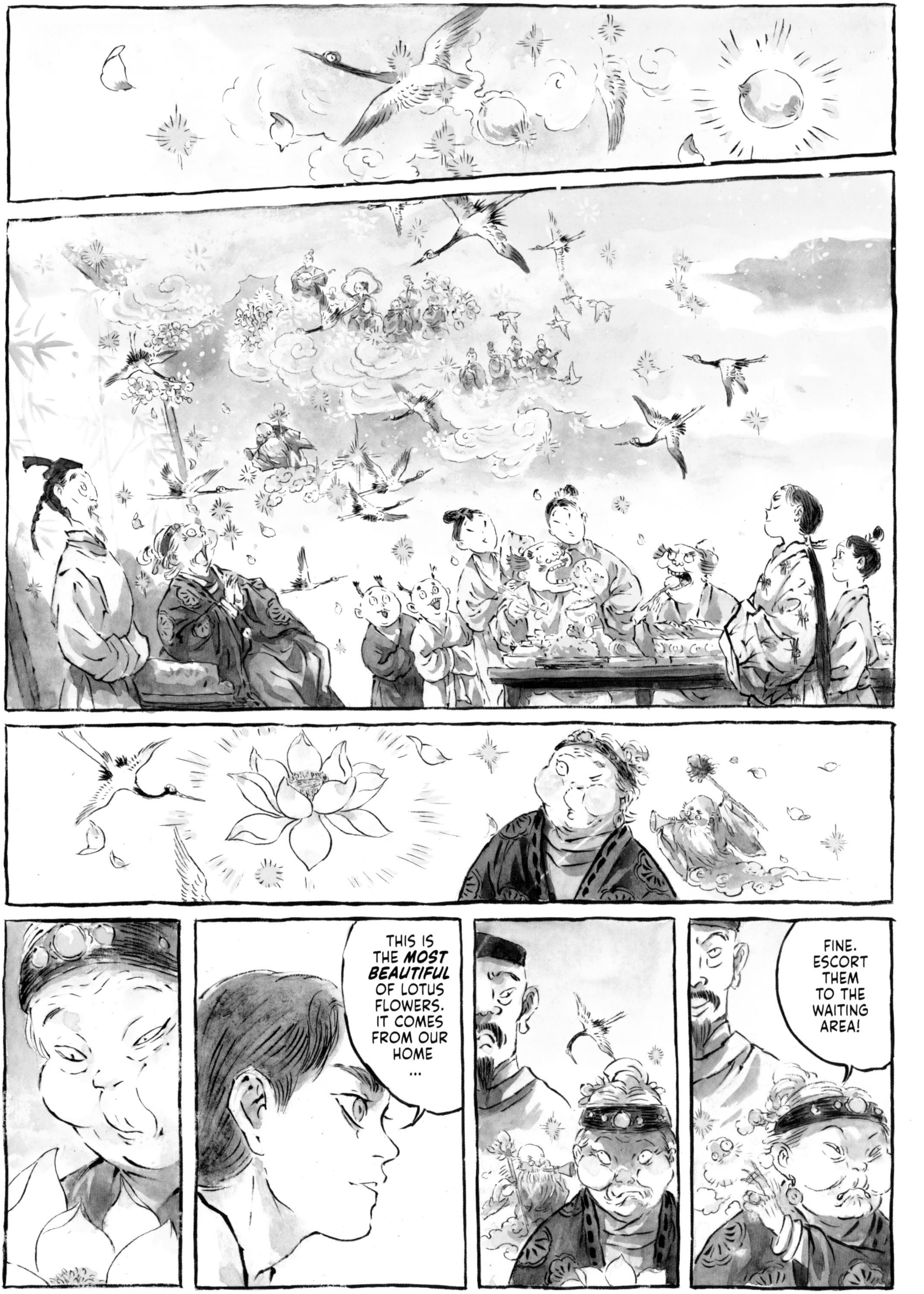
THIS IS THE **MOST BEAUTIFUL** OF LOTUS FLOWERS. IT COMES FROM OUR HOME ...
FINE. ESCORT THEM TO THE WAITING AREA!

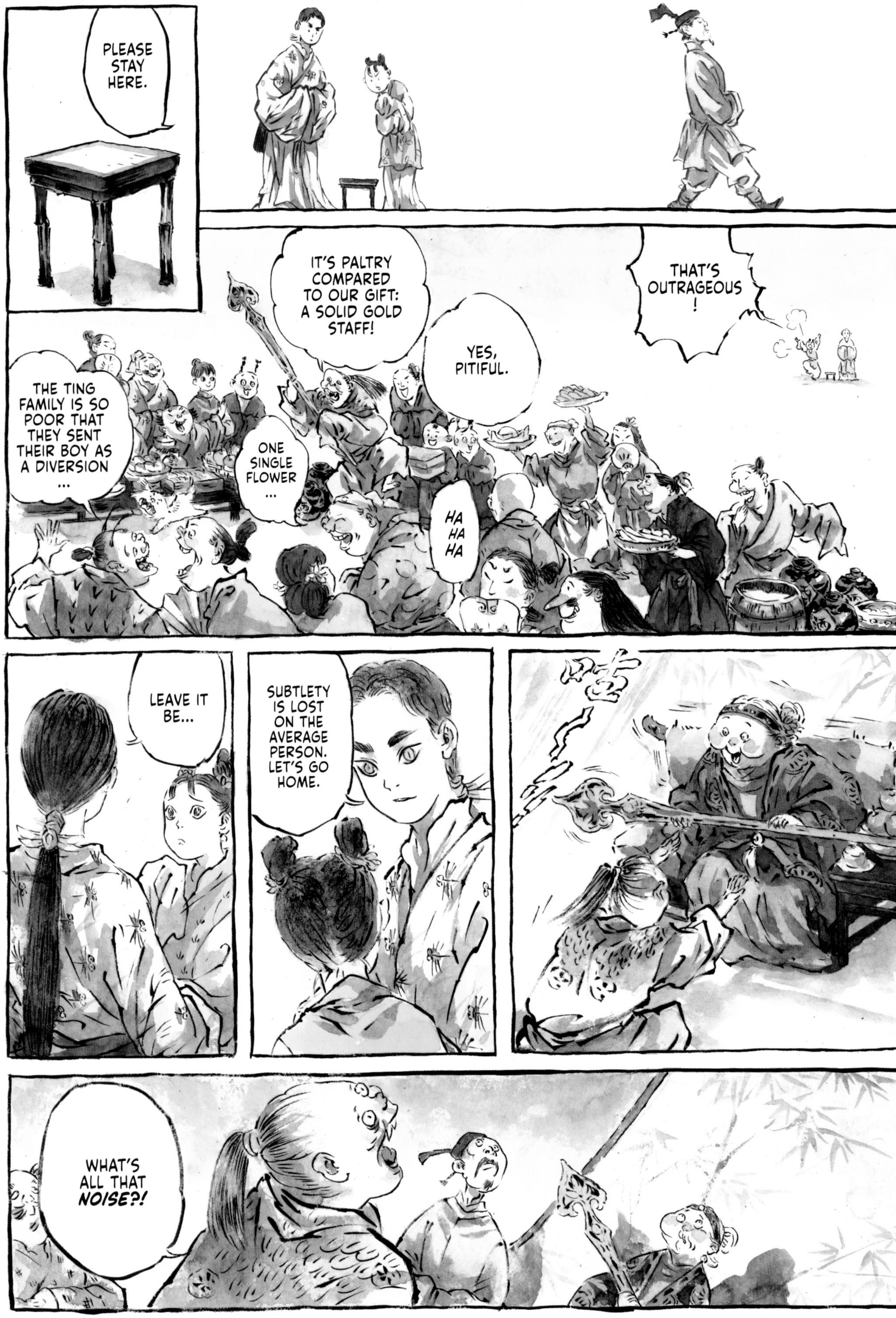
PLEASE STAY HERE.
IT'S PALTRY COMPARED TO OUR GIFT: A SOLID GOLD STAFF!
THAT'S OUTRAGEOUS!
THE TING FAMILY IS SO POOR THAT THEY SENT THEIR BOY AS A DIVERSION ...
YES, PITIFUL.
ONE SINGLE FLOWER ...
HA HA HA
LEAVE IT BE...
SUBTLETY IS LOST ON THE AVERAGE PERSON. LET'S GO HOME.
WHAT'S ALL THAT *NOISE?!*

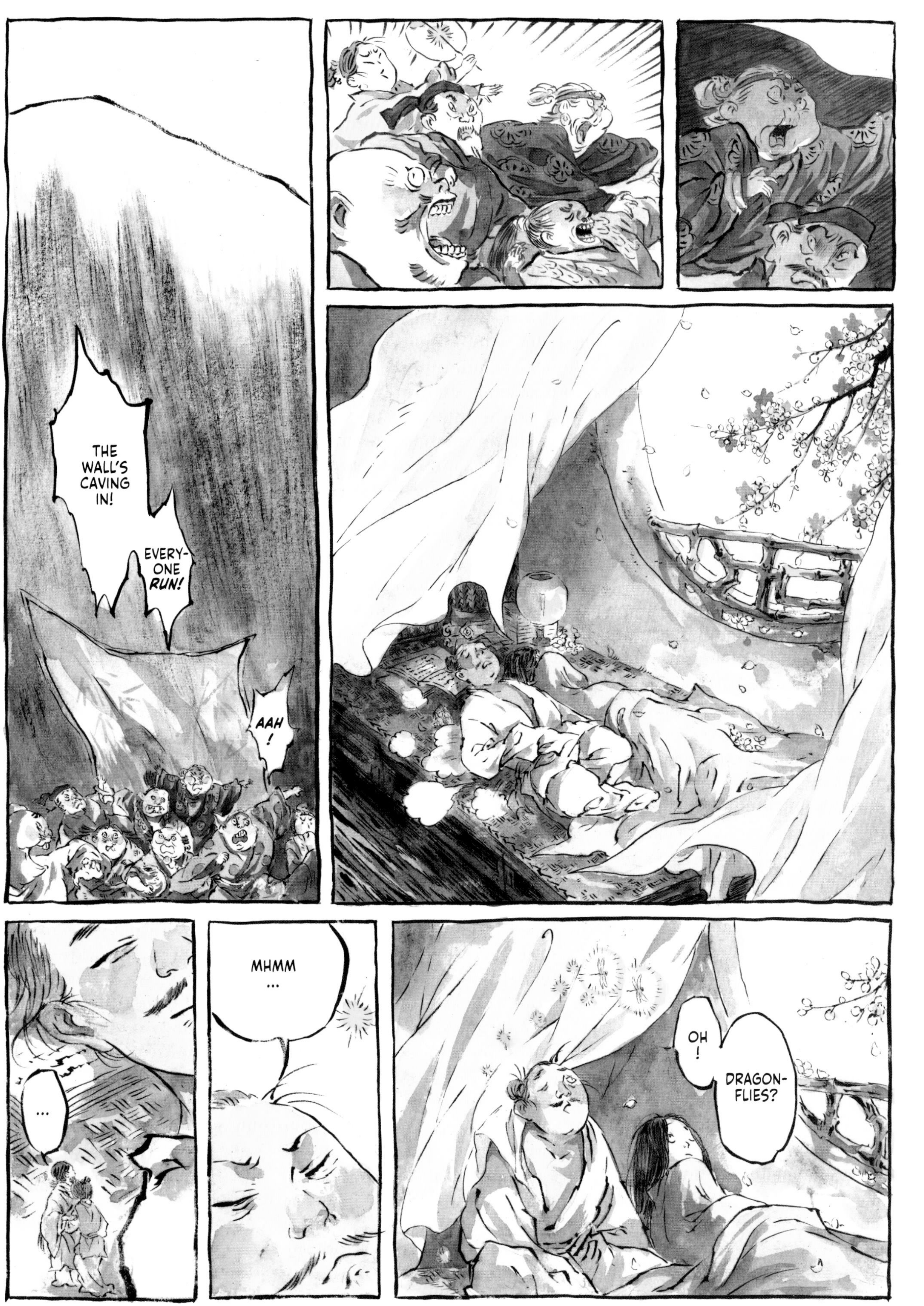
THE WALL'S CAVING IN!
EVERY-ONE RUN!
AAH!
...
MHMM ...
OH!
DRAGON-FLIES?

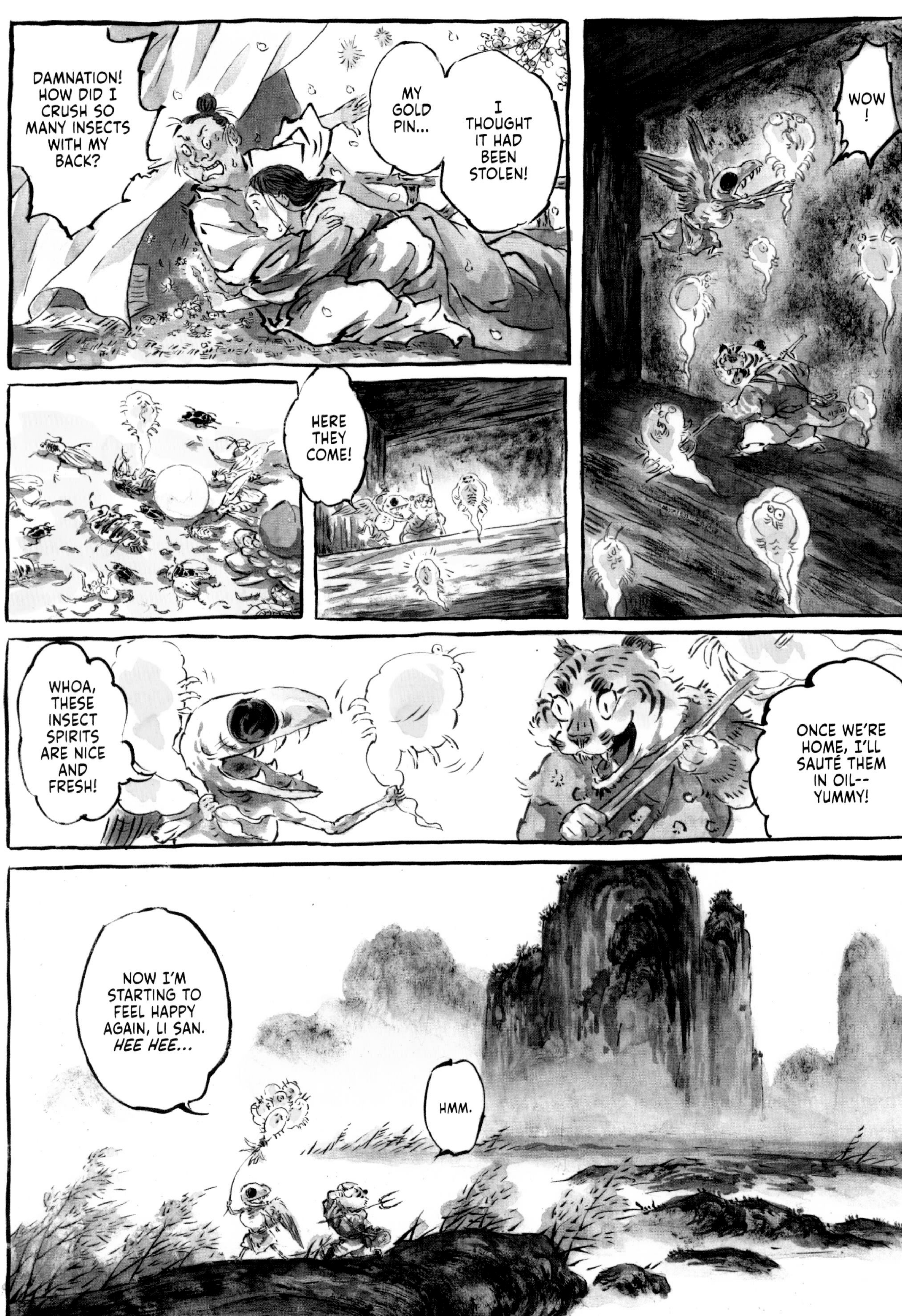
DAMNATION! HOW DID I CRUSH SO MANY INSECTS WITH MY BACK?
MY GOLD PIN...
I THOUGHT IT HAD BEEN STOLEN!
WOW!
HERE THEY COME!
WHOA, THESE INSECT SPIRITS ARE NICE AND FRESH!
ONCE WE'RE HOME, I'LL SAUTÉ THEM IN OIL-- YUMMY!
NOW I'M STARTING TO FEEL HAPPY AGAIN, LI SAN. *HEE HEE...*
HMM.

ENTOMOLOGY

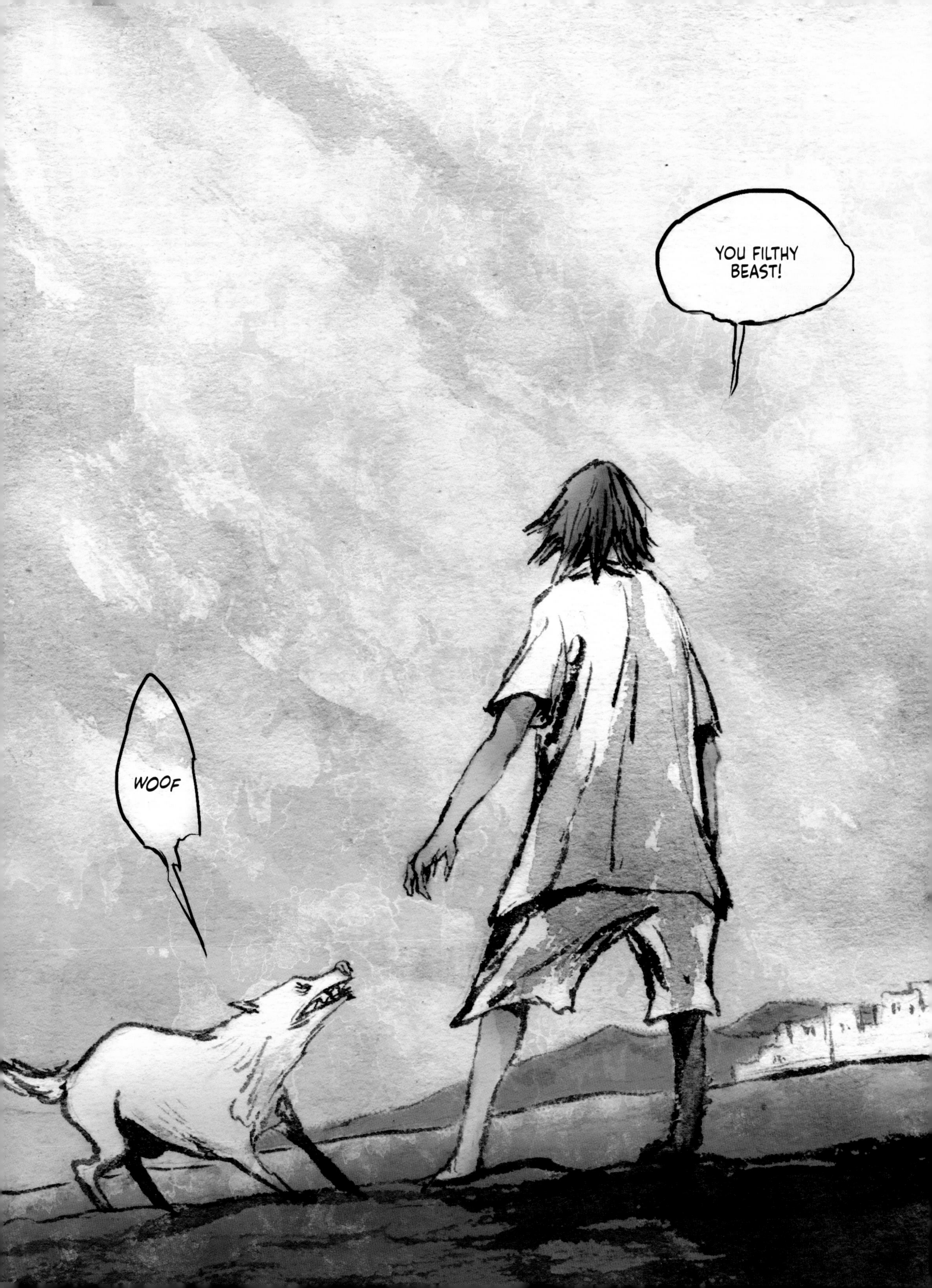
YOU FILTHY BEAST!
WOOF

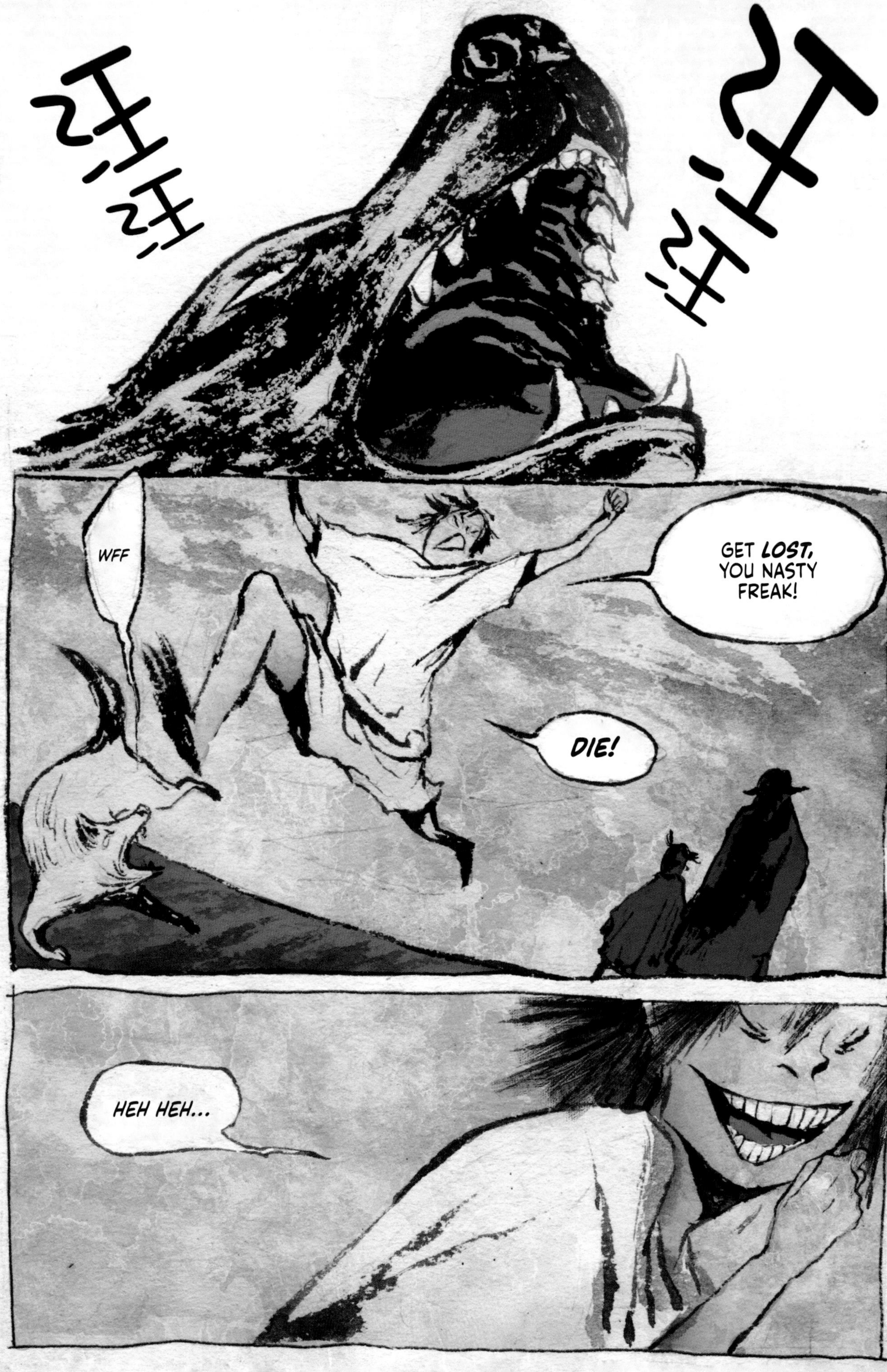
WFF
GET LOST, YOU NASTY FREAK!
DIE!
HEH HEH...

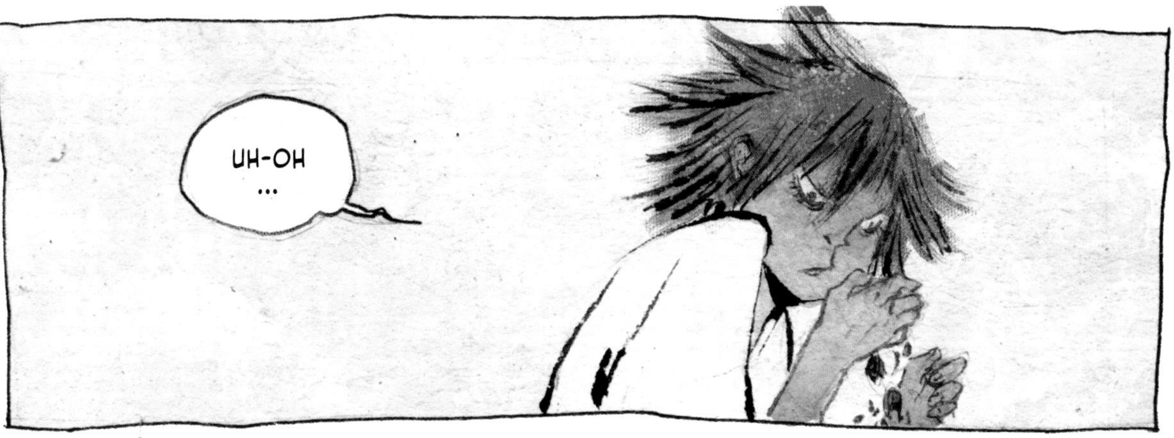
UH-OH
...

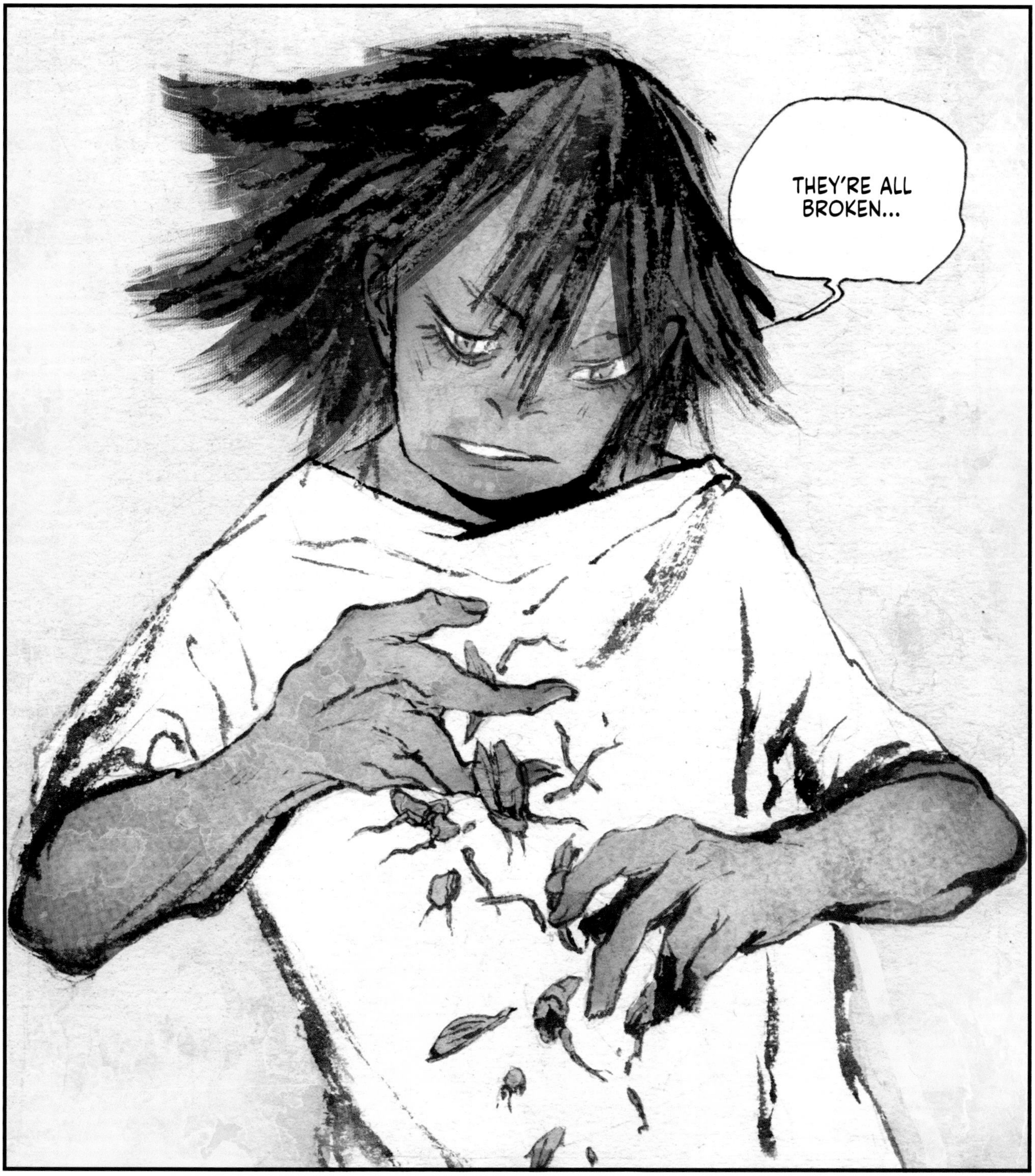
THEY'RE ALL
BROKEN...

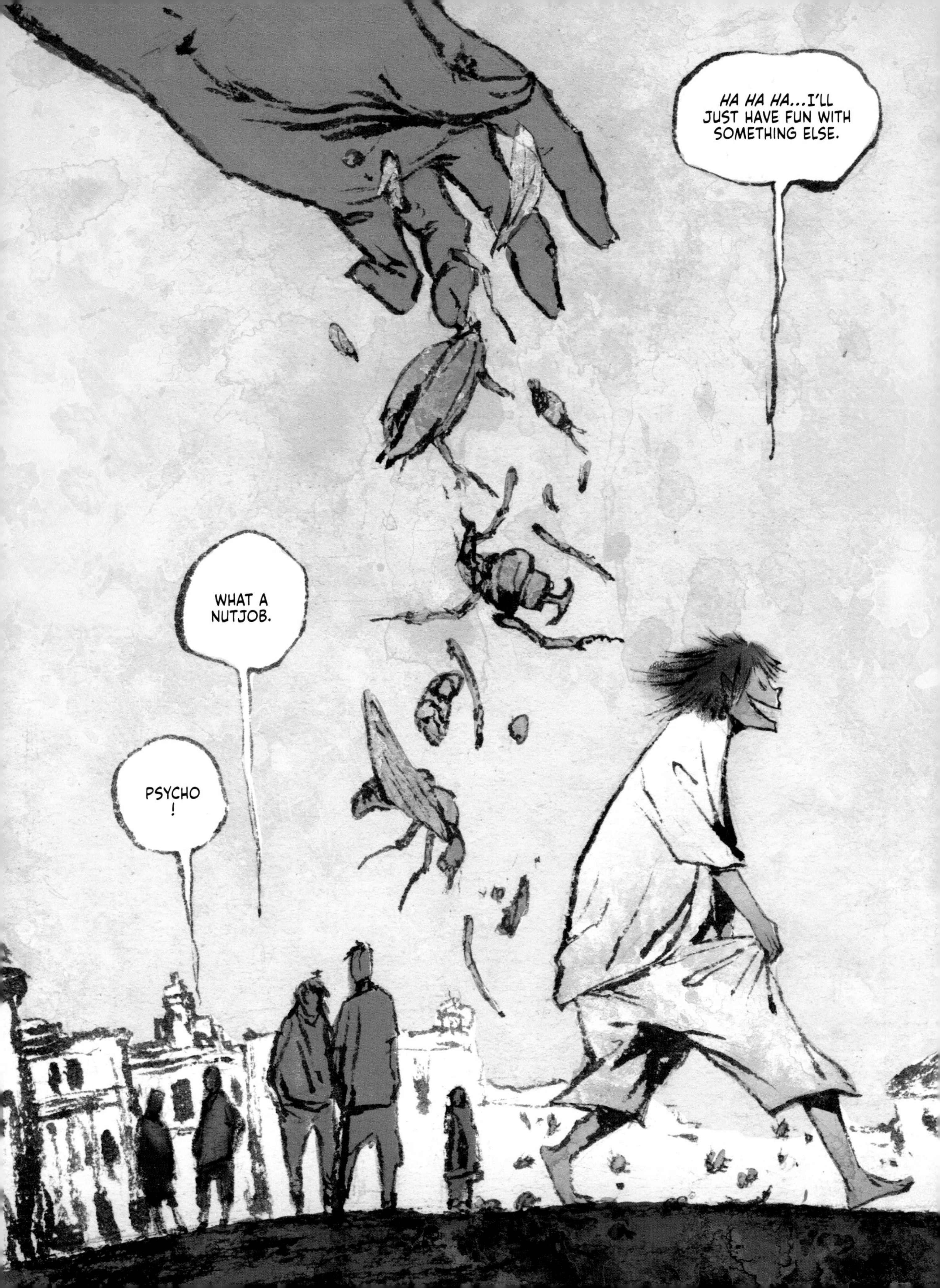
HA HA HA...I'LL JUST HAVE FUN WITH SOMETHING ELSE.
WHAT A NUTJOB.
PSYCHO!

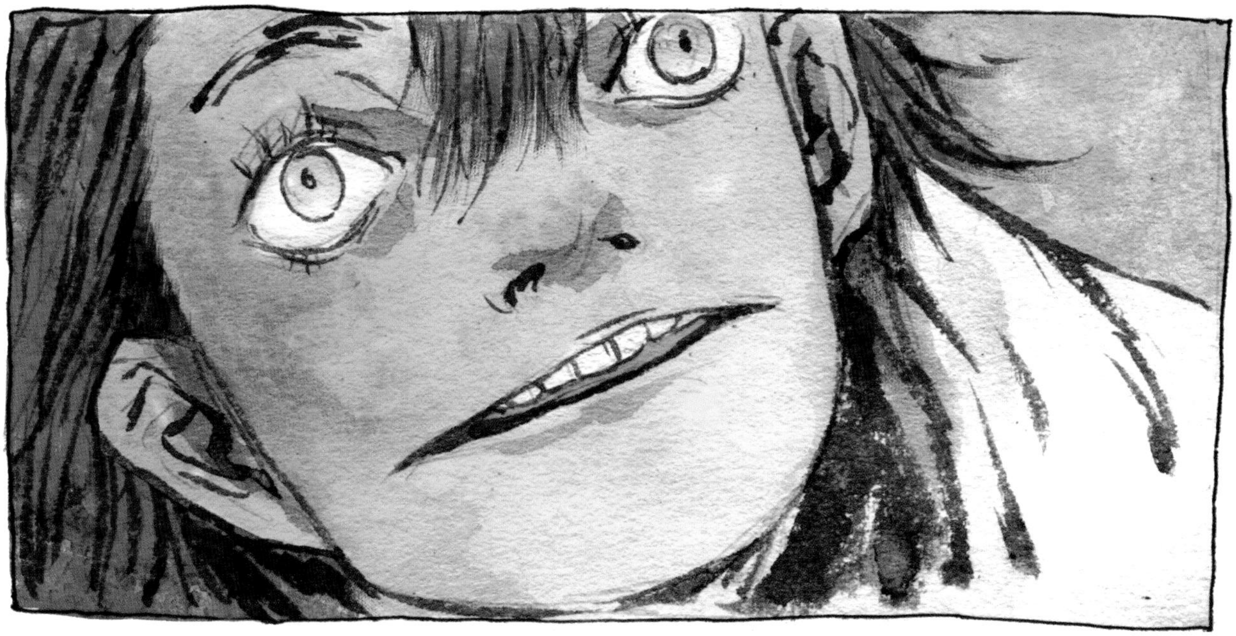

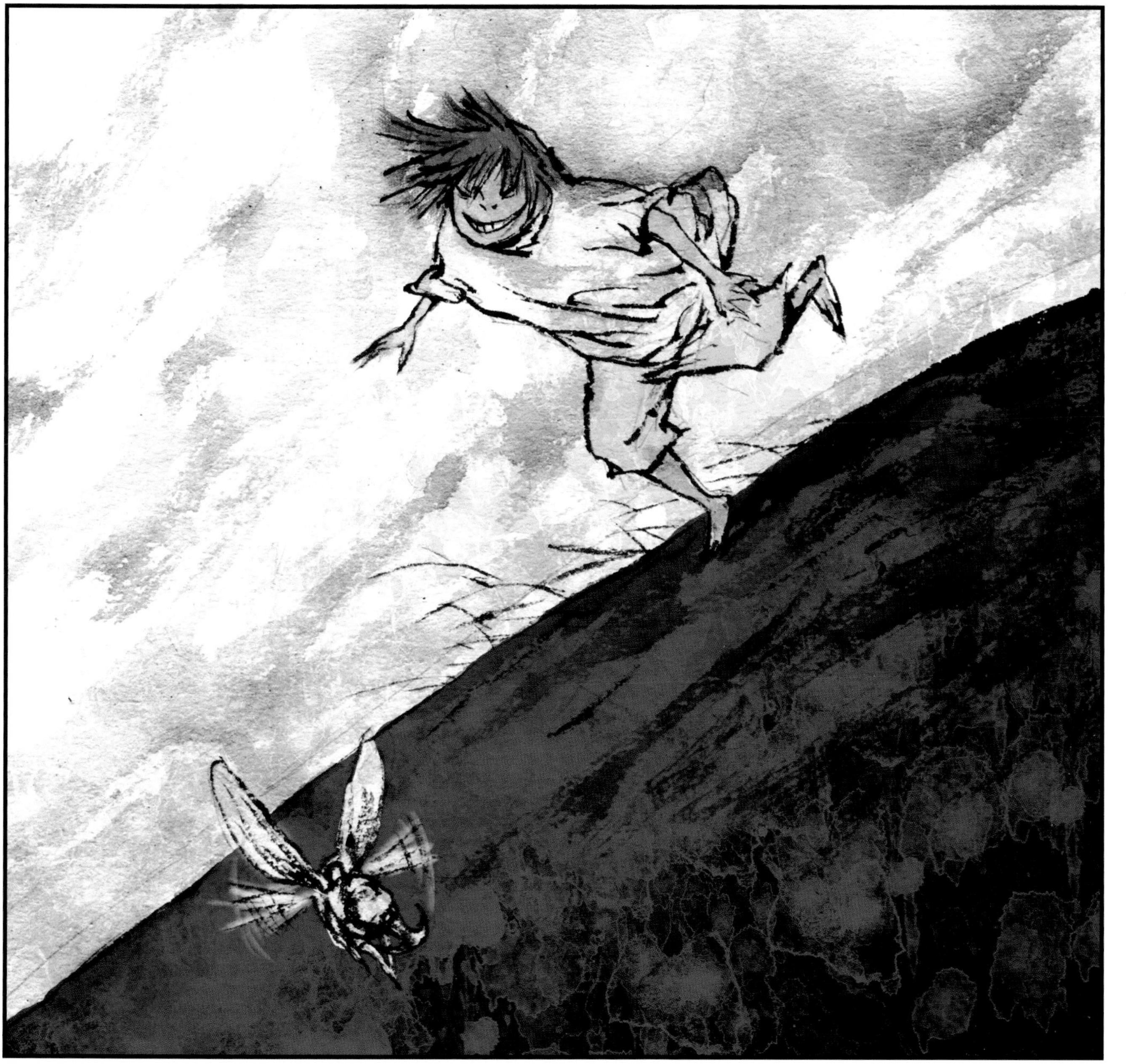

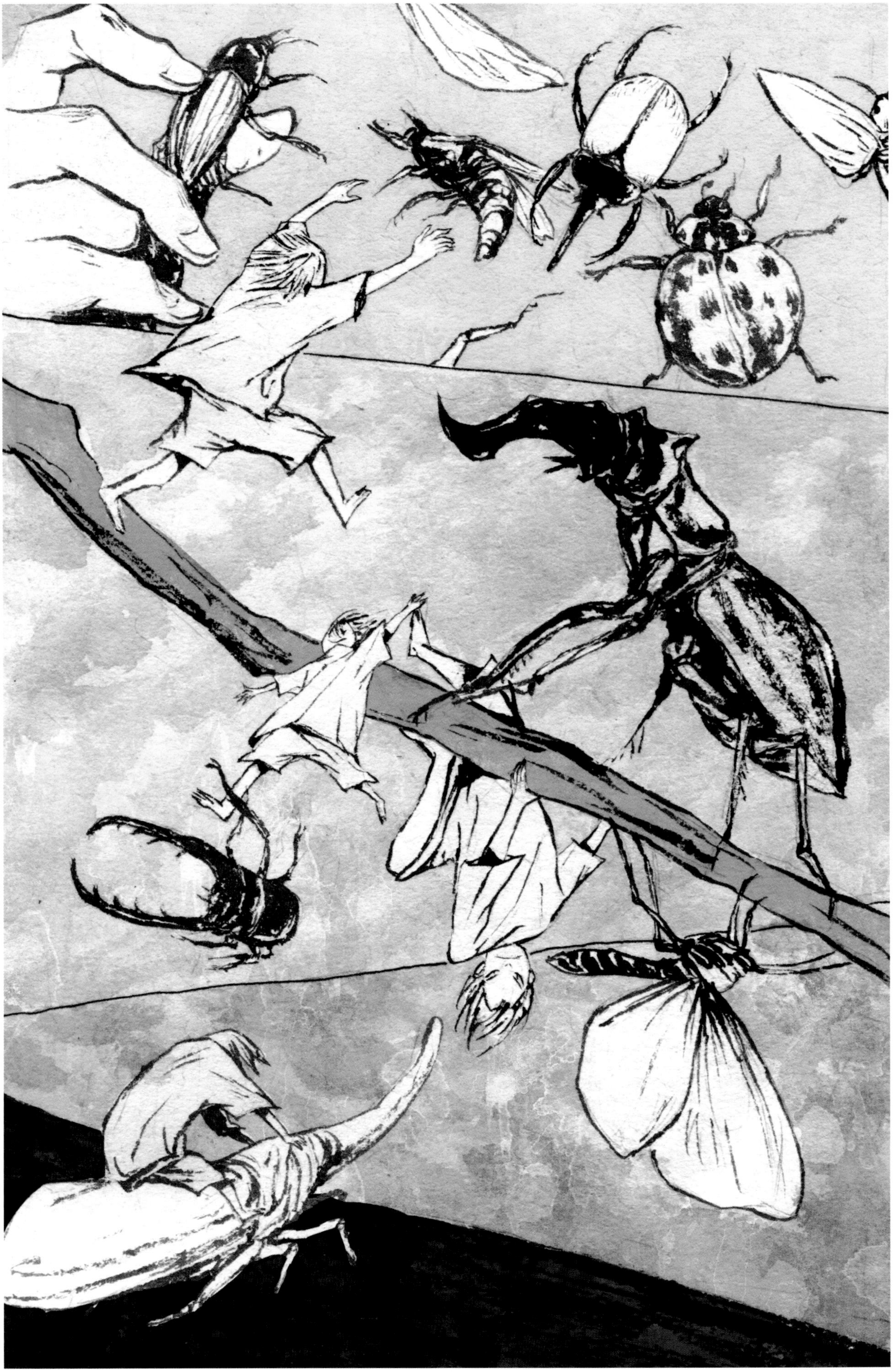

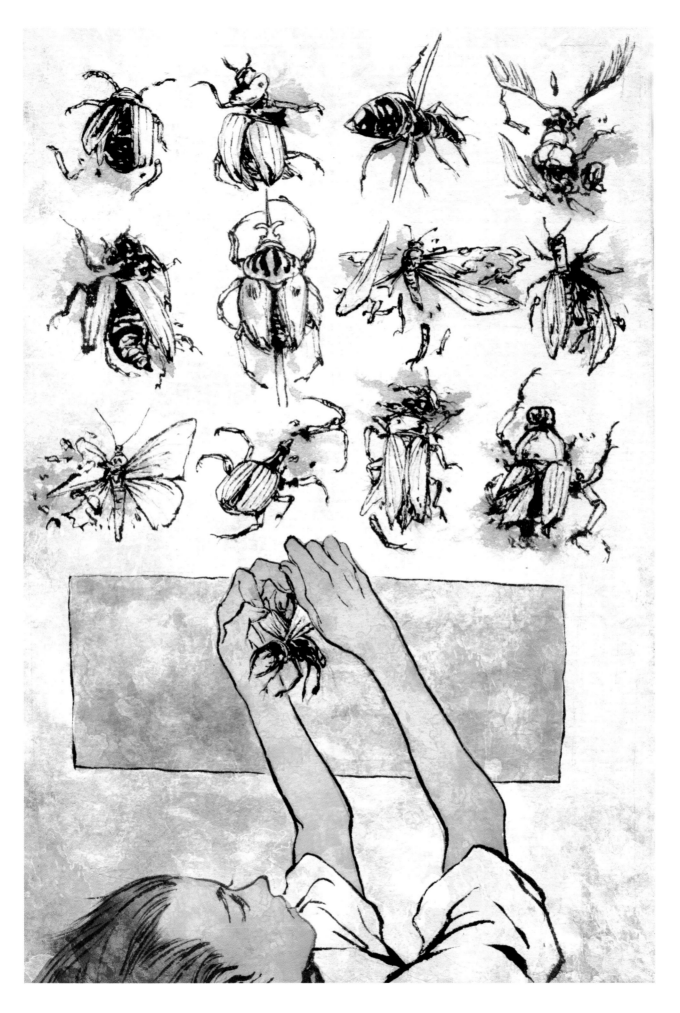

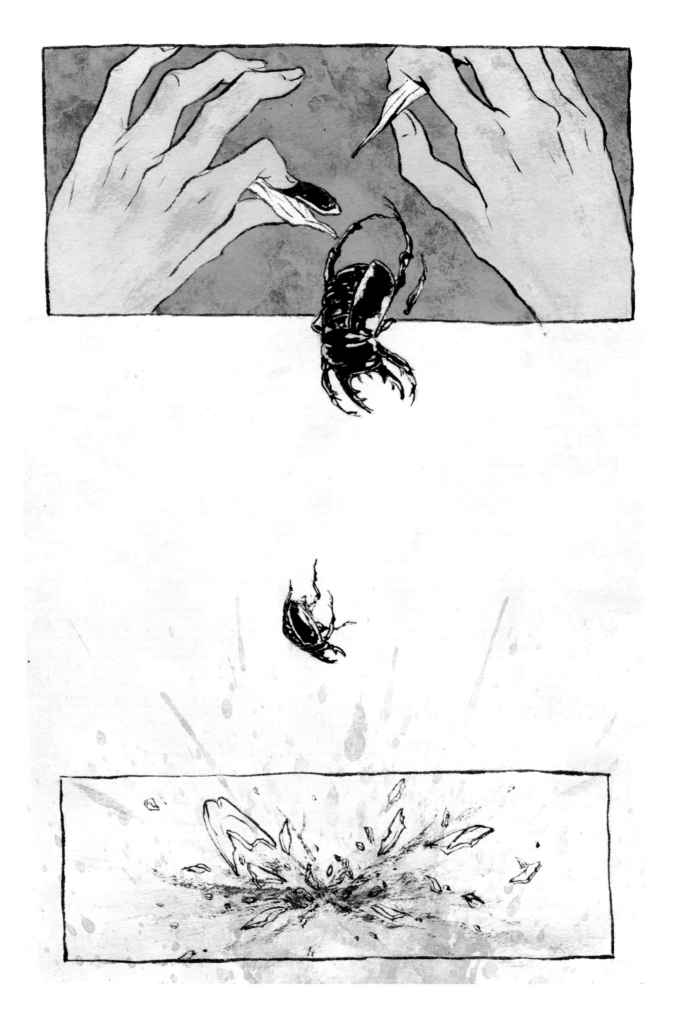

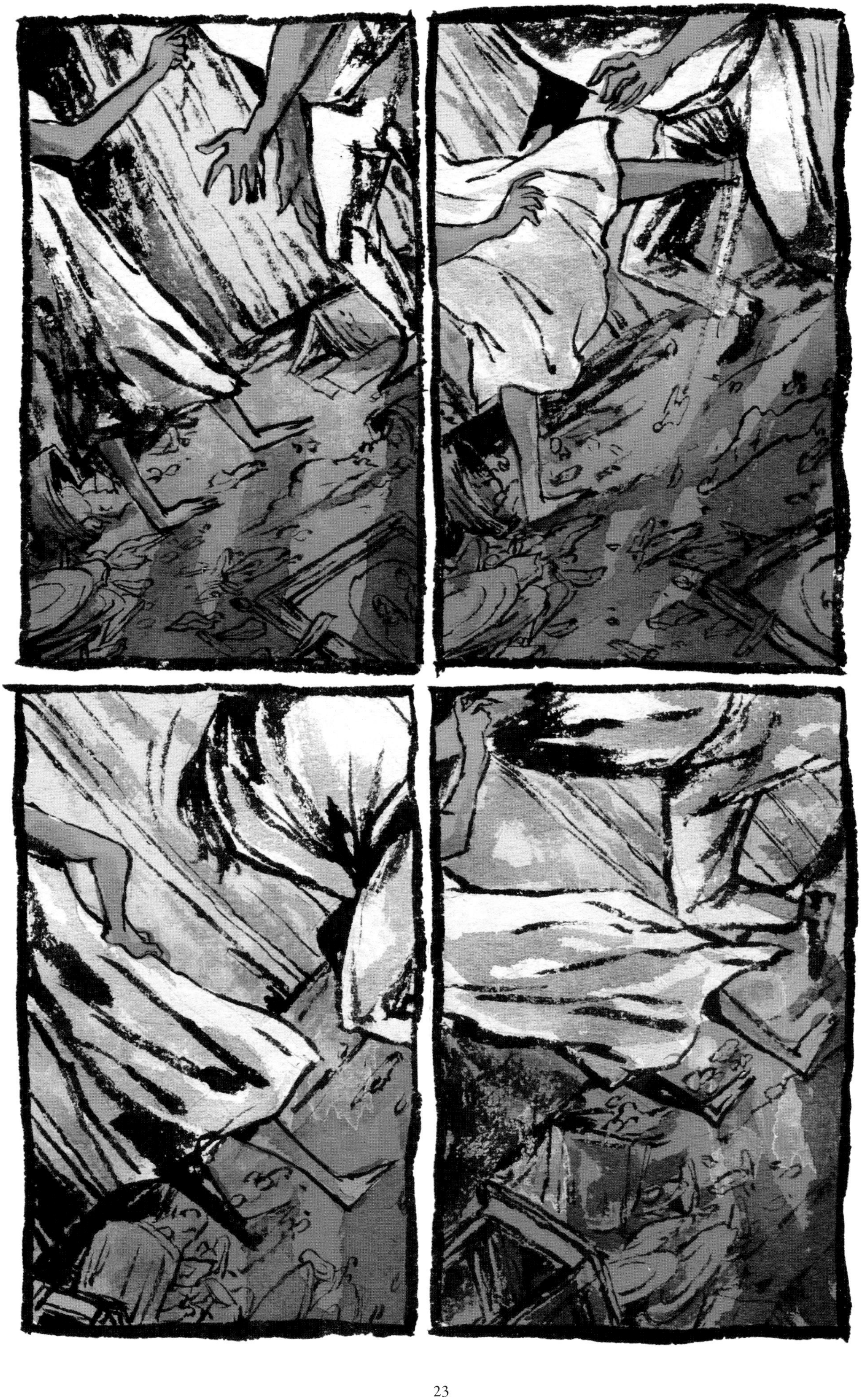

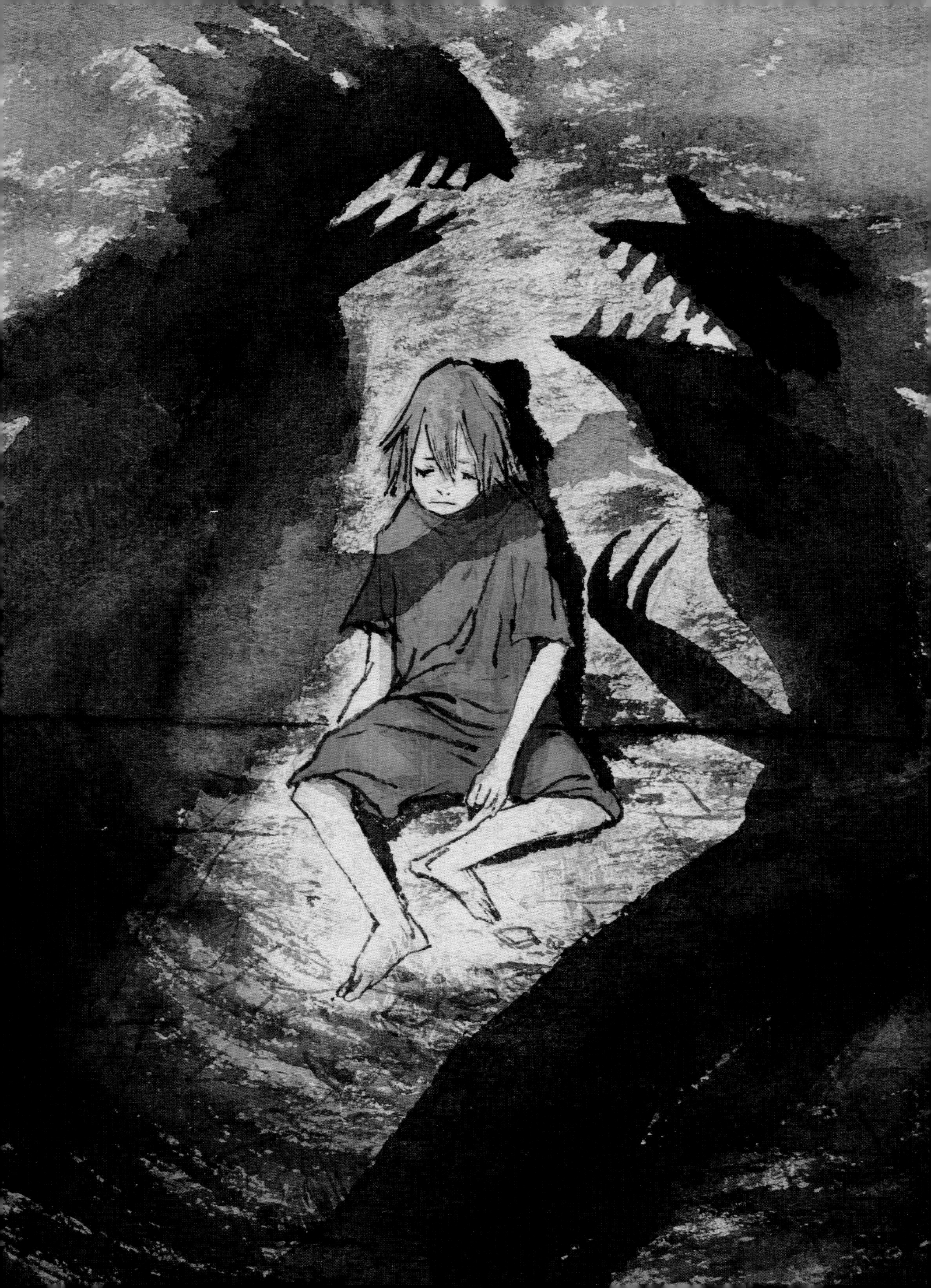

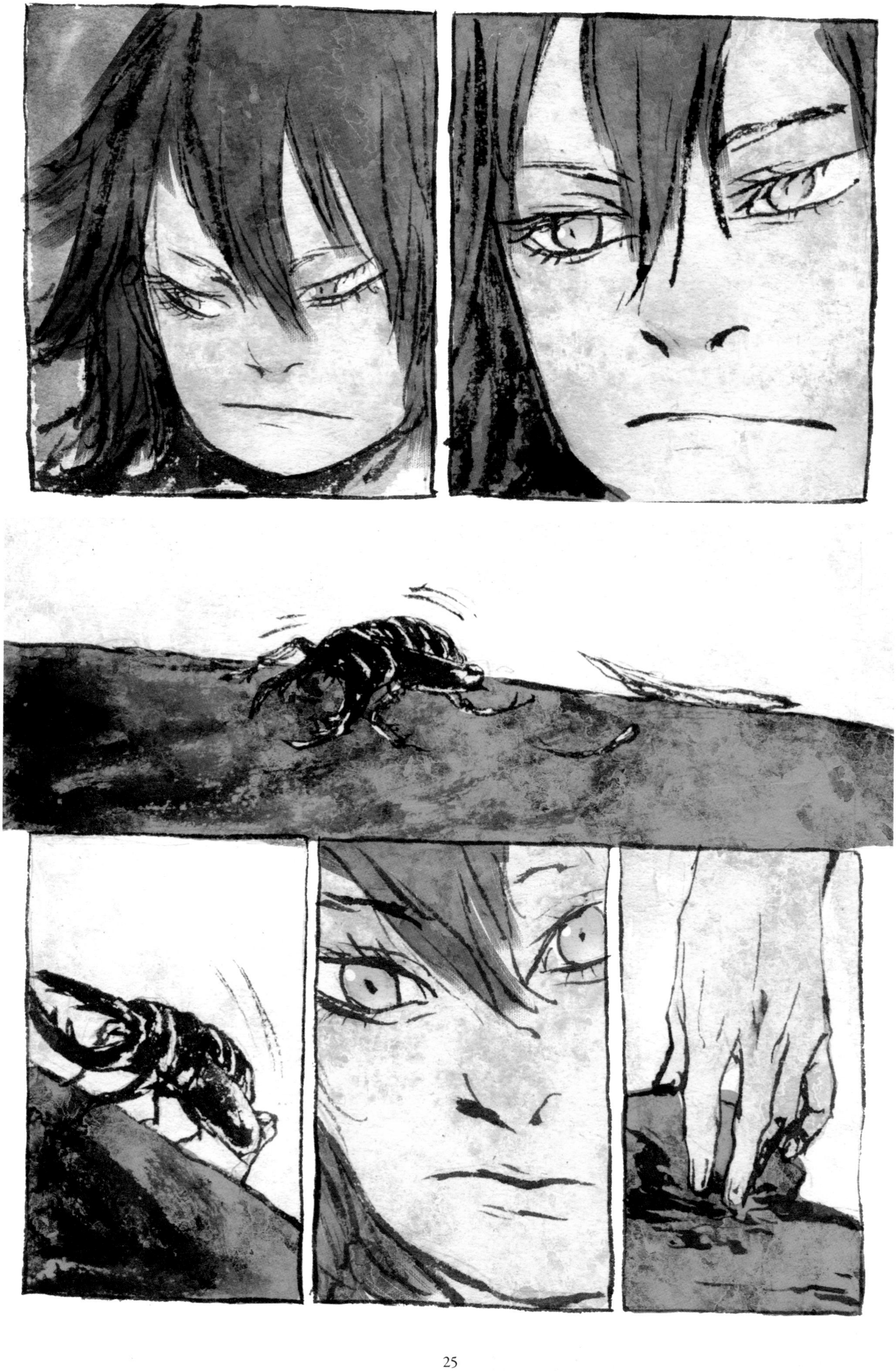

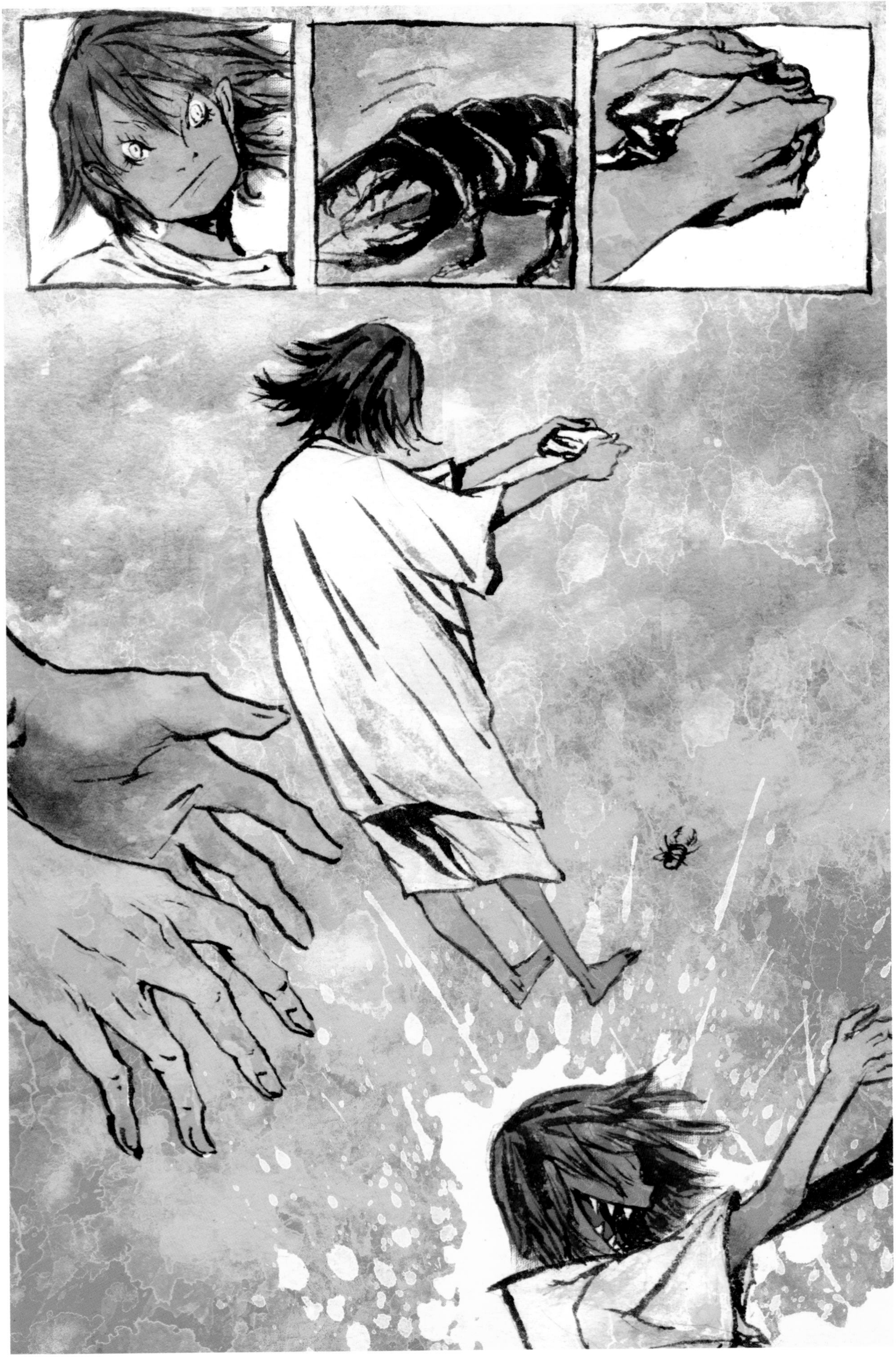

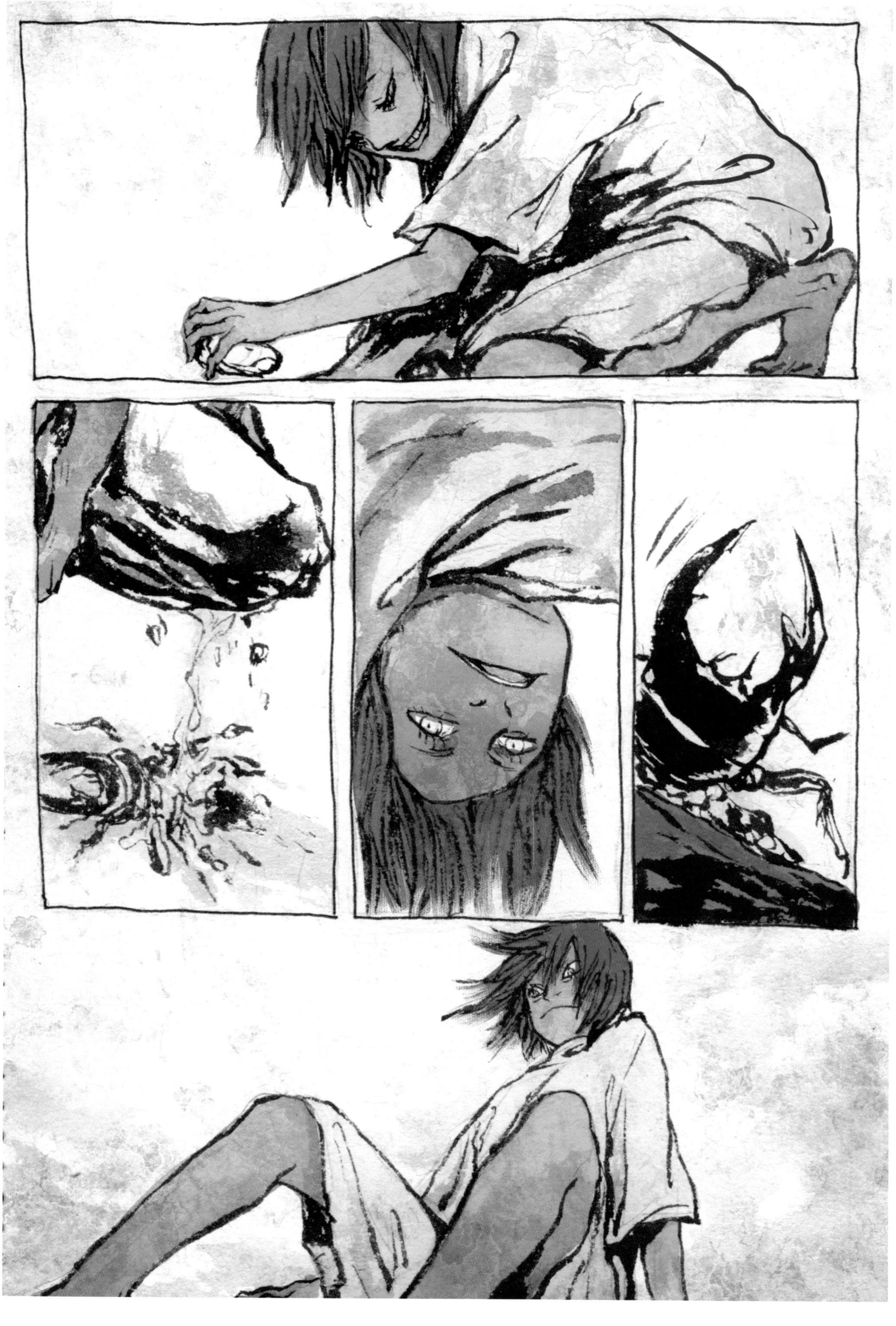

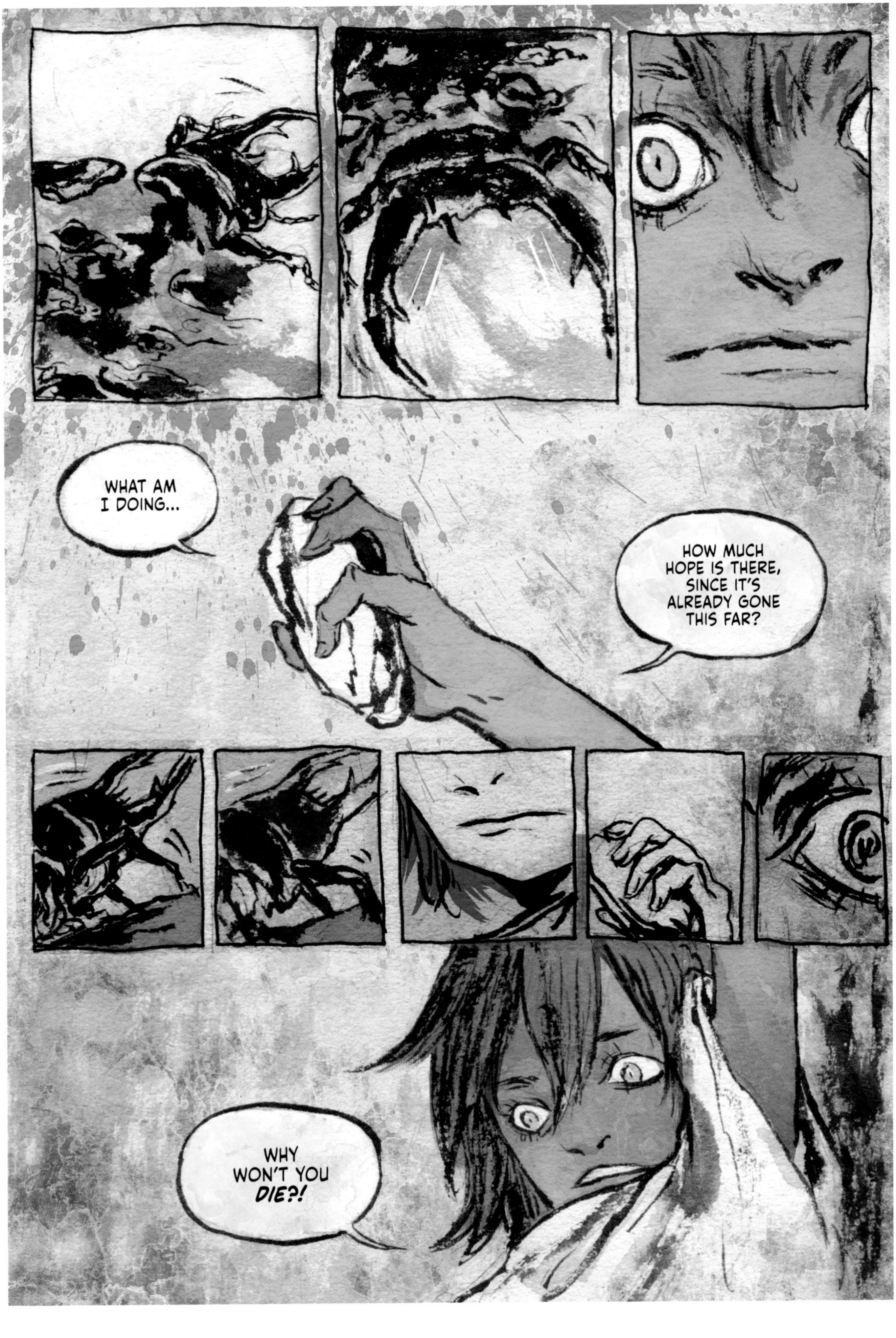
WHAT AM I DOING...
HOW MUCH HOPE IS THERE, SINCE IT'S ALREADY GONE THIS FAR?
WHY WON'T YOU *DIE?!*

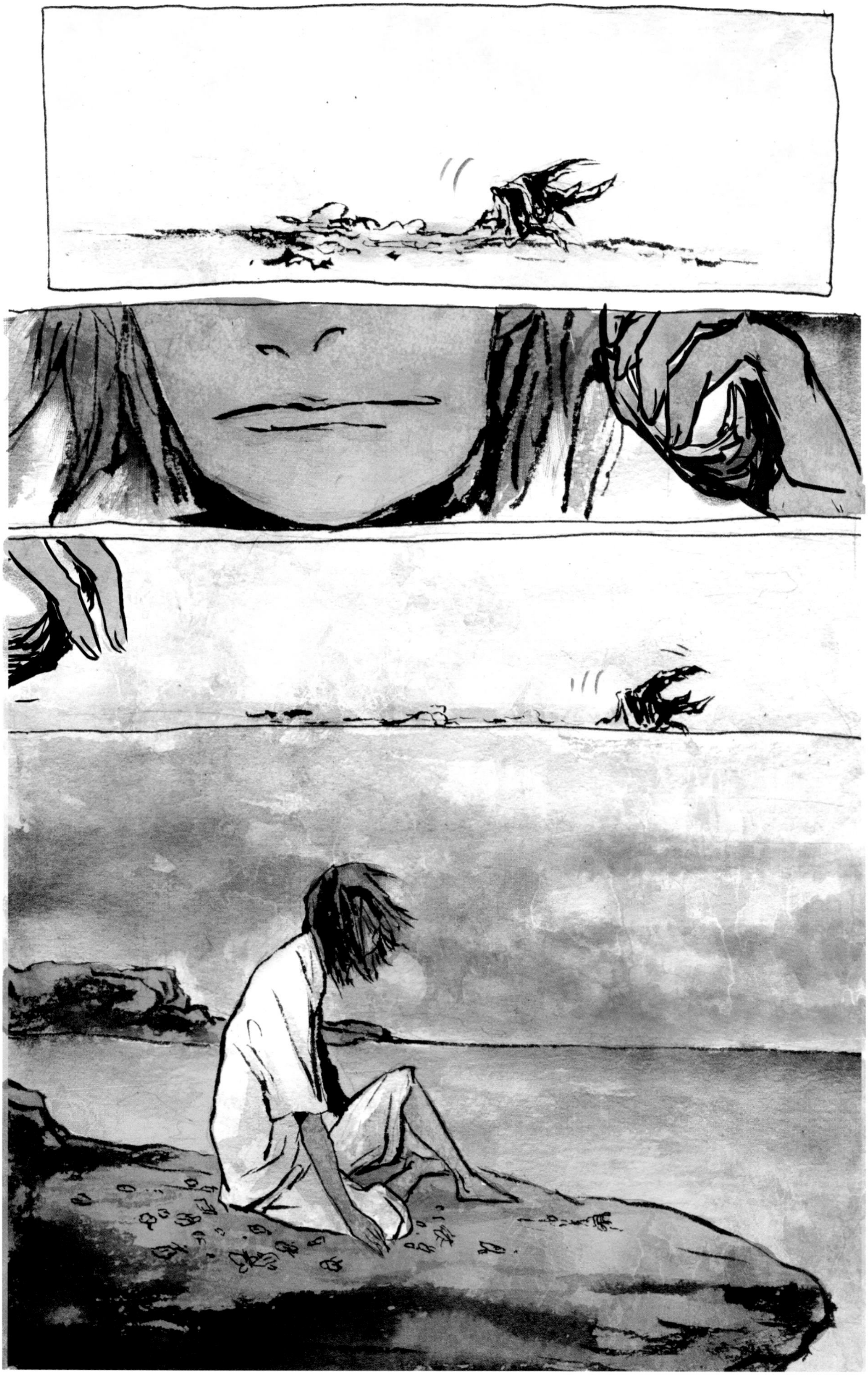

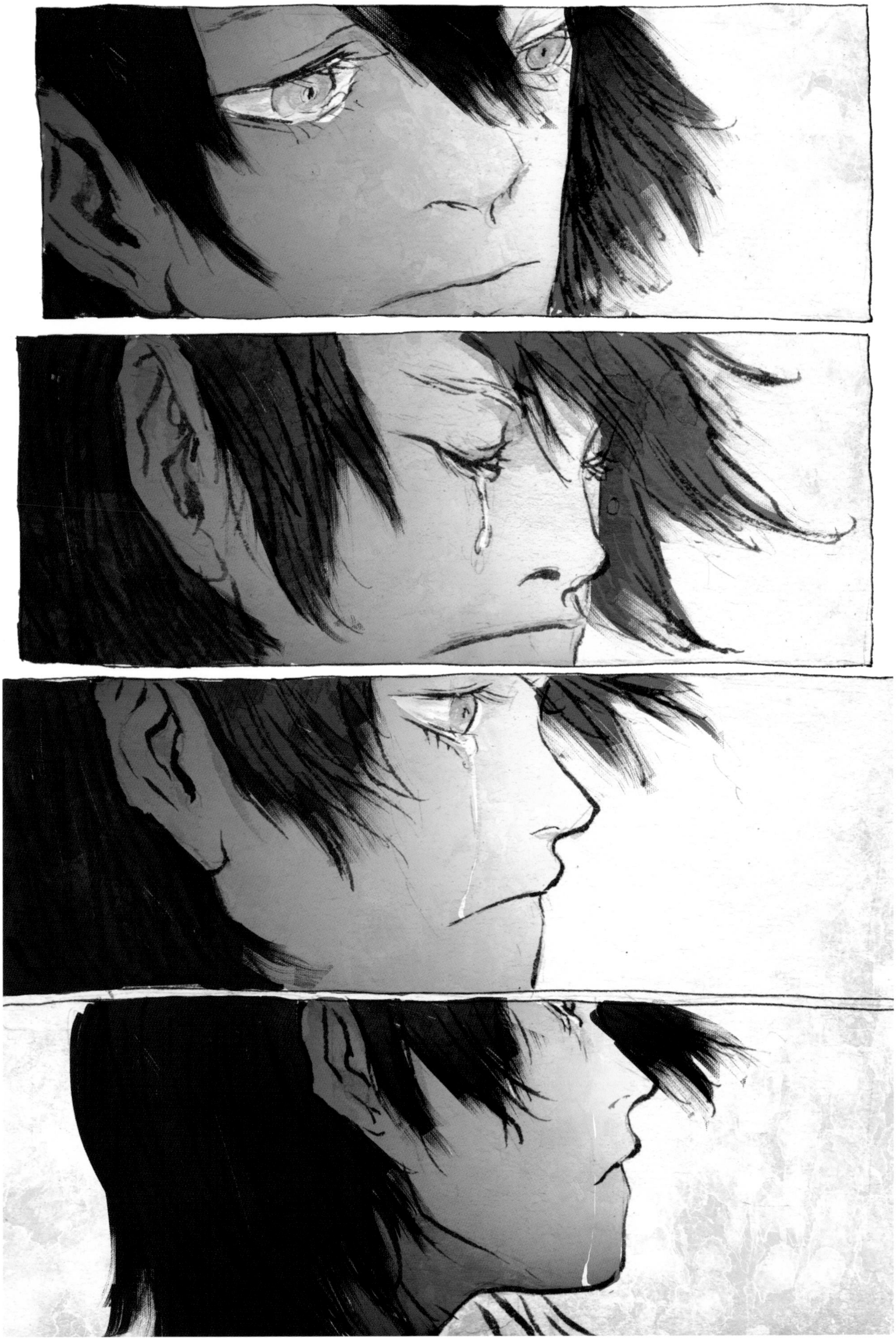

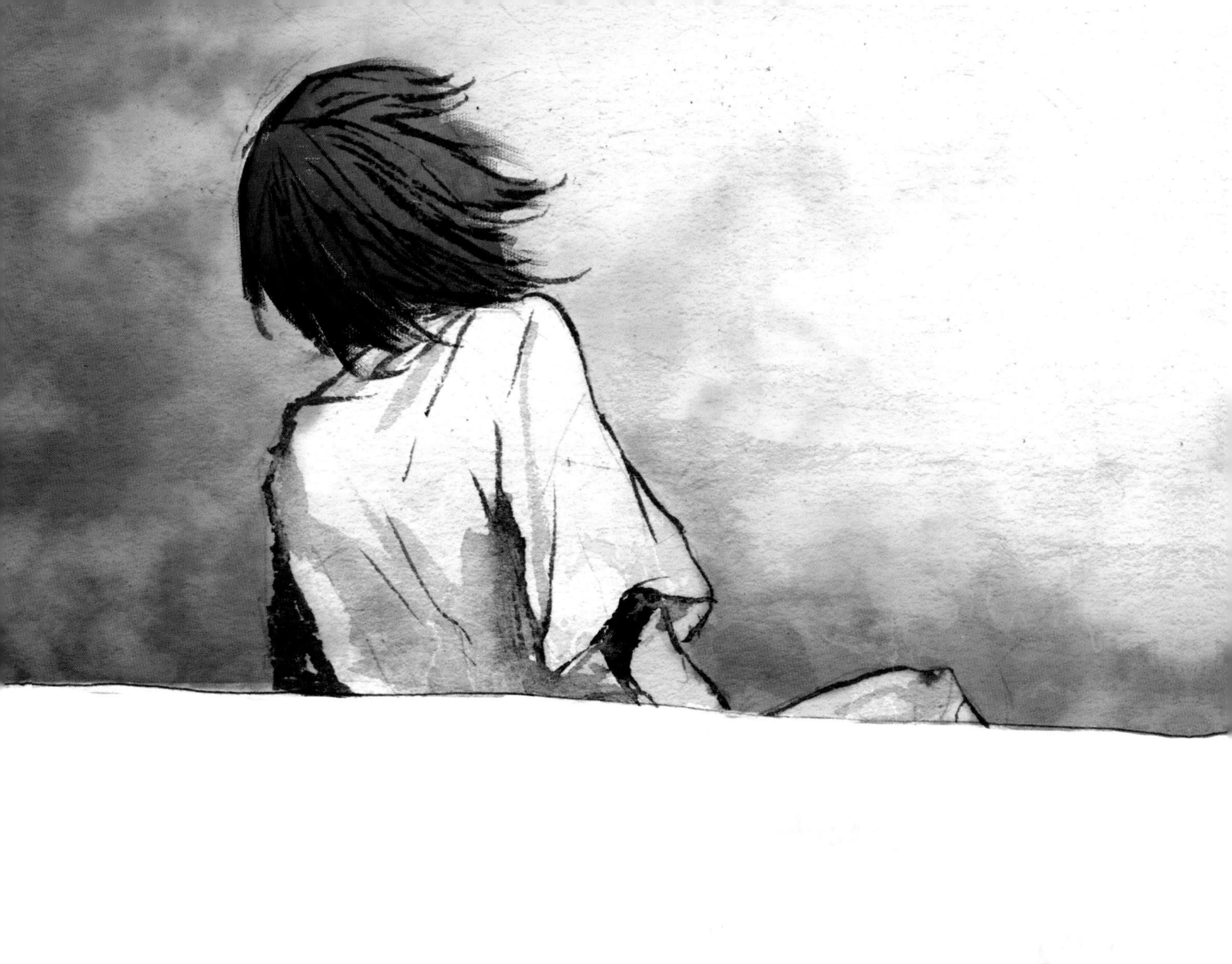

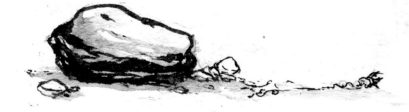

HAI ZI

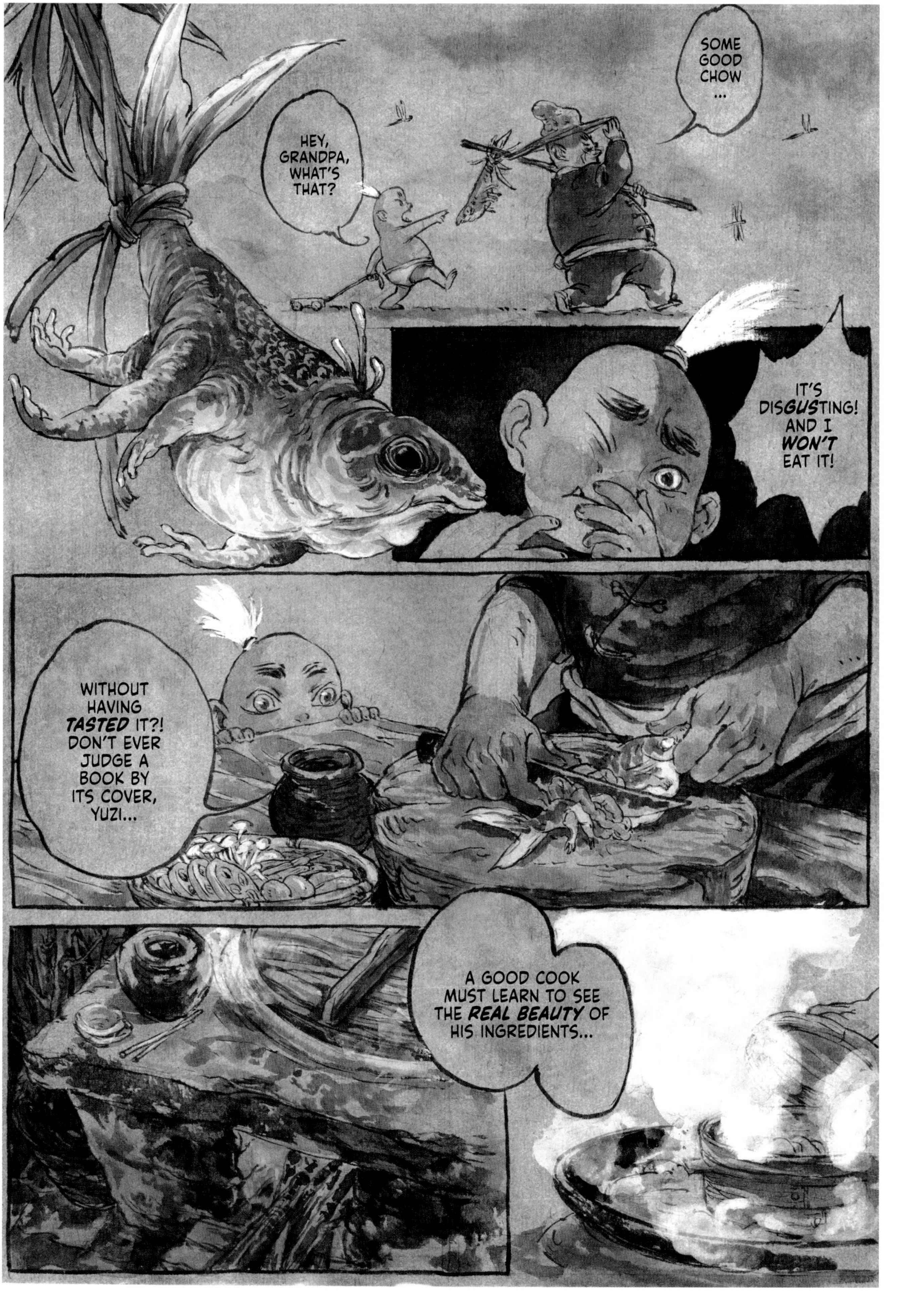
HEY, GRANDPA, WHAT'S THAT?
SOME GOOD CHOW ...
IT'S DISGUSTING! AND I WON'T EAT IT!
WITHOUT HAVING TASTED IT?! DON'T EVER JUDGE A BOOK BY ITS COVER, YUZI...
A GOOD COOK MUST LEARN TO SEE THE REAL BEAUTY OF HIS INGREDIENTS...

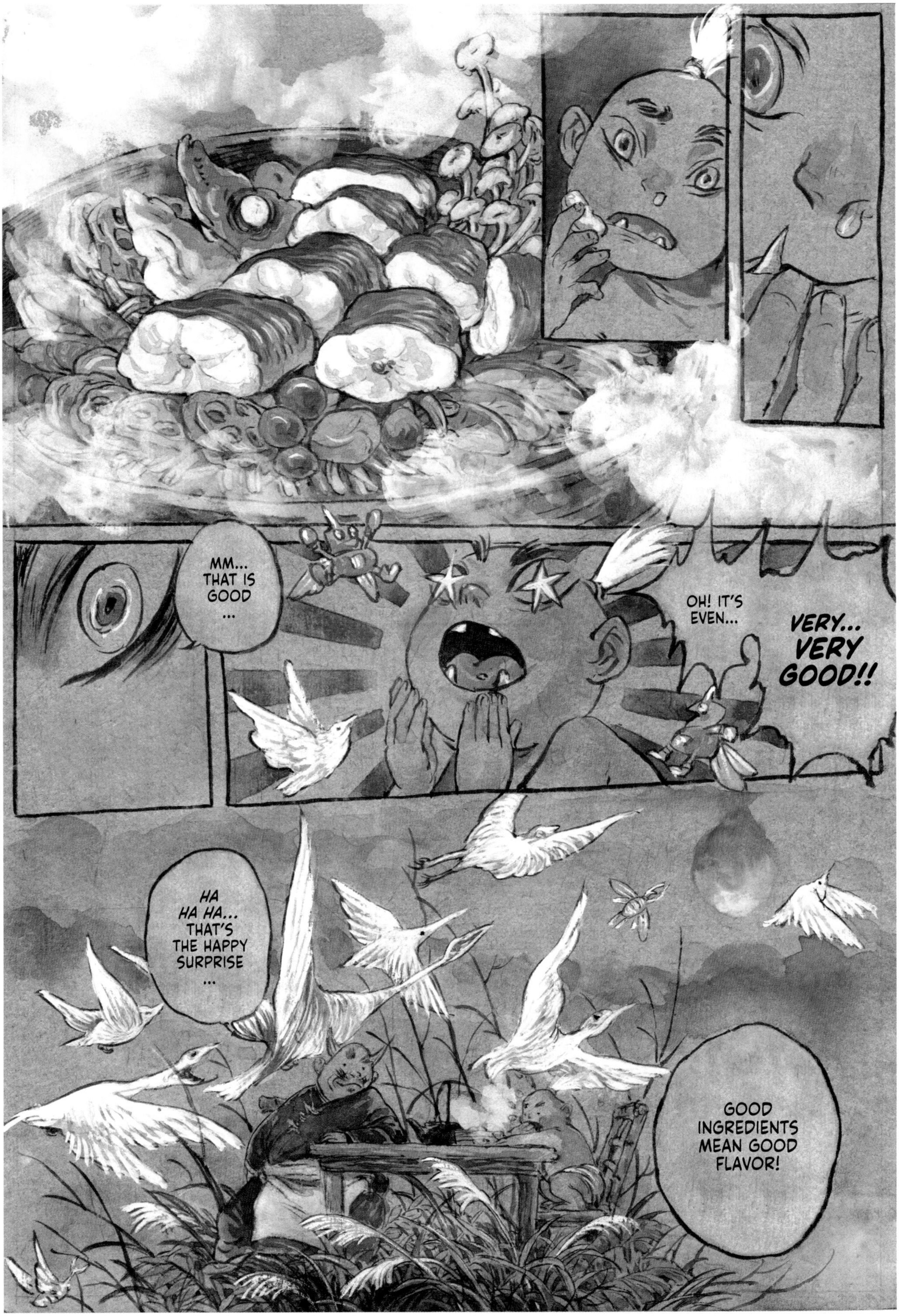
MM... THAT IS GOOD ...
OH! IT'S EVEN...
VERY... VERY GOOD!!
HA HA HA... THAT'S THE HAPPY SURPRISE ...
GOOD INGREDIENTS MEAN GOOD FLAVOR!

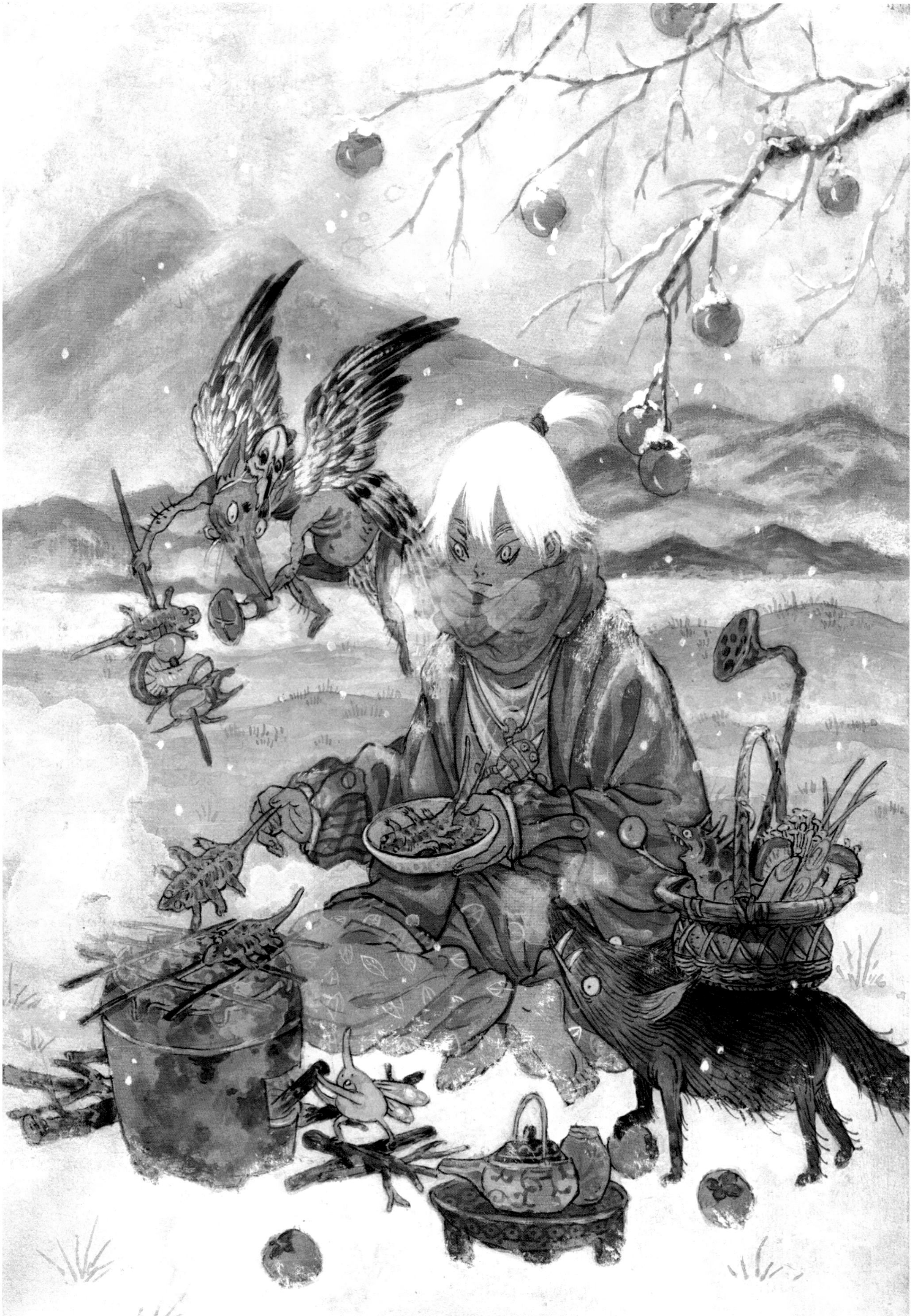

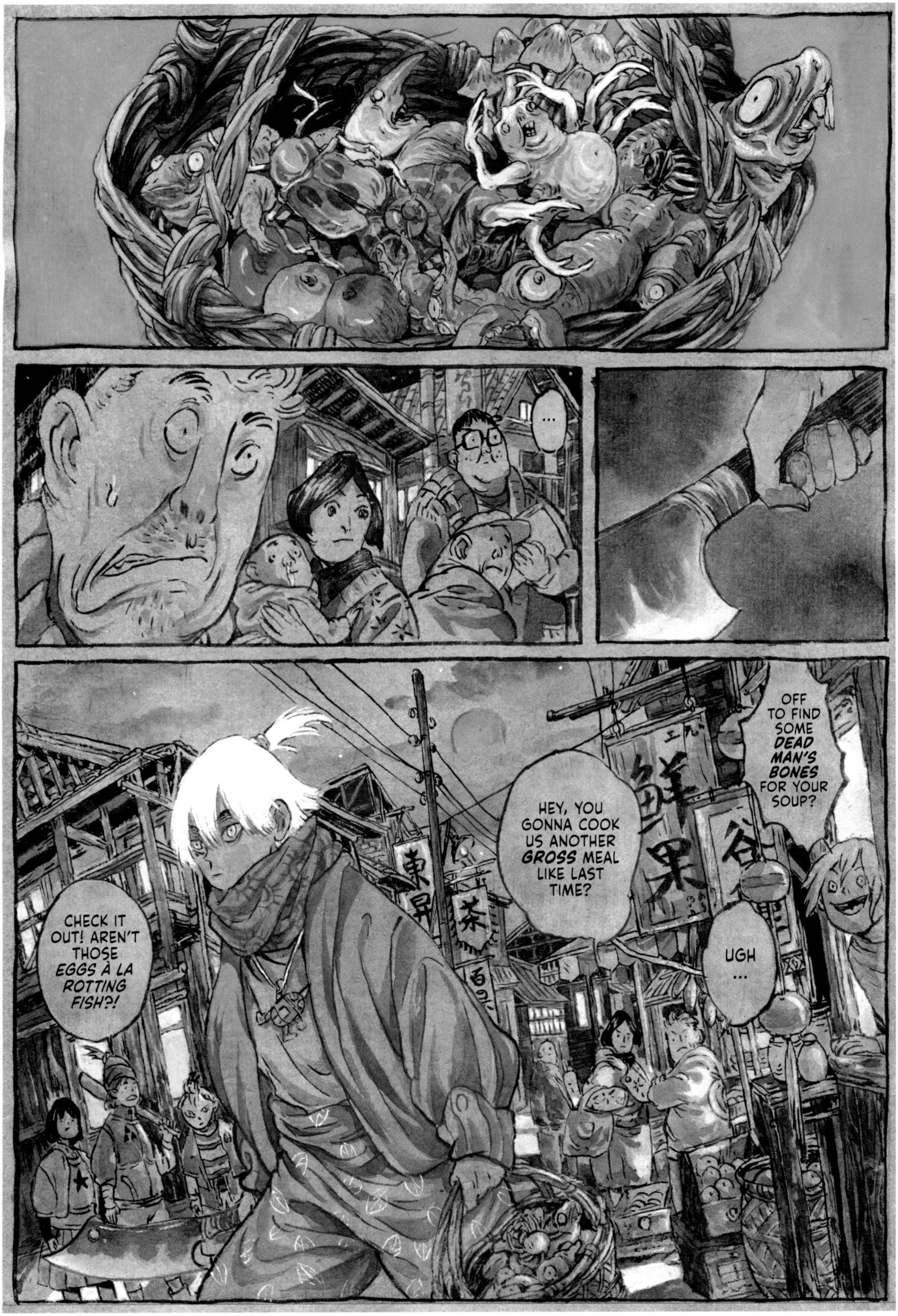
...
CHECK IT OUT! AREN'T THOSE *EGGS À LA ROTTING FISH*?!
HEY, YOU GONNA COOK US ANOTHER **GROSS** MEAL LIKE LAST TIME?
OFF TO FIND SOME ***DEAD MAN'S BONES*** FOR YOUR SOUP?
UGH ...

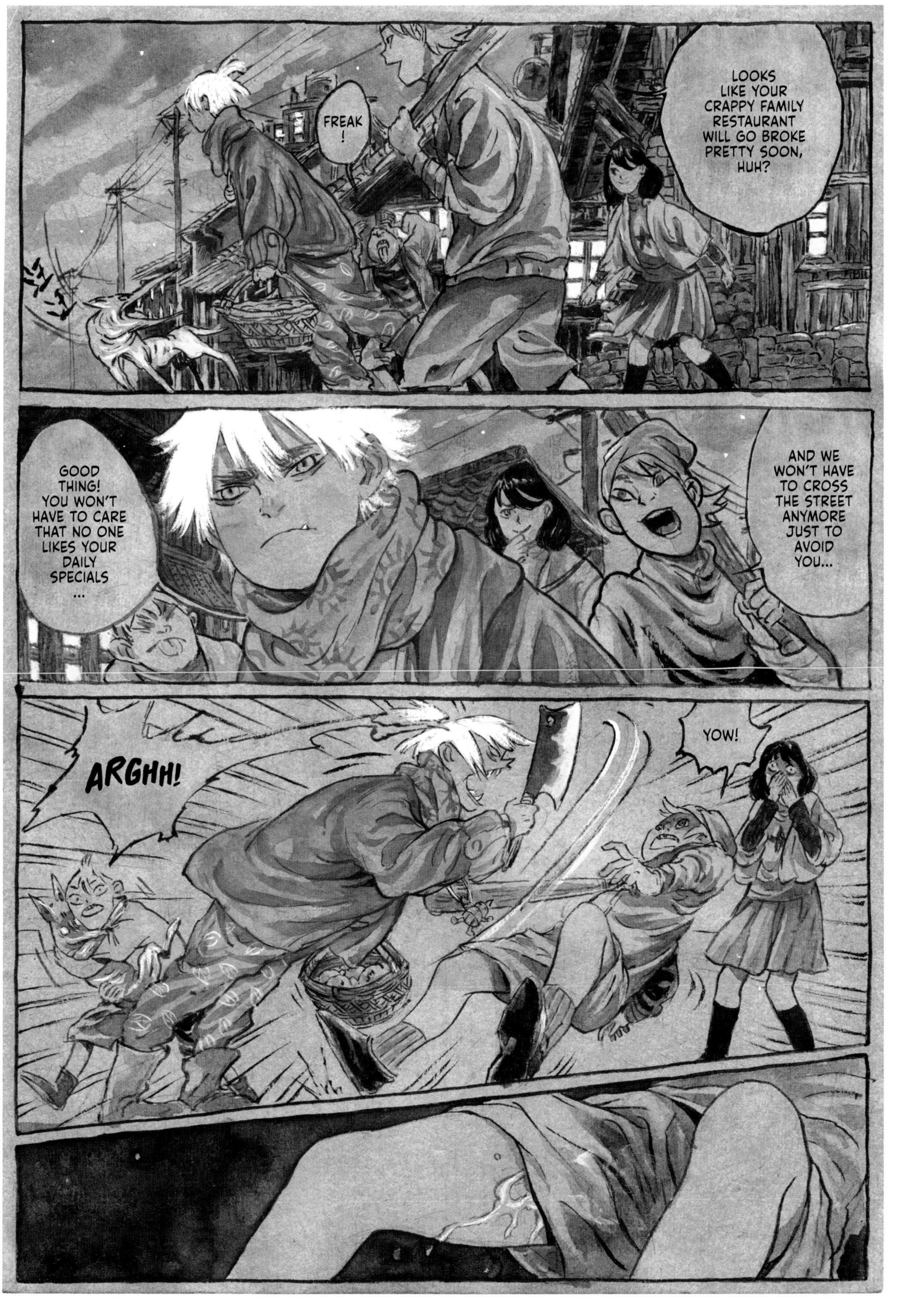
FREAK!
LOOKS LIKE YOUR CRAPPY FAMILY RESTAURANT WILL GO BROKE PRETTY SOON, HUH?
GOOD THING! YOU WON'T HAVE TO CARE THAT NO ONE LIKES YOUR DAILY SPECIALS...
AND WE WON'T HAVE TO CROSS THE STREET ANYMORE JUST TO AVOID YOU...
ARGHH!
YOW!

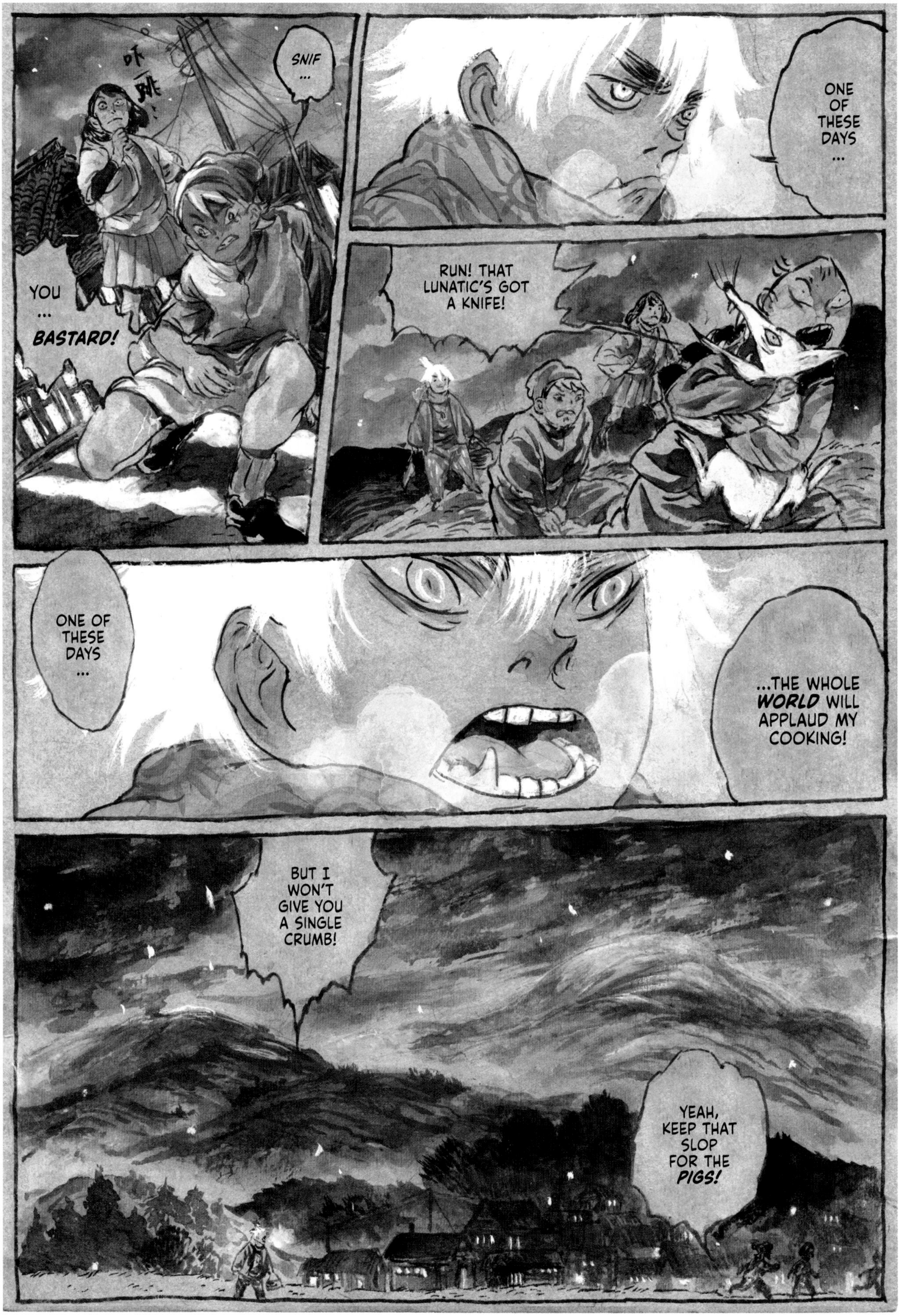
SNIF
...
YOU
...
BASTARD!
ONE OF THESE DAYS ...
RUN! THAT LUNATIC'S GOT A KNIFE!
ONE OF THESE DAYS ...
...THE WHOLE WORLD WILL APPLAUD MY COOKING!
BUT I WON'T GIVE YOU A SINGLE CRUMB!
YEAH, KEEP THAT SLOP FOR THE PIGS!

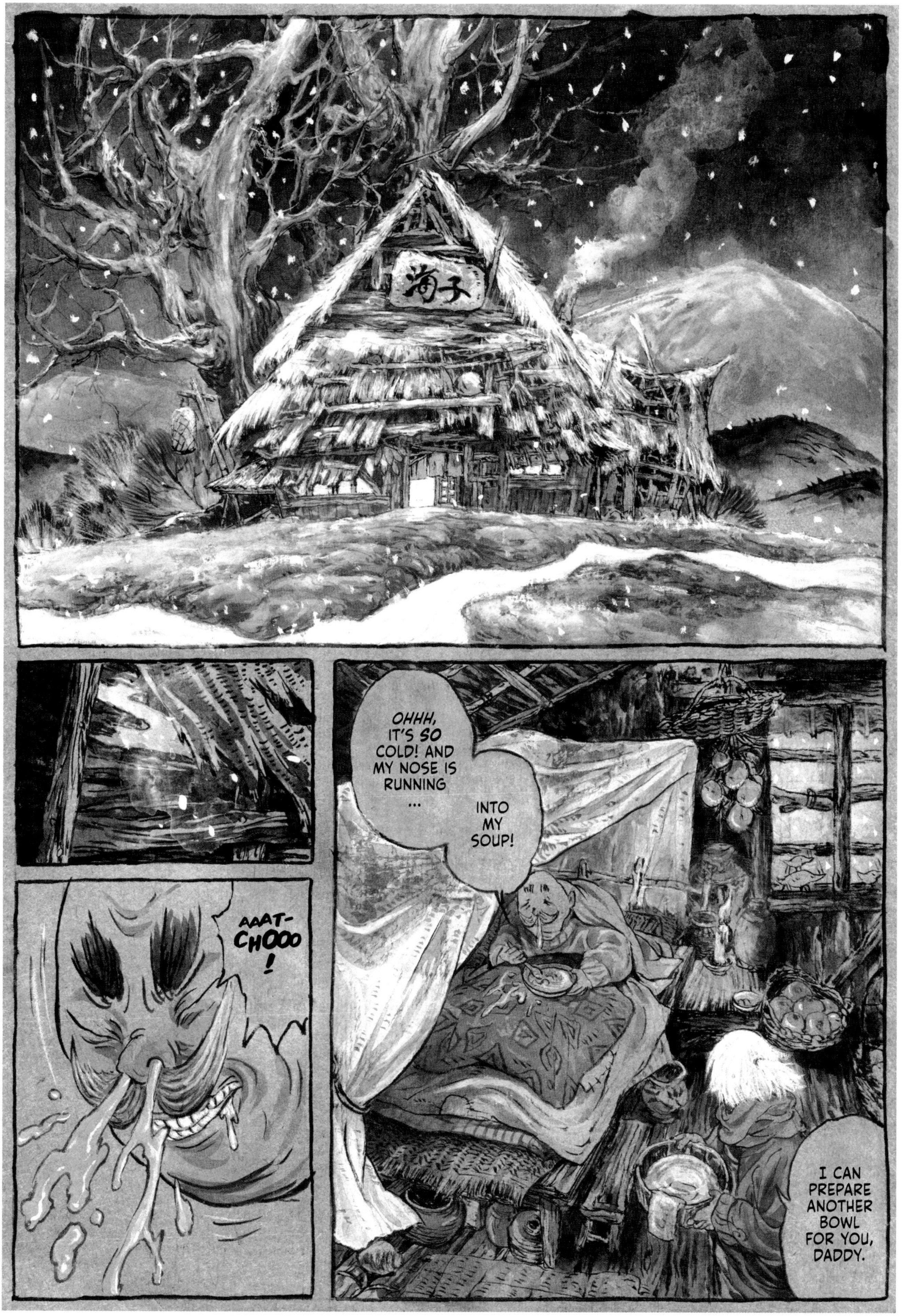
OHHH, IT'S SO COLD! AND MY NOSE IS RUNNING ...
INTO MY SOUP!
AAAT-CHOOO!
I CAN PREPARE ANOTHER BOWL FOR YOU, DADDY.

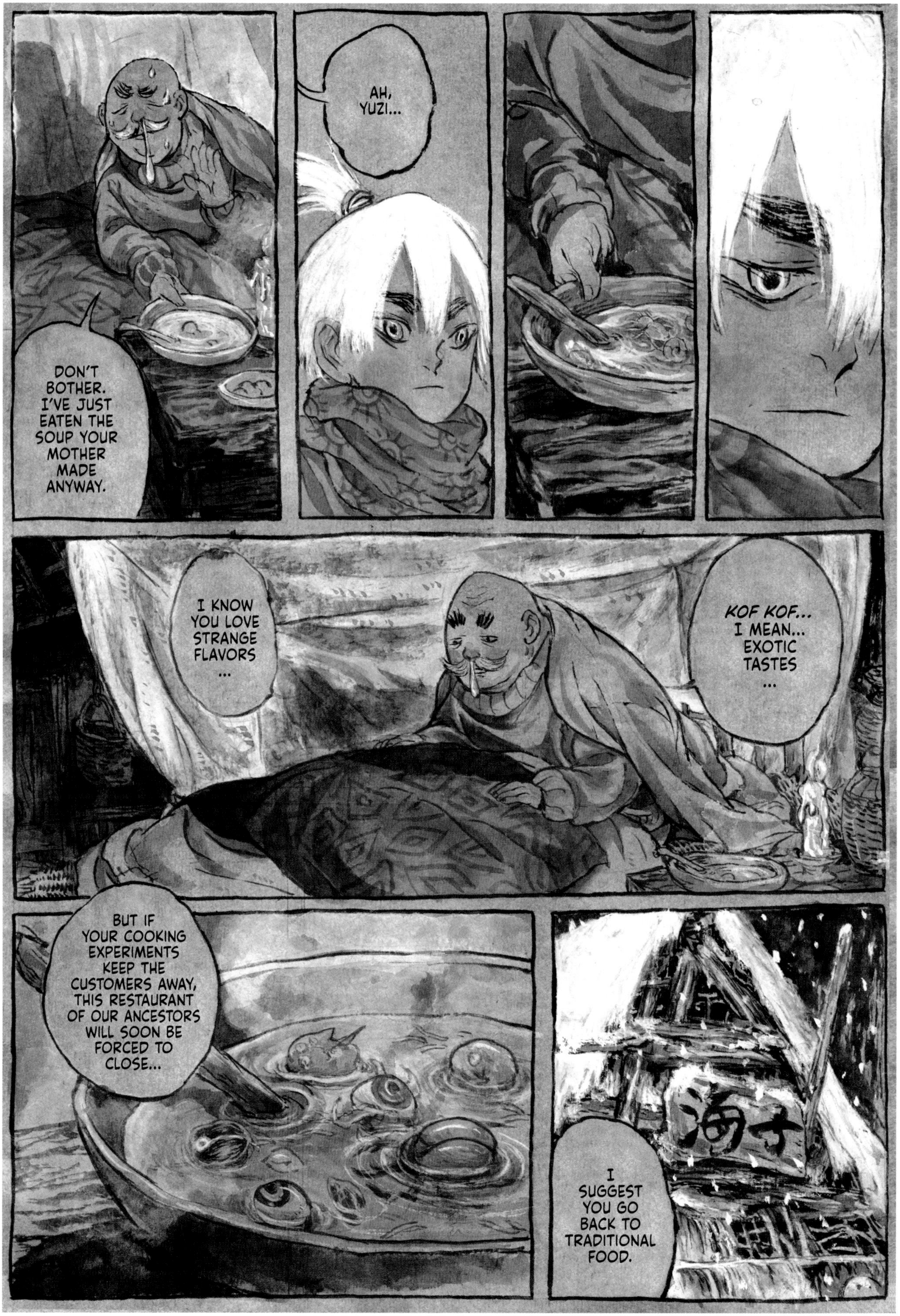
DON'T BOTHER. I'VE JUST EATEN THE SOUP YOUR MOTHER MADE ANYWAY.
AH, YUZI...
I KNOW YOU LOVE STRANGE FLAVORS ...
KOF KOF... I MEAN... EXOTIC TASTES ...
BUT IF YOUR COOKING EXPERIMENTS KEEP THE CUSTOMERS AWAY, THIS RESTAURANT OF OUR ANCESTORS WILL SOON BE FORCED TO CLOSE...
I SUGGEST YOU GO BACK TO TRADITIONAL FOOD.

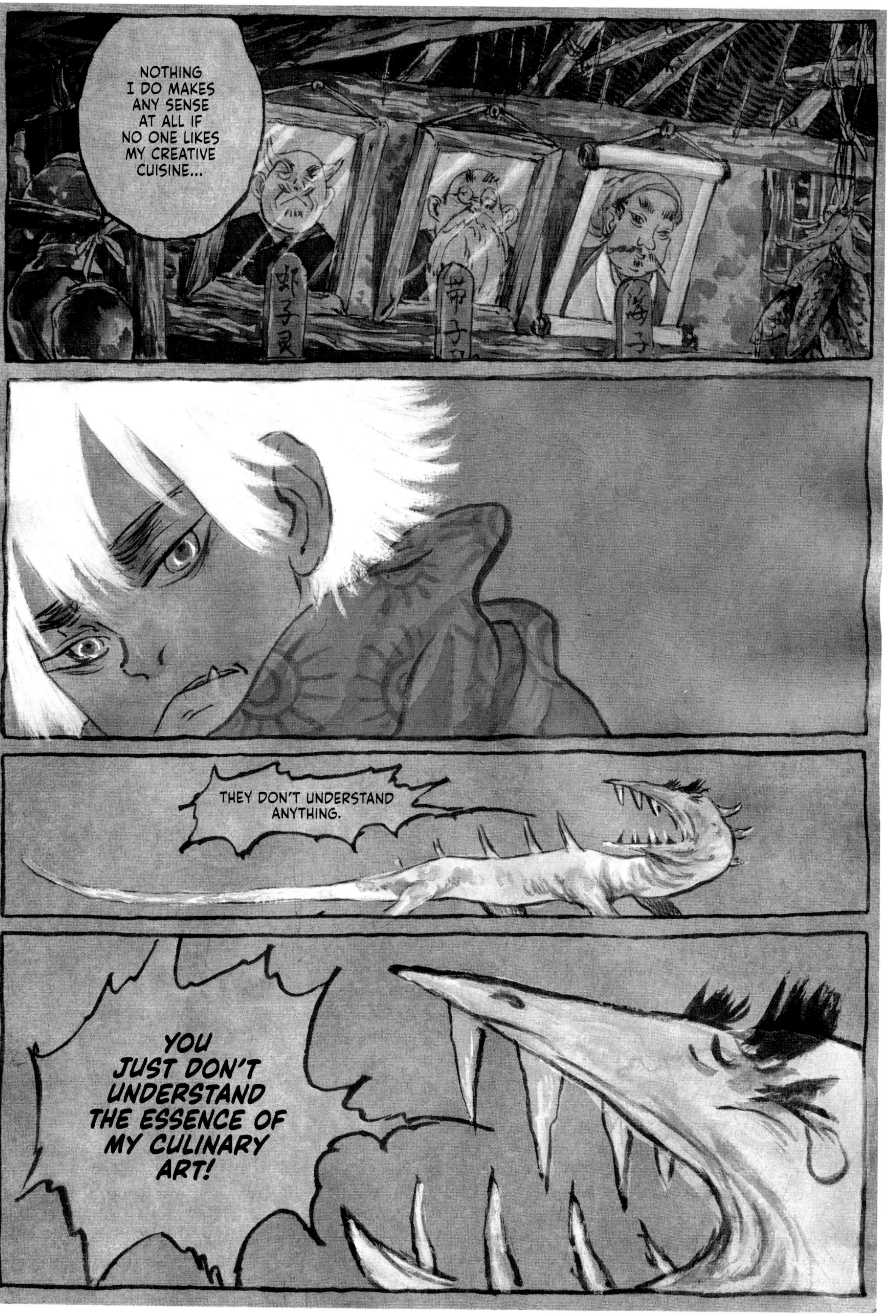
NOTHING I DO MAKES ANY SENSE AT ALL IF NO ONE LIKES MY CREATIVE CUISINE...
THEY DON'T UNDERSTAND ANYTHING.
YOU JUST DON'T UNDERSTAND THE ESSENCE OF MY CULINARY ART!

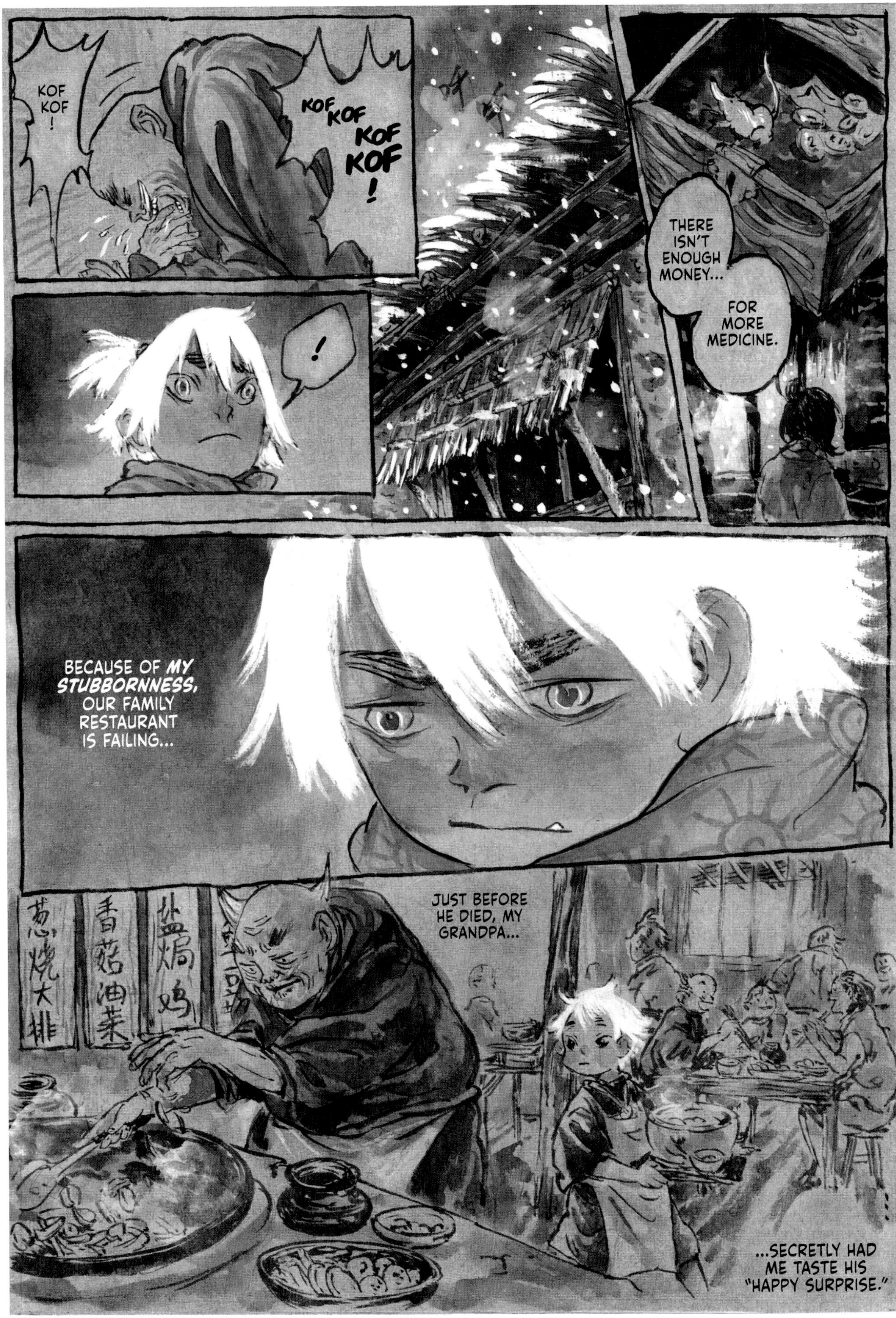
KOF KOF !
KOF KOF KOF KOF !
!
THERE ISN'T ENOUGH MONEY...
FOR MORE MEDICINE.
BECAUSE OF MY STUBBORNNESS, OUR FAMILY RESTAURANT IS FAILING...
葱烧大排
香菇油菜
盐焗鸡
JUST BEFORE HE DIED, MY GRANDPA...
...SECRETLY HAD ME TASTE HIS "HAPPY SURPRISE."

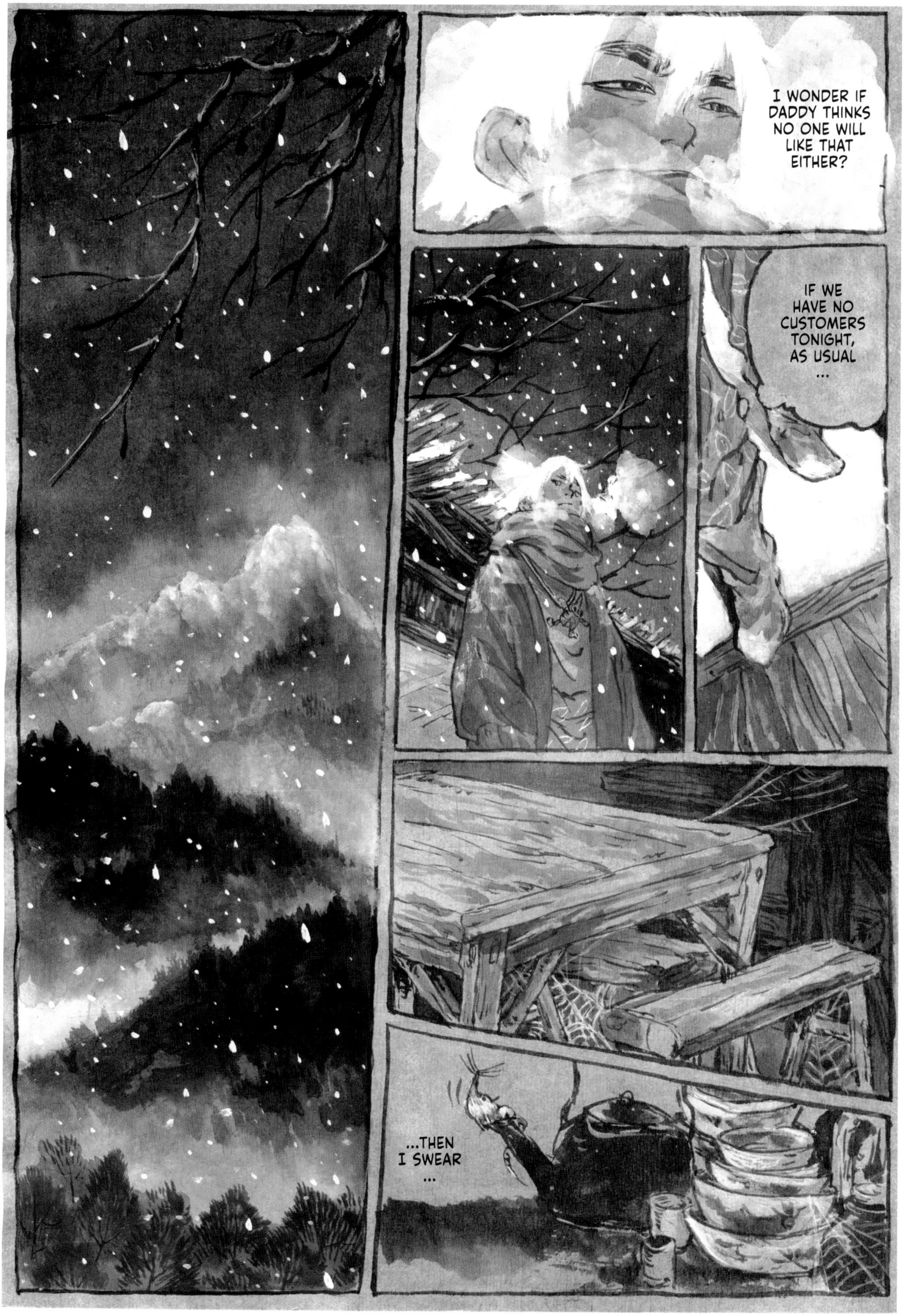
I WONDER IF DADDY THINKS NO ONE WILL LIKE THAT EITHER?
IF WE HAVE NO CUSTOMERS TONIGHT, AS USUAL ...
...THEN I SWEAR ...

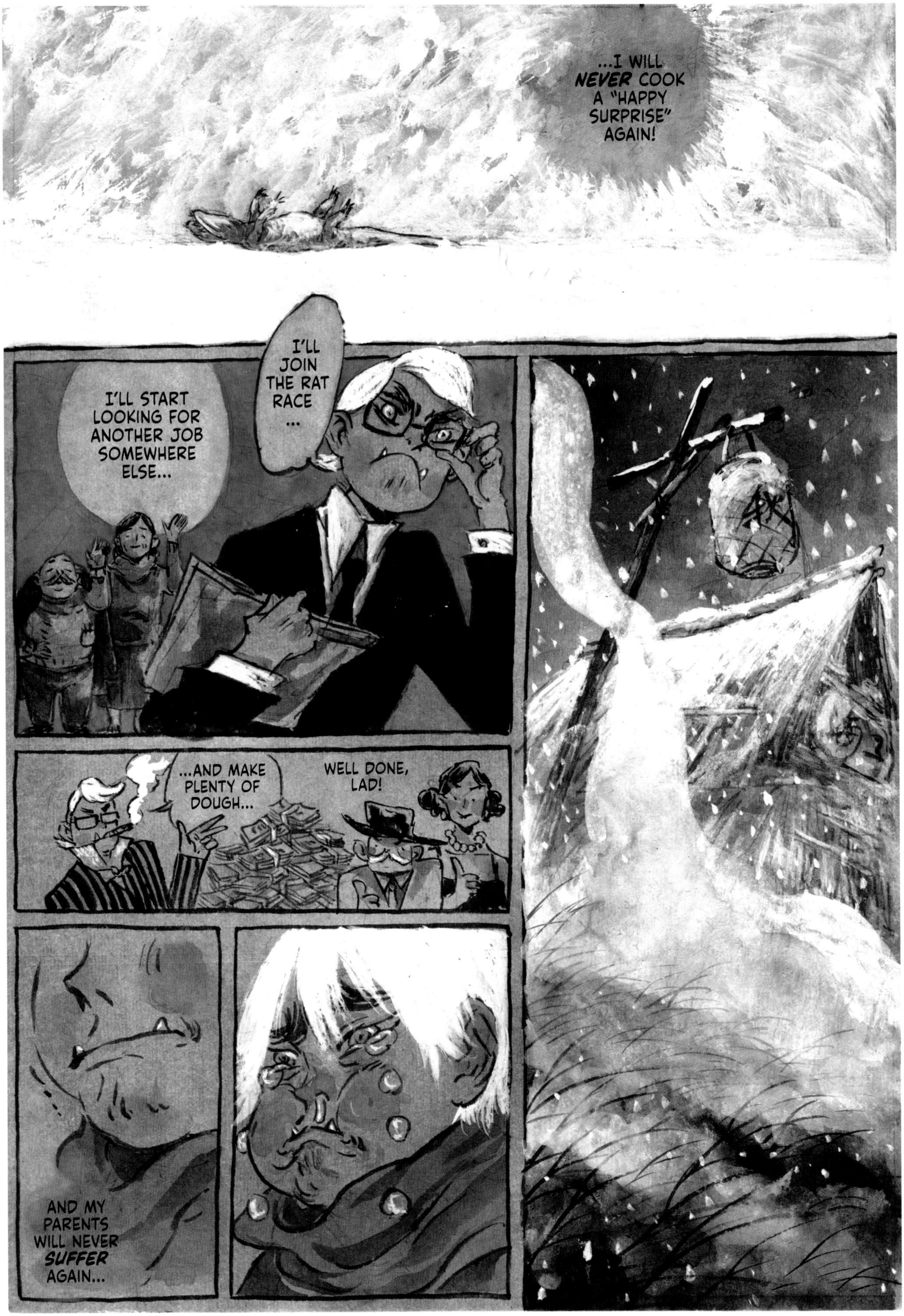
...I WILL NEVER COOK A "HAPPY SURPRISE" AGAIN!
I'LL START LOOKING FOR ANOTHER JOB SOMEWHERE ELSE...
I'LL JOIN THE RAT RACE ...
...AND MAKE PLENTY OF DOUGH...
WELL DONE, LAD!
AND MY PARENTS WILL NEVER SUFFER AGAIN...

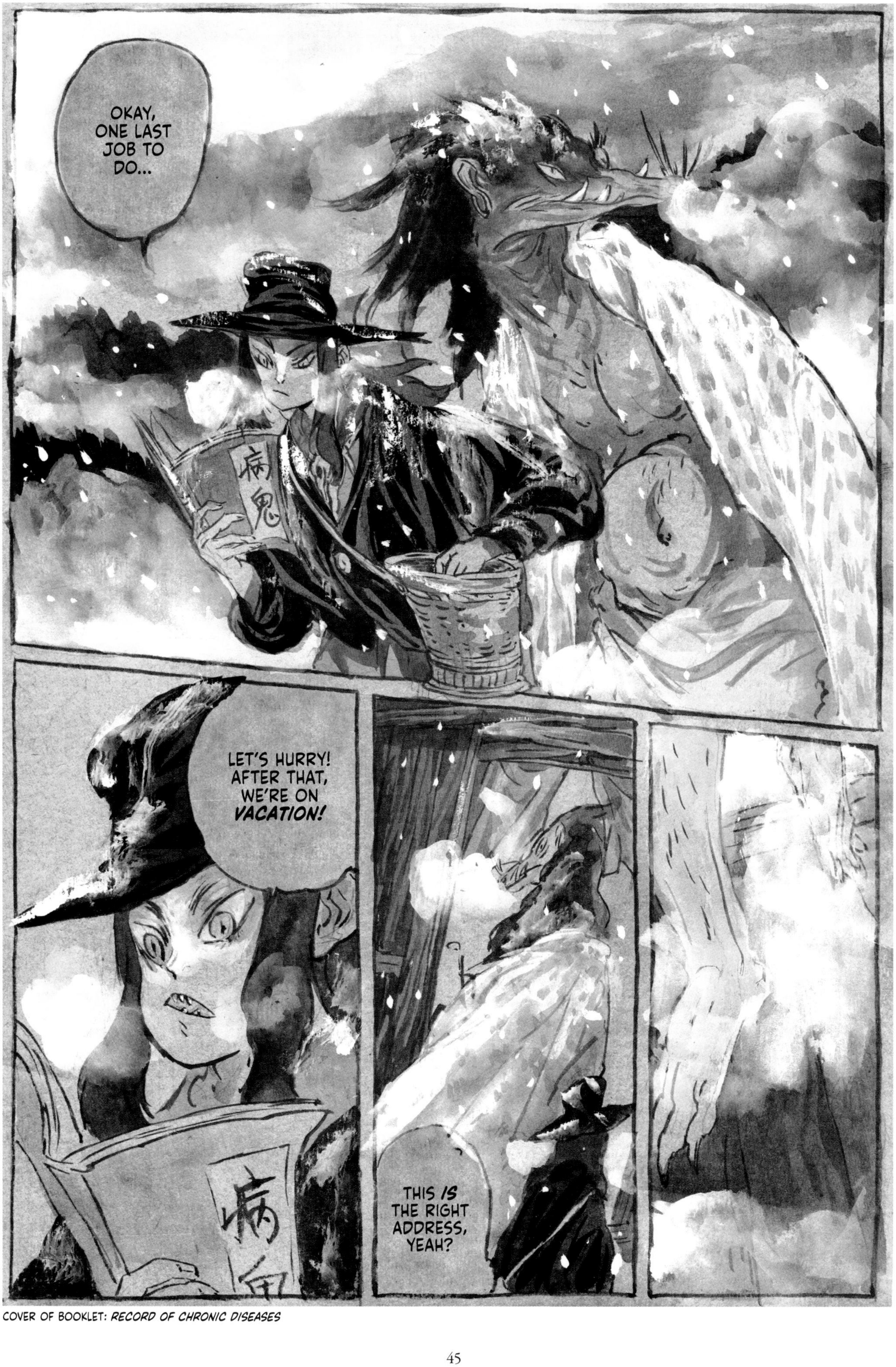
OKAY, ONE LAST JOB TO DO...
病鬼
LET'S HURRY! AFTER THAT, WE'RE ON *VACATION!*
THIS *IS* THE RIGHT ADDRESS, YEAH?

COVER OF BOOKLET: *RECORD OF CHRONIC DISEASES*

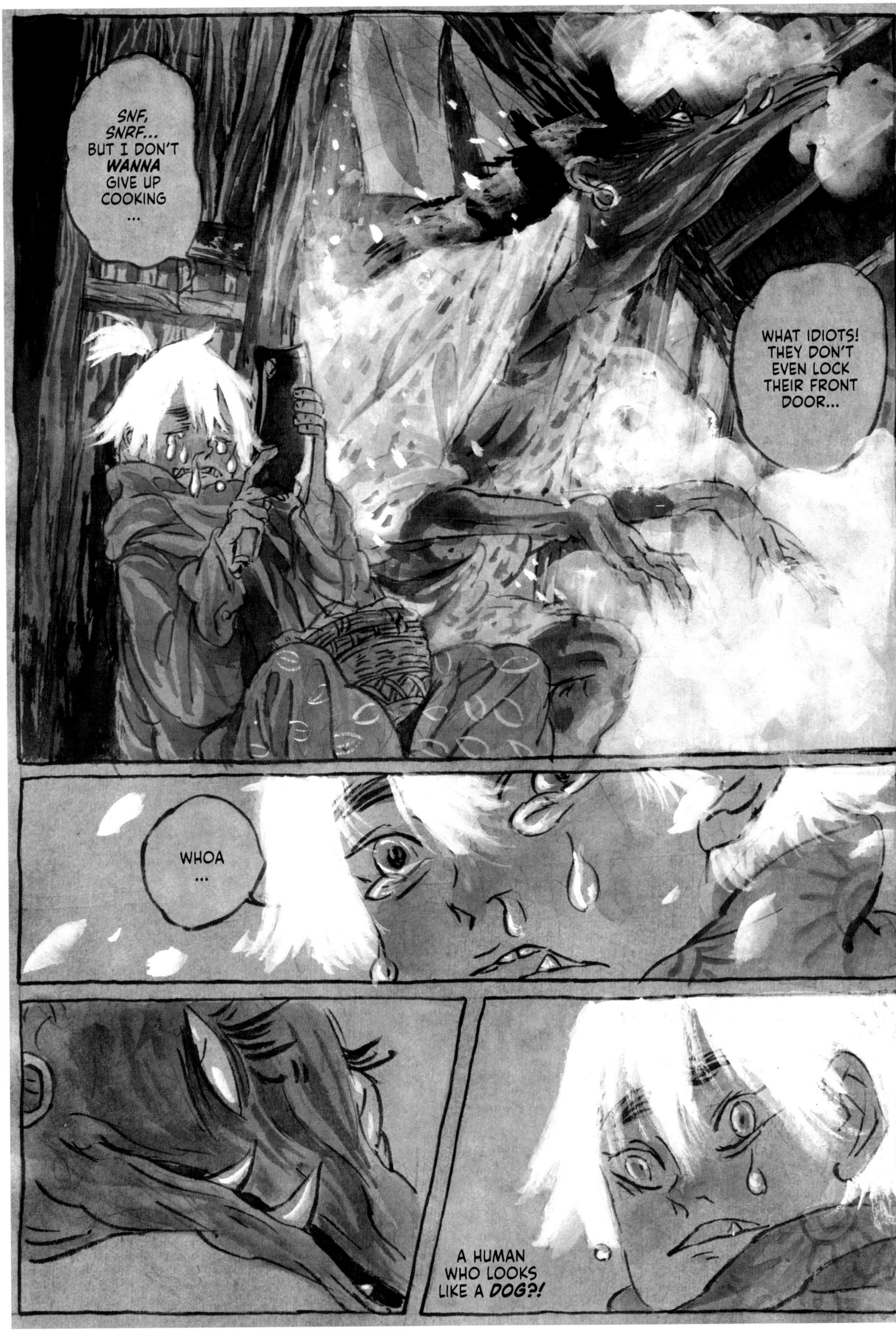
SNF, SNRF... BUT I DON'T WANNA GIVE UP COOKING ...
WHAT IDIOTS! THEY DON'T EVEN LOCK THEIR FRONT DOOR...
WHOA ...
A HUMAN WHO LOOKS LIKE A DOG?!

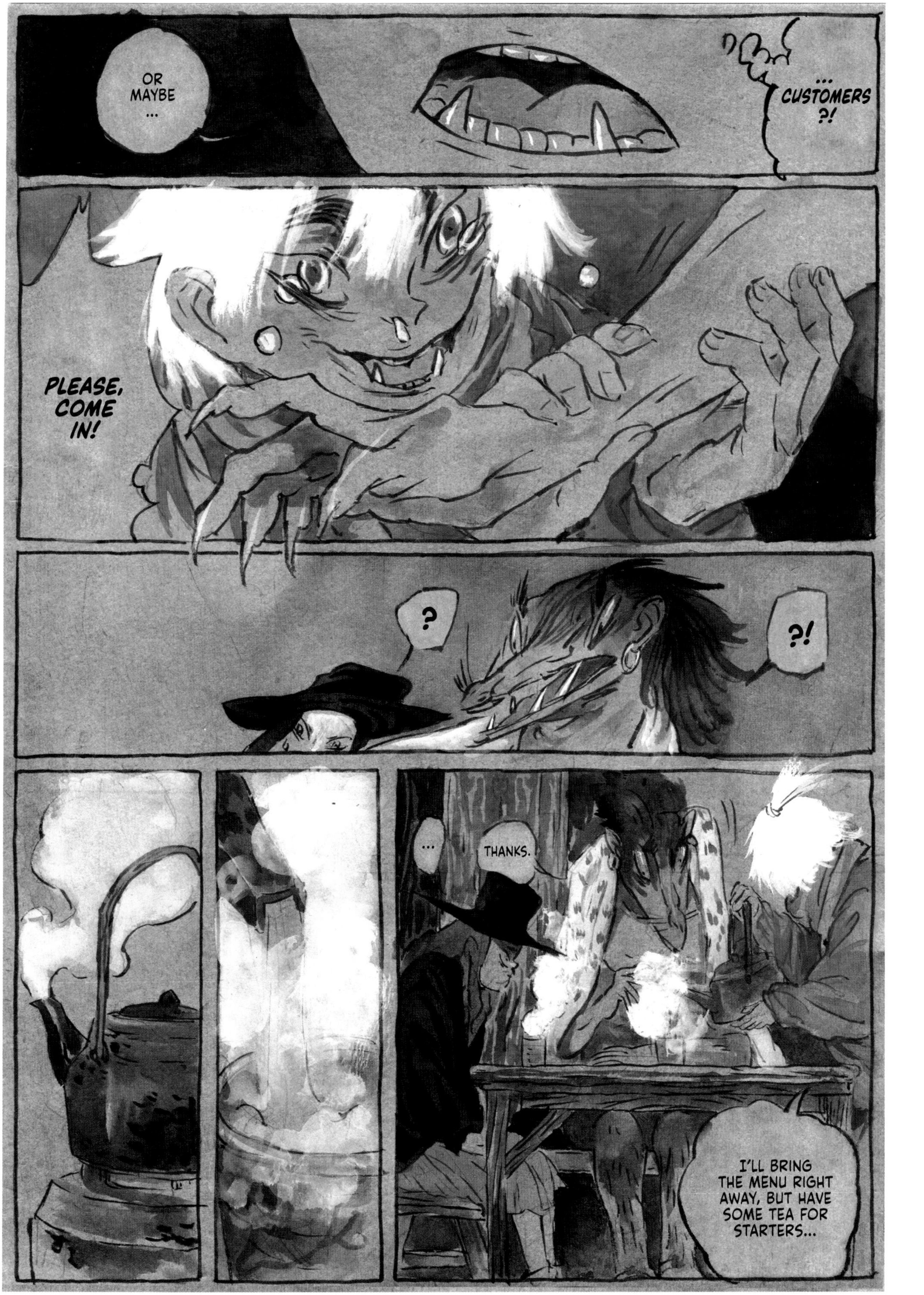

OR MAYBE ...
... CUSTOMERS ?!
PLEASE, COME IN!
?
?!
...
THANKS.
I'LL BRING THE MENU RIGHT AWAY, BUT HAVE SOME TEA FOR STARTERS...

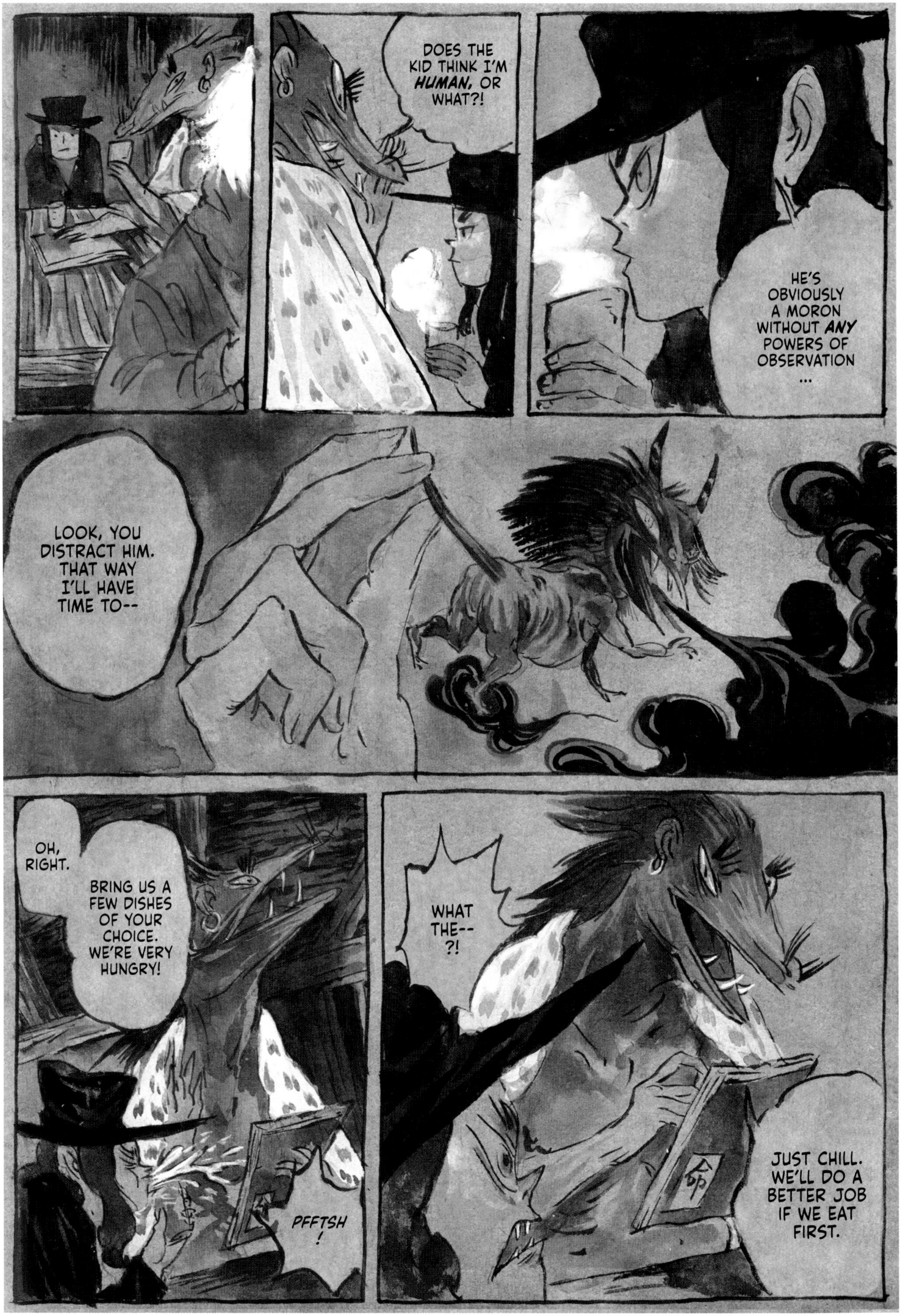

DOES THE KID THINK I'M *HUMAN,* OR WHAT?!
HE'S OBVIOUSLY A MORON WITHOUT *ANY* POWERS OF OBSERVATION ...
LOOK, YOU DISTRACT HIM. THAT WAY I'LL HAVE TIME TO--
OH, RIGHT.
BRING US A FEW DISHES OF YOUR CHOICE. WE'RE VERY HUNGRY!
PFFTSH!
WHAT THE--?!
JUST CHILL. WE'LL DO A BETTER JOB IF WE EAT FIRST.

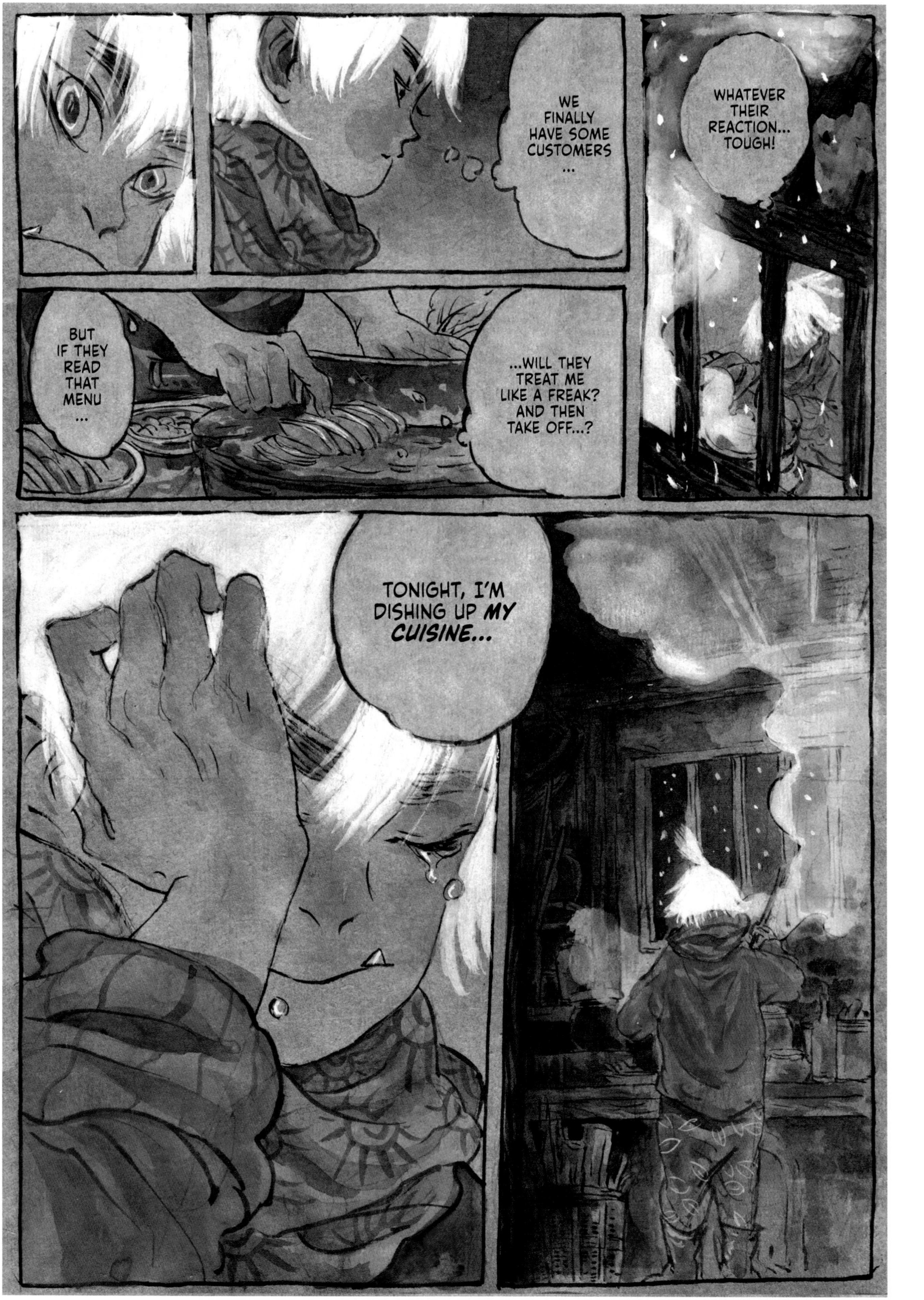
WE FINALLY HAVE SOME CUSTOMERS ...
WHATEVER THEIR REACTION... TOUGH!
BUT IF THEY READ THAT MENU ...
...WILL THEY TREAT ME LIKE A FREAK? AND THEN TAKE OFF...?
TONIGHT, I'M DISHING UP ***MY CUISINE...***

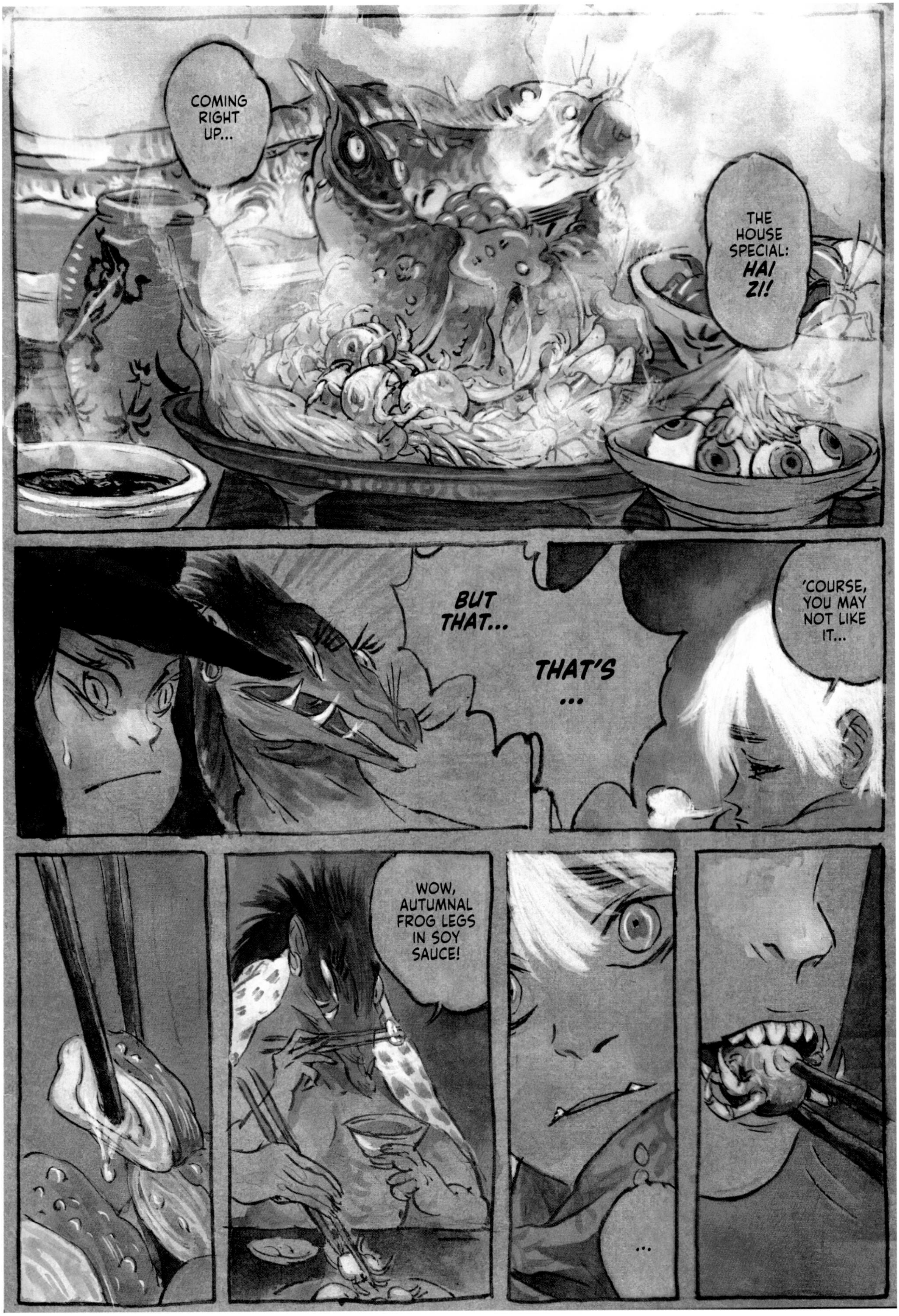
COMING RIGHT UP...
THE HOUSE SPECIAL: HAI ZI!
'COURSE, YOU MAY NOT LIKE IT...
BUT THAT...
THAT'S ...
WOW, AUTUMNAL FROG LEGS IN SOY SAUCE!
...

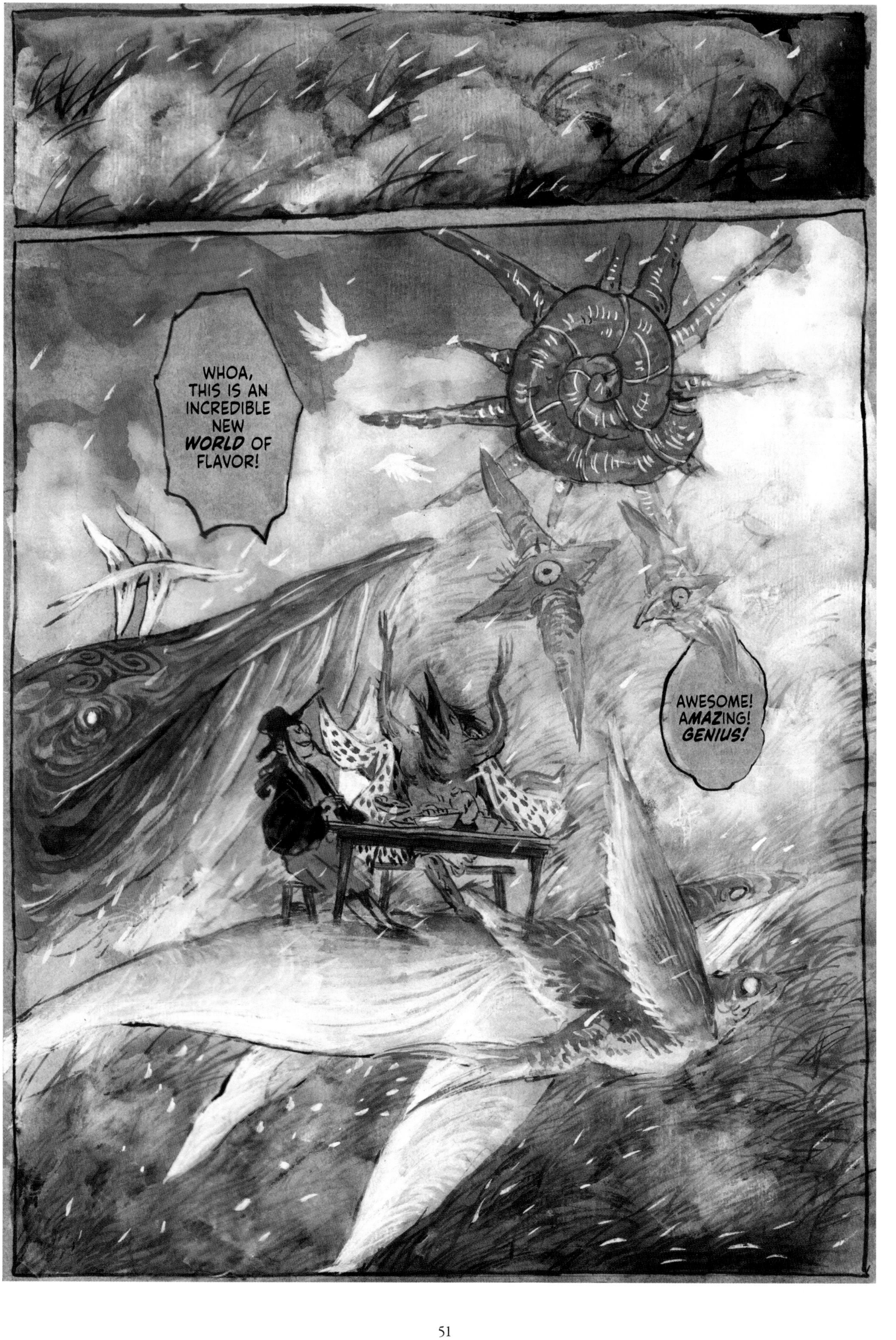
WHOA, THIS IS AN INCREDIBLE NEW WORLD OF FLAVOR!
AWESOME! AMAZING! GENIUS!

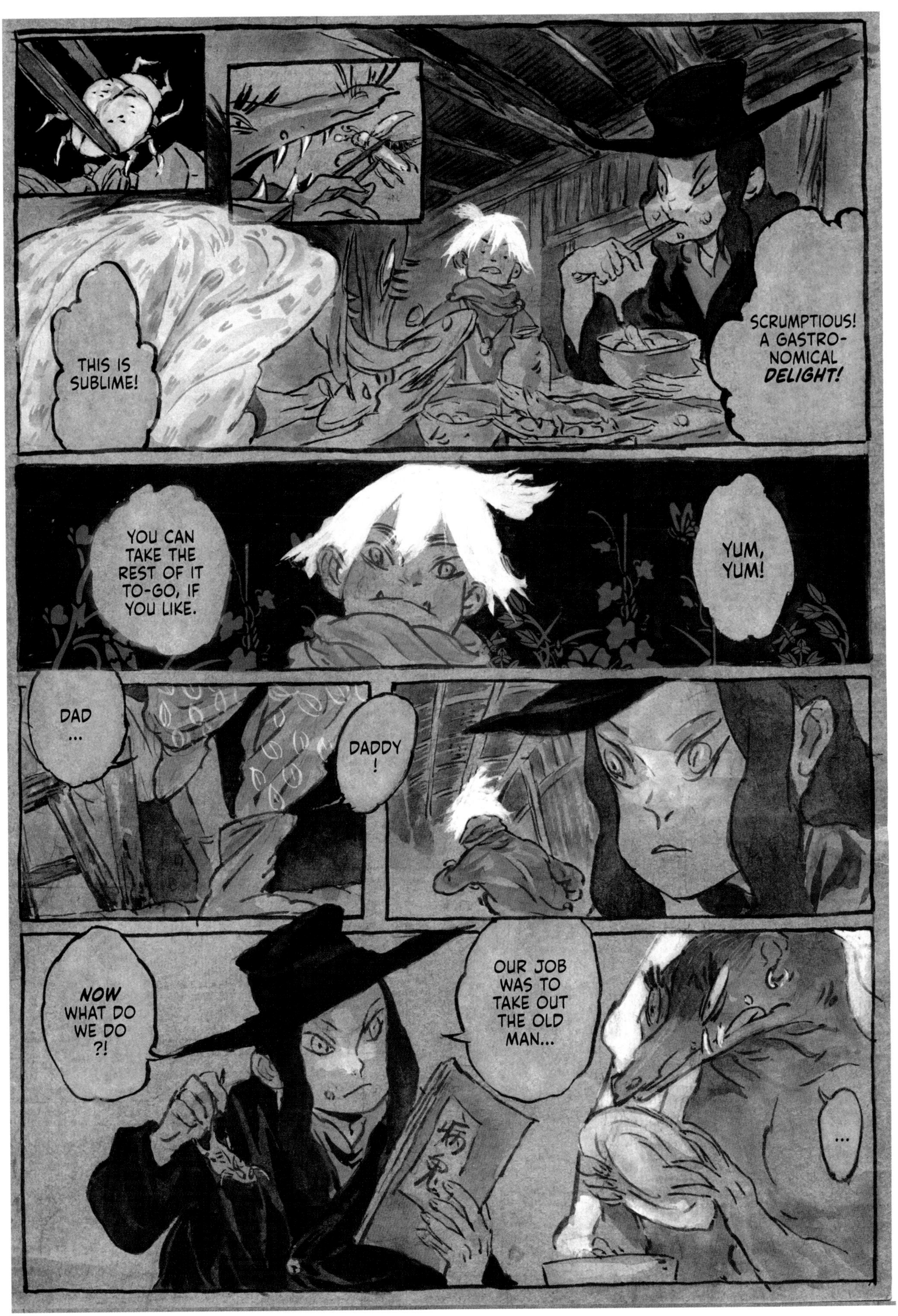
THIS IS SUBLIME!
SCRUMPTIOUS! A GASTRONOMICAL DELIGHT!
YOU CAN TAKE THE REST OF IT TO-GO, IF YOU LIKE.
YUM, YUM!
DAD ...
DADDY !
NOW WHAT DO WE DO ?!
OUR JOB WAS TO TAKE OUT THE OLD MAN...
...

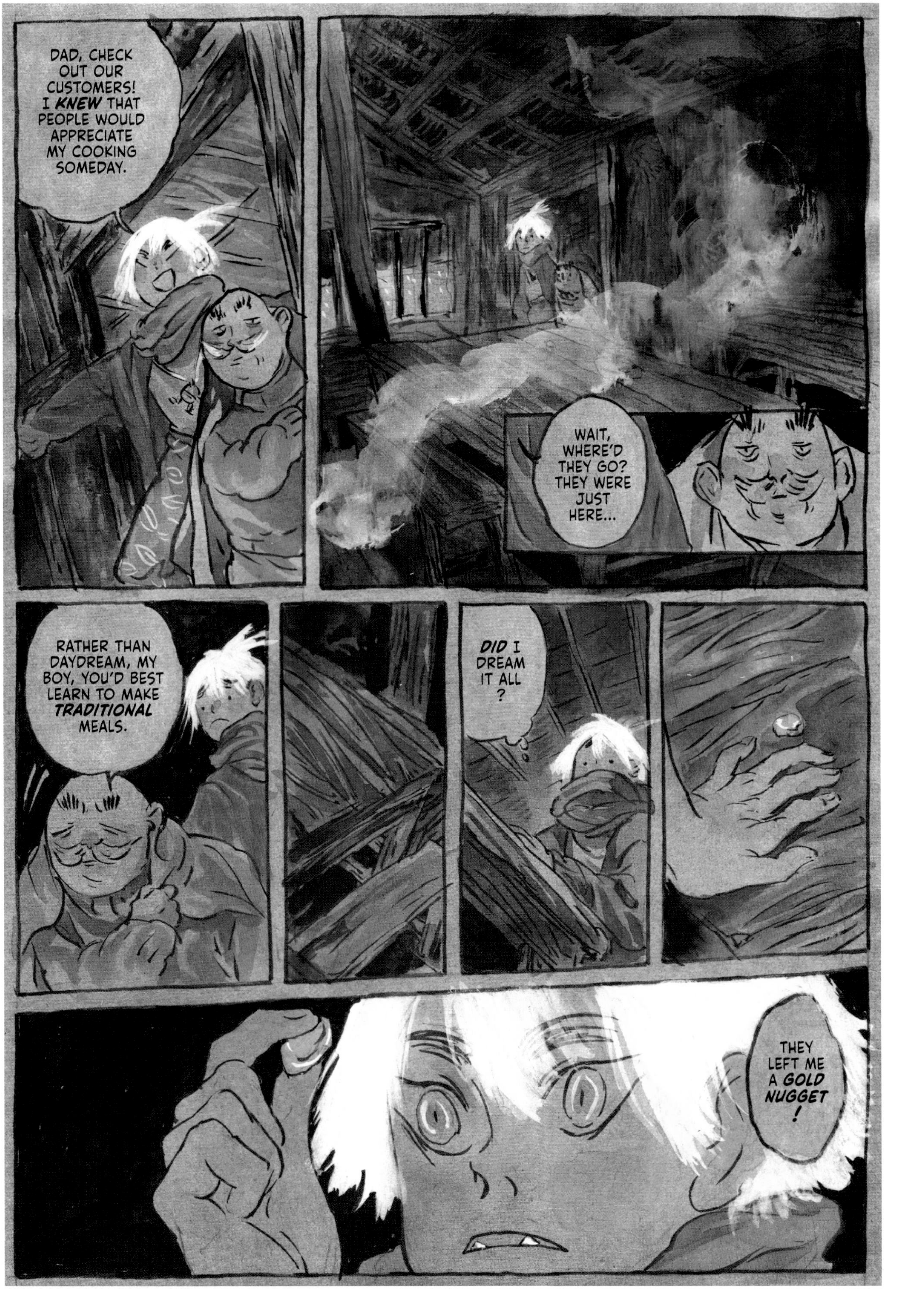
DAD, CHECK OUT OUR CUSTOMERS! I KNEW THAT PEOPLE WOULD APPRECIATE MY COOKING SOMEDAY.
WAIT, WHERE'D THEY GO? THEY WERE JUST HERE...
RATHER THAN DAYDREAM, MY BOY, YOU'D BEST LEARN TO MAKE TRADITIONAL MEALS.
DID I DREAM IT ALL ?
THEY LEFT ME A GOLD NUGGET !

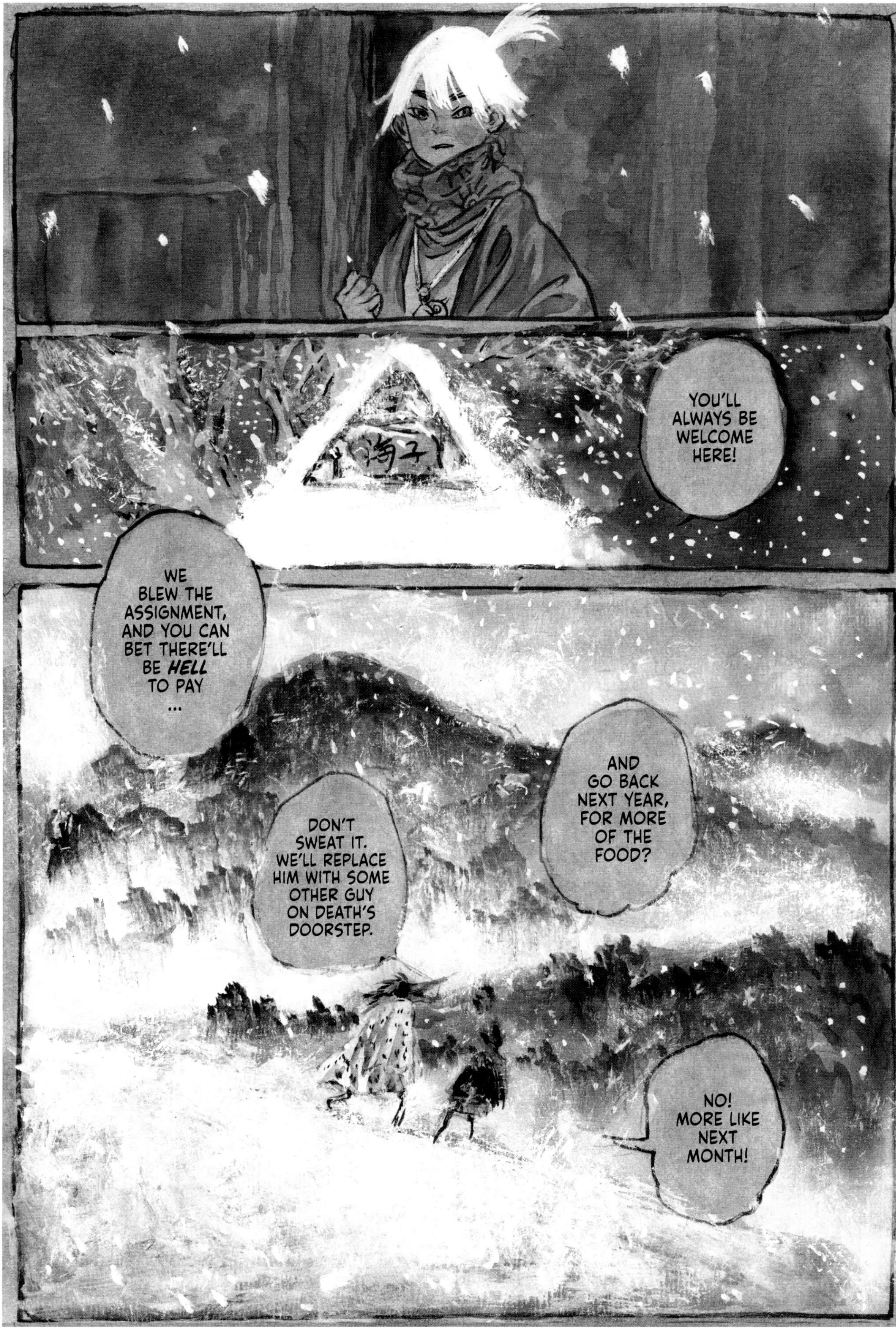

海子
YOU'LL ALWAYS BE WELCOME HERE!
WE BLEW THE ASSIGNMENT, AND YOU CAN BET THERE'LL BE **HELL** TO PAY ...
AND GO BACK NEXT YEAR, FOR MORE OF THE FOOD?
DON'T SWEAT IT. WE'LL REPLACE HIM WITH SOME OTHER GUY ON DEATH'S DOORSTEP.
NO! MORE LIKE NEXT MONTH!

UNTITLED

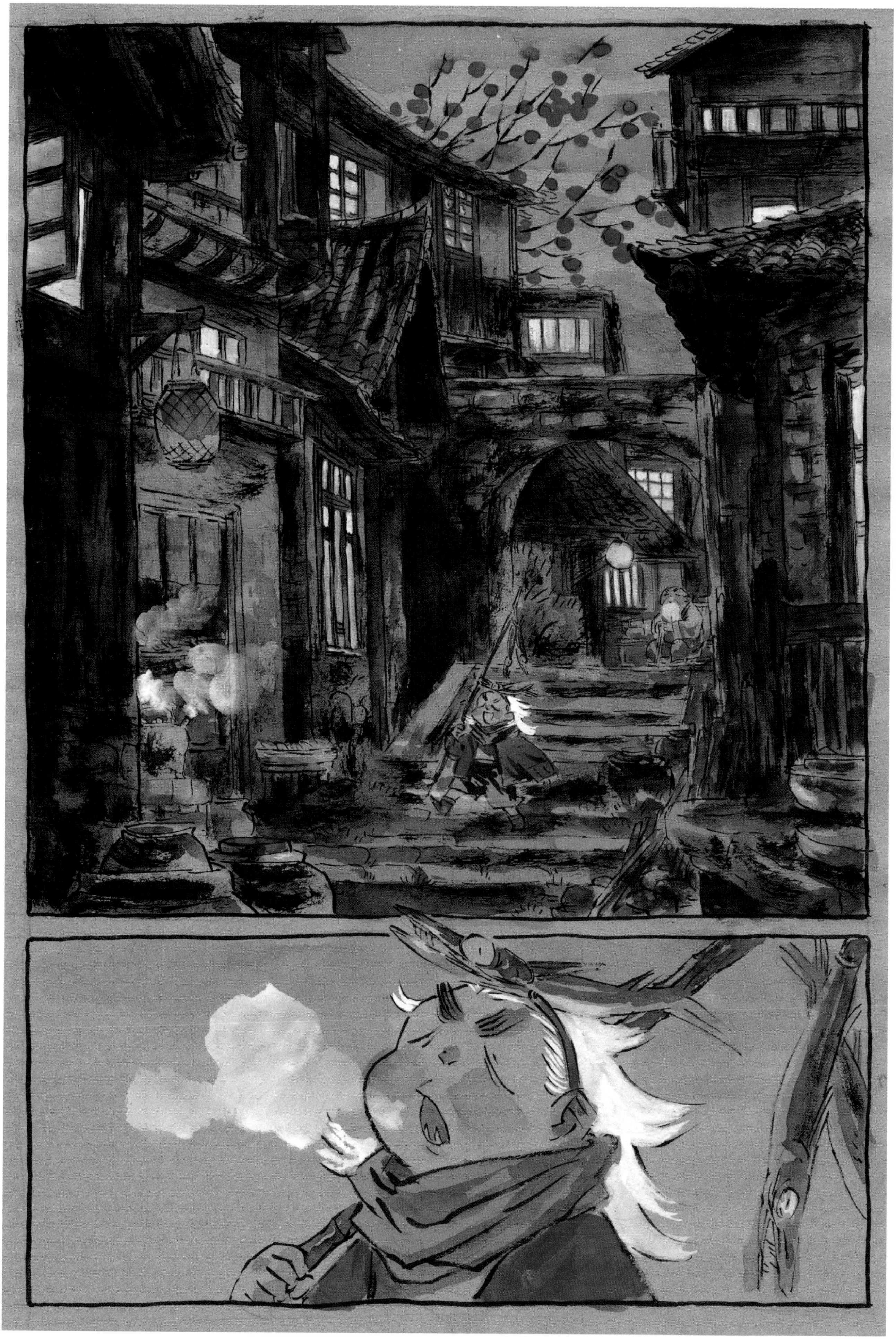

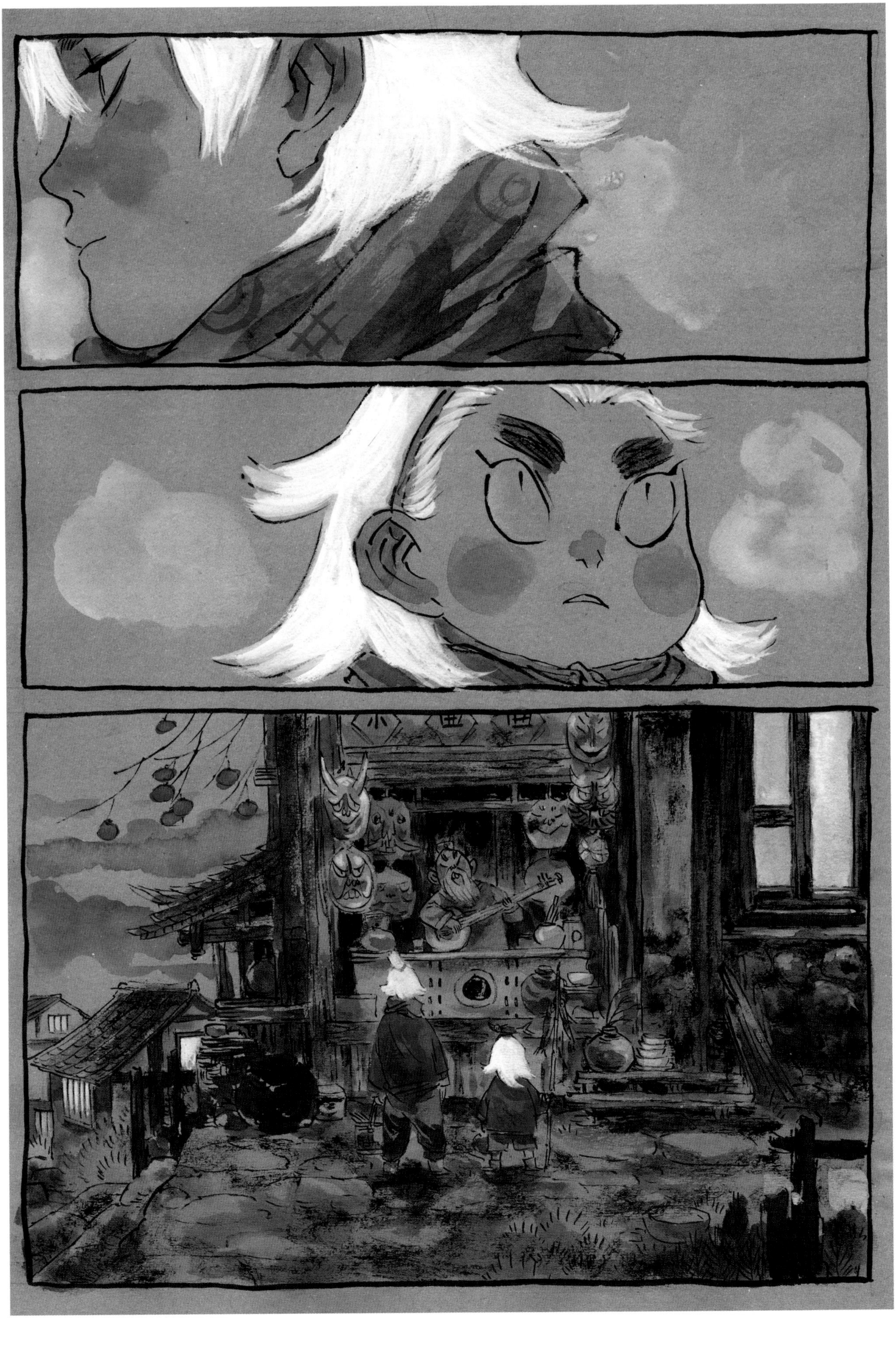

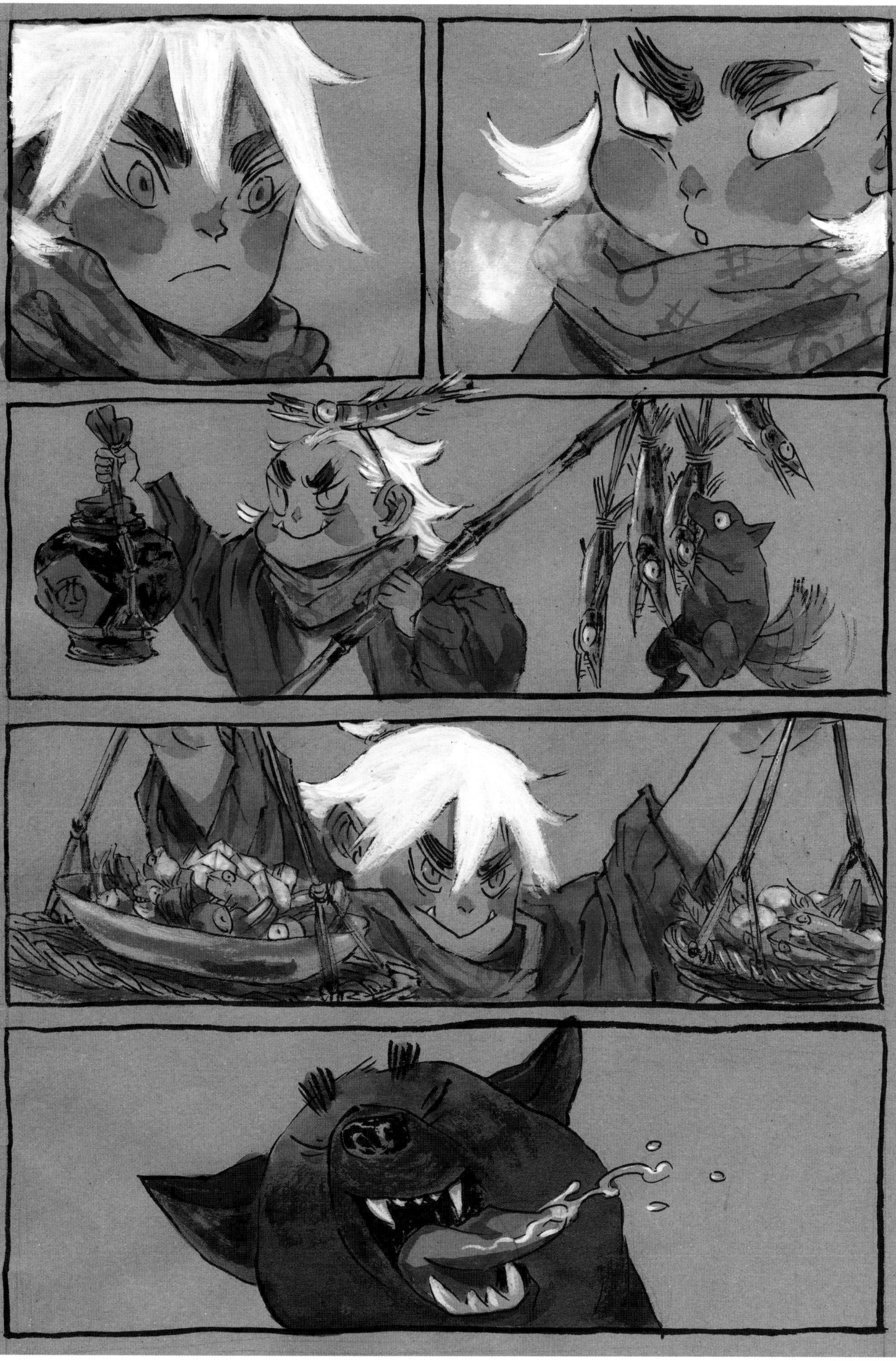

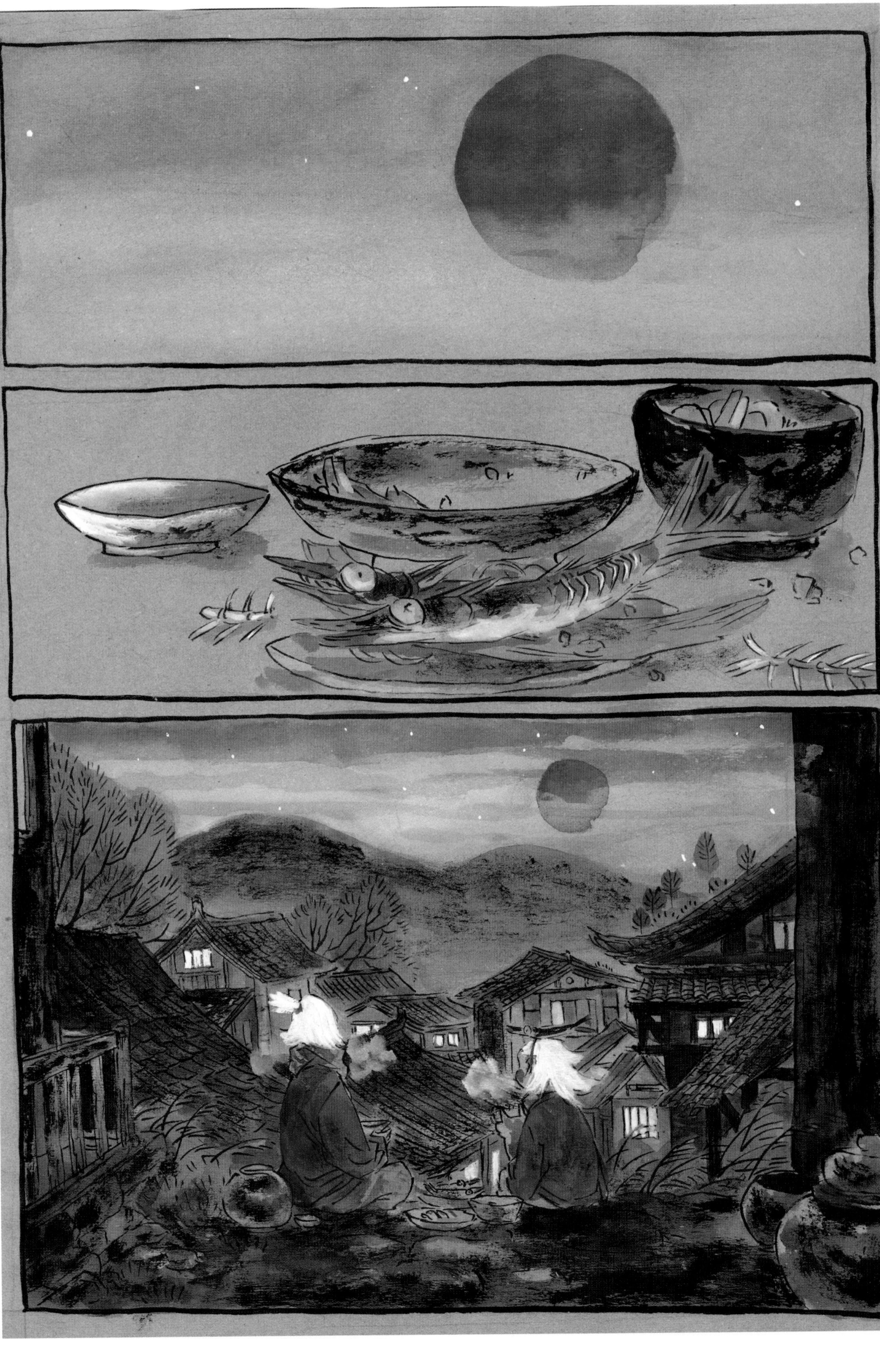

IMMORTAL BREATH

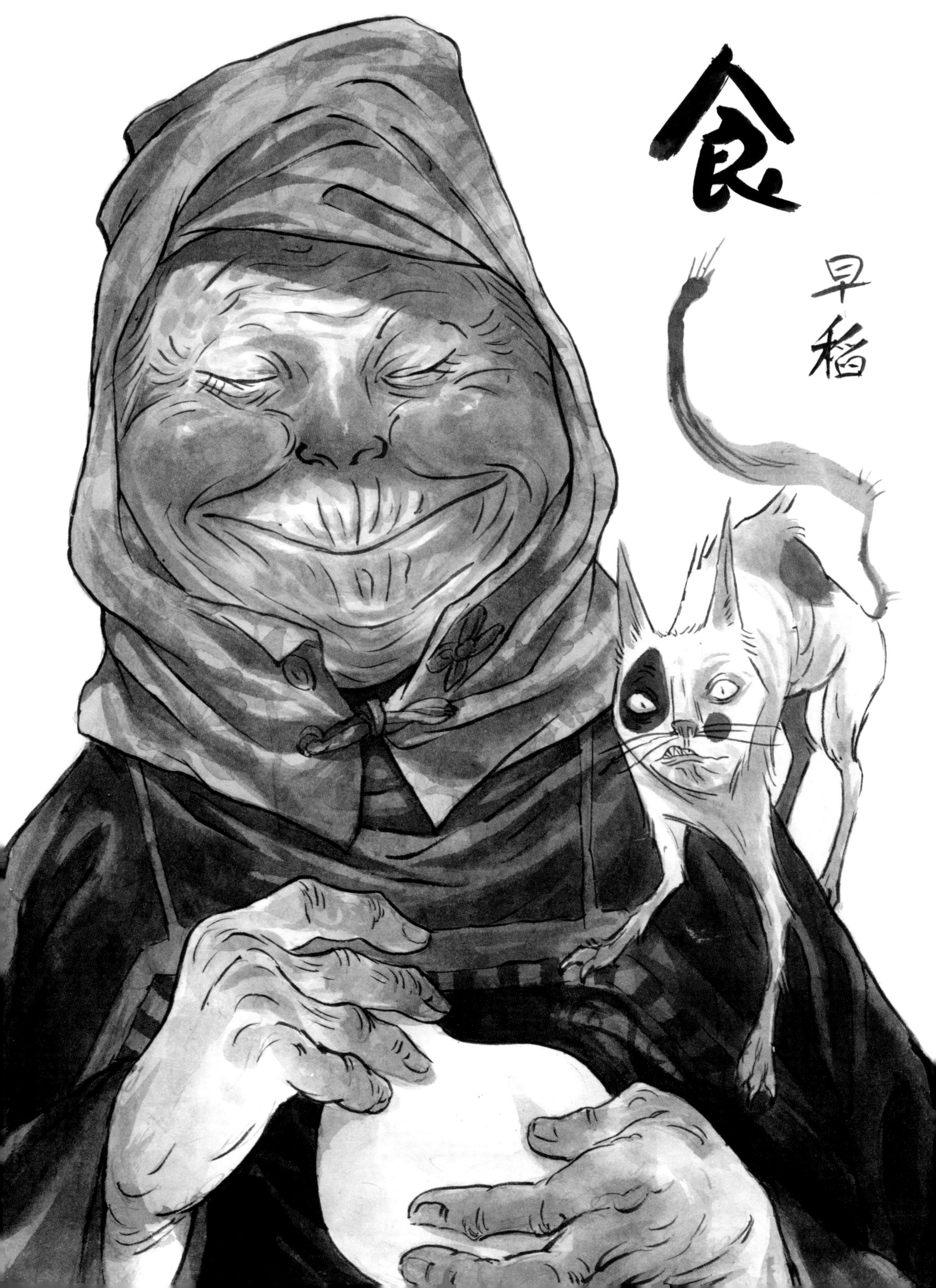
食
早稲

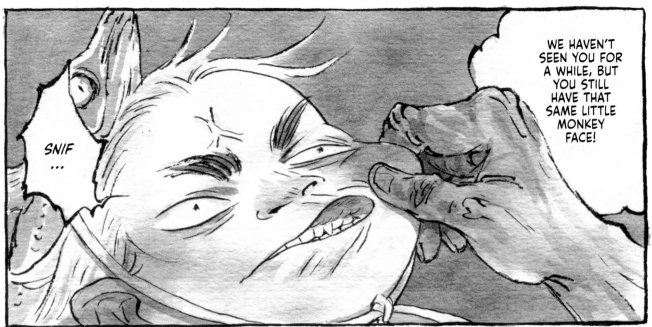

SNIF ...

WE HAVEN'T SEEN YOU FOR A WHILE, BUT YOU STILL HAVE THAT SAME LITTLE MONKEY FACE!

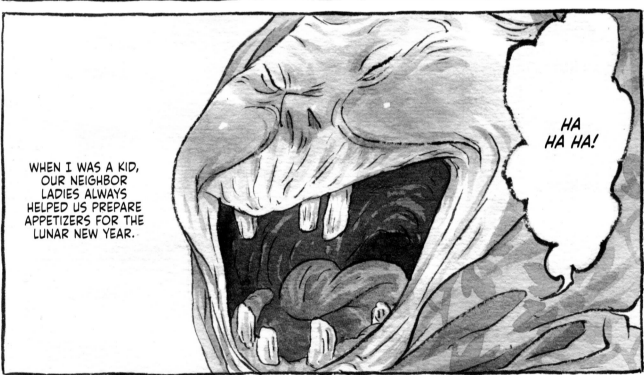

WHEN I WAS A KID, OUR NEIGHBOR LADIES ALWAYS HELPED US PREPARE APPETIZERS FOR THE LUNAR NEW YEAR.

HA HA HA!

STOP! OR I'LL *KILL* YOU, MADAM SIX!*

...THOSE OLD WOMEN USED TO PINCH ME ALL THE TIME, AND IT REALLY HURT!

BECAUSE I WAS A REAL BRAT...

* TRADITIONALLY, NAMES IN ANCIENT CHINA WERE DERIVED FROM SIBLING RANK.

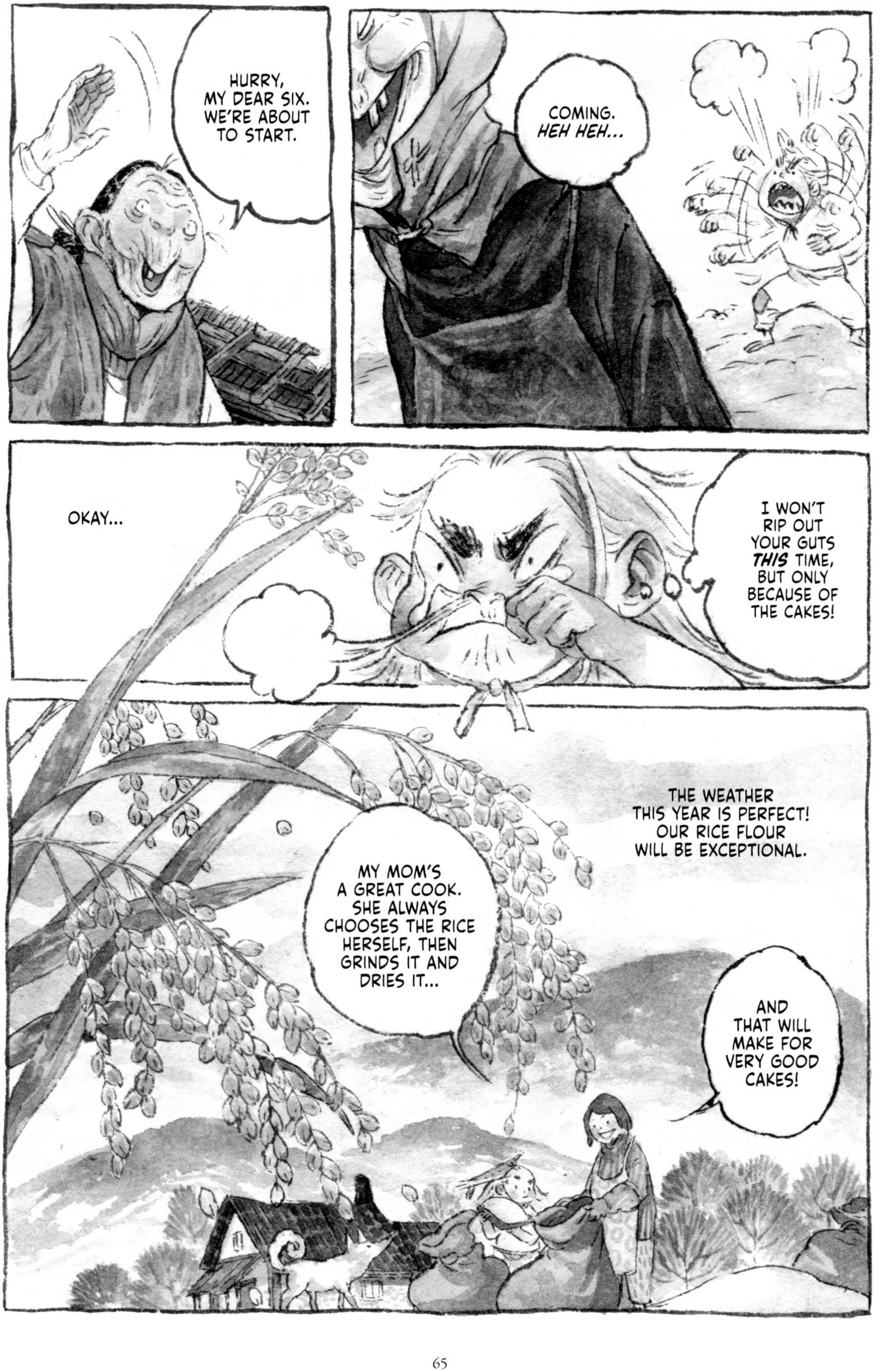
HURRY, MY DEAR SIX. WE'RE ABOUT TO START.
COMING. *HEH HEH...*
OKAY...
I WON'T RIP OUT YOUR GUTS ***THIS*** TIME, BUT ONLY BECAUSE OF THE CAKES!
THE WEATHER THIS YEAR IS PERFECT! OUR RICE FLOUR WILL BE EXCEPTIONAL.
MY MOM'S A GREAT COOK. SHE ALWAYS CHOOSES THE RICE HERSELF, THEN GRINDS IT AND DRIES IT...
AND THAT WILL MAKE FOR VERY GOOD CAKES!

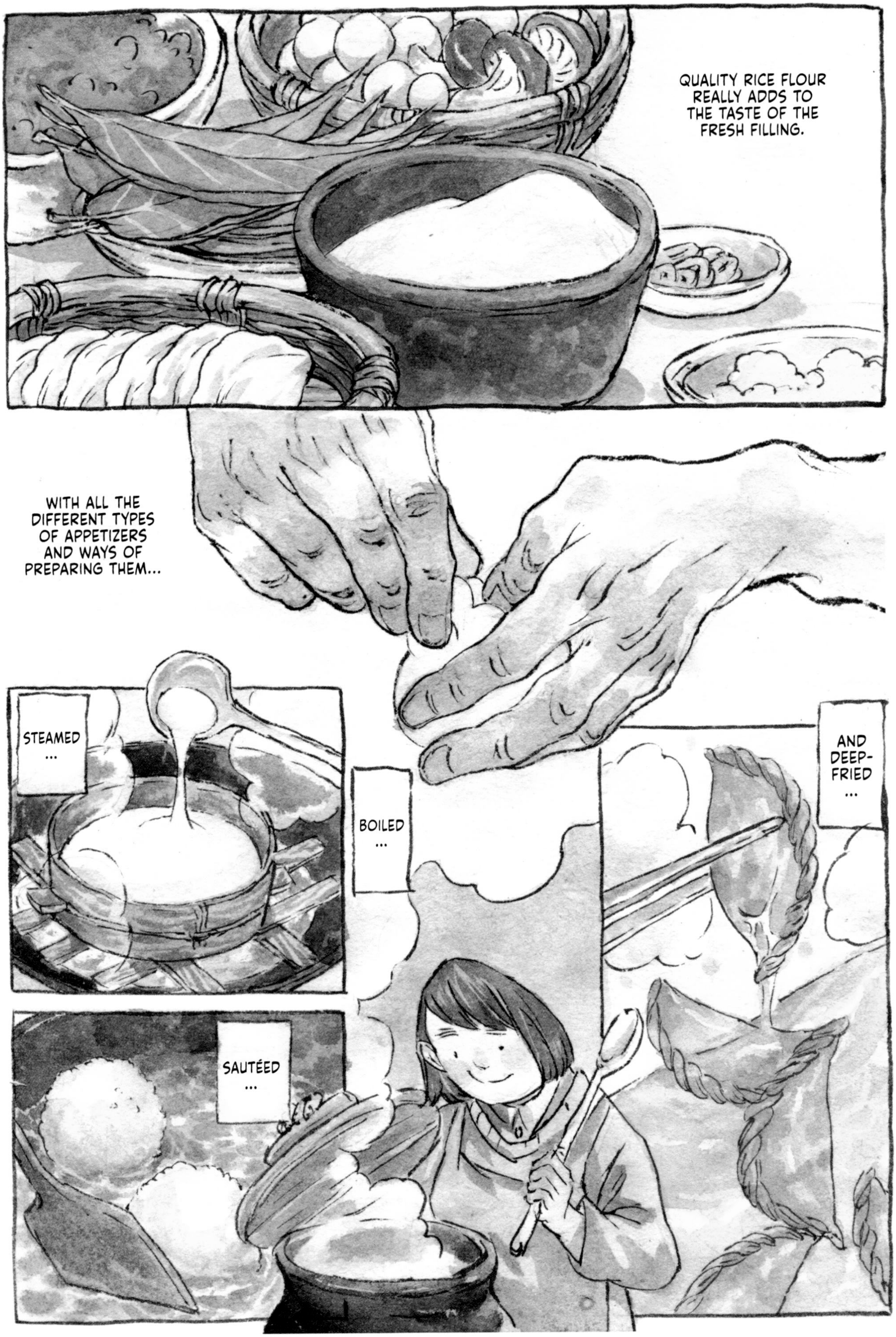
QUALITY RICE FLOUR REALLY ADDS TO THE TASTE OF THE FRESH FILLING.
WITH ALL THE DIFFERENT TYPES OF APPETIZERS AND WAYS OF PREPARING THEM...
STEAMED ...
BOILED ...
AND DEEP-FRIED ...
SAUTÉED ...

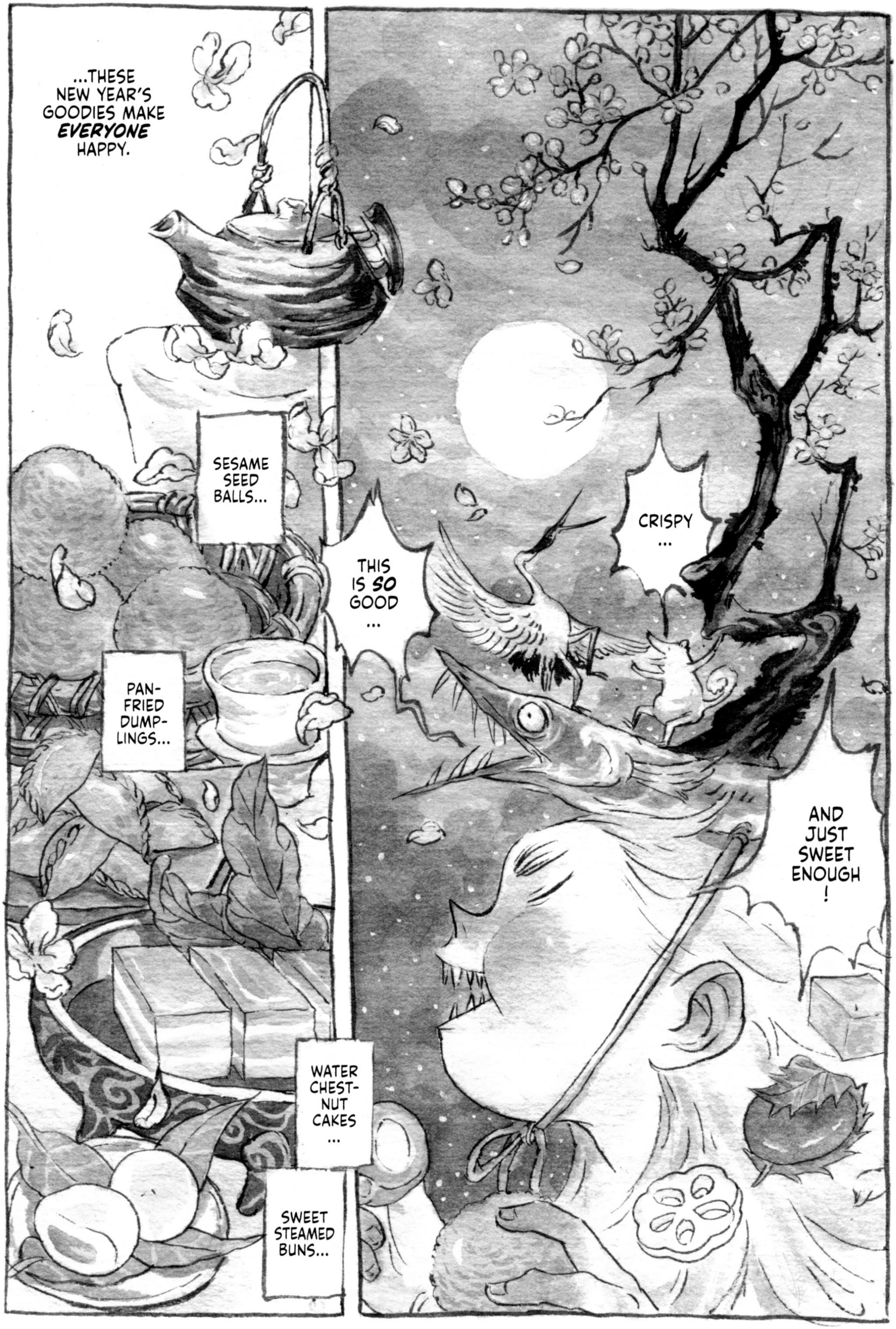
...THESE NEW YEAR'S GOODIES MAKE *EVERYONE* HAPPY.
SESAME SEED BALLS...
PAN-FRIED DUMP-LINGS...
WATER CHEST-NUT CAKES ...
SWEET STEAMED BUNS...
THIS IS *SO* GOOD ...
CRISPY ...
AND JUST SWEET ENOUGH !

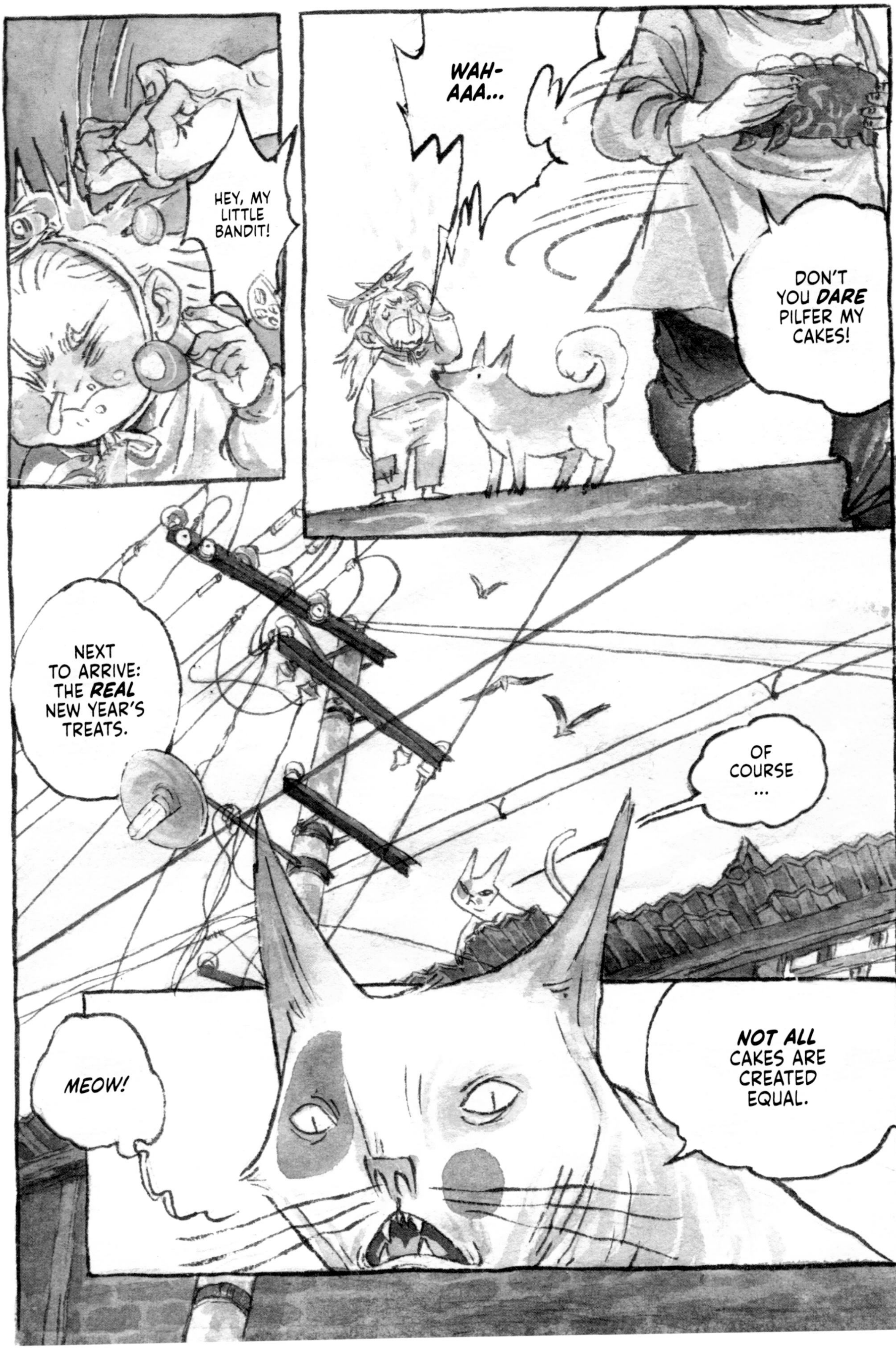
HEY, MY LITTLE BANDIT!
WAH-AAA...
DON'T YOU DARE PILFER MY CAKES!
NEXT TO ARRIVE: THE REAL NEW YEAR'S TREATS.
OF COURSE ...
MEOW!
NOT ALL CAKES ARE CREATED EQUAL.

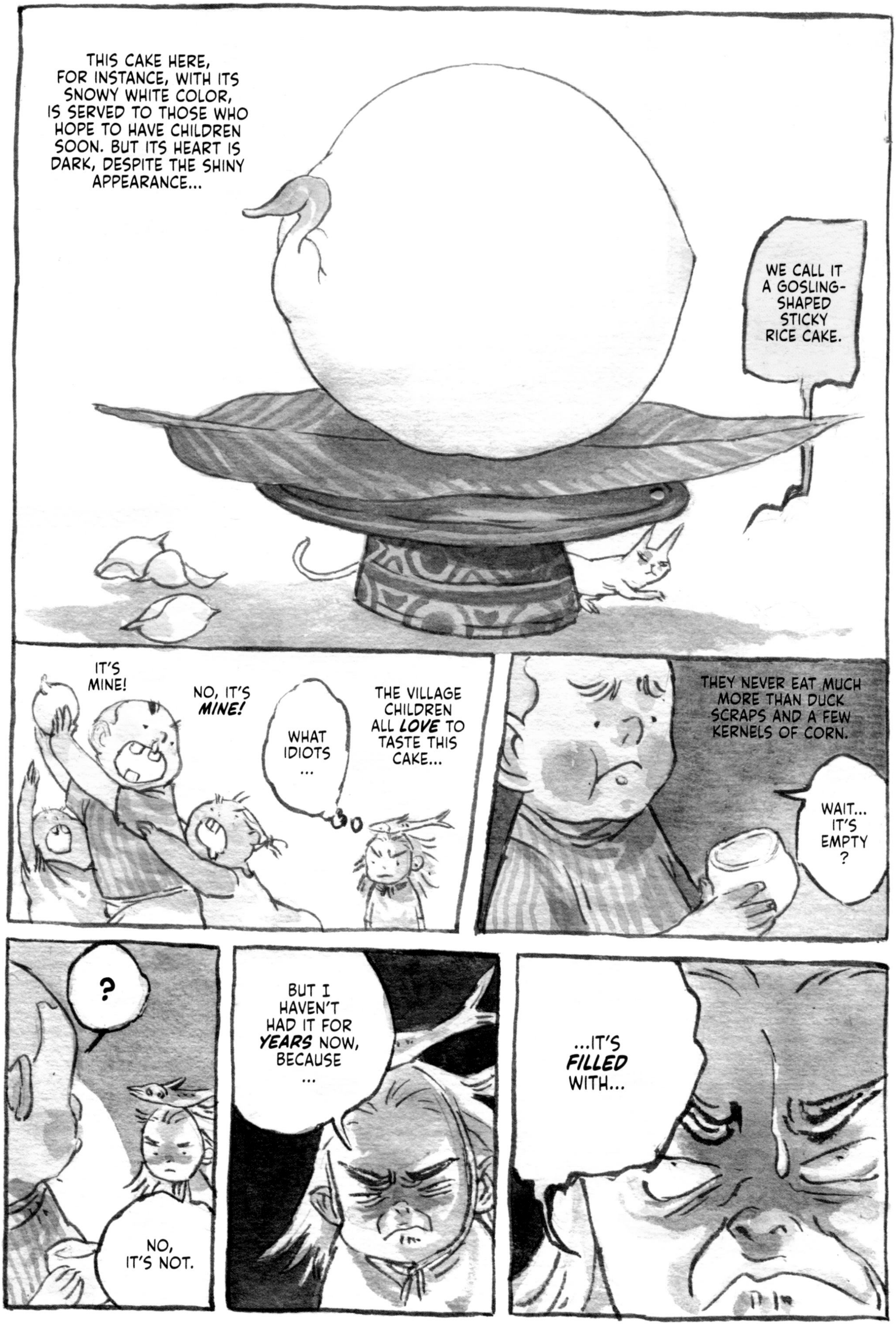
THIS CAKE HERE, FOR INSTANCE, WITH ITS SNOWY WHITE COLOR, IS SERVED TO THOSE WHO HOPE TO HAVE CHILDREN SOON. BUT ITS HEART IS DARK, DESPITE THE SHINY APPEARANCE...
WE CALL IT A GOSLING-SHAPED STICKY RICE CAKE.
IT'S MINE!
NO, IT'S MINE!
WHAT IDIOTS ...
THE VILLAGE CHILDREN ALL LOVE TO TASTE THIS CAKE...
THEY NEVER EAT MUCH MORE THAN DUCK SCRAPS AND A FEW KERNELS OF CORN.
WAIT... IT'S EMPTY ?
?
NO, IT'S NOT.
BUT I HAVEN'T HAD IT FOR YEARS NOW, BECAUSE ...
...IT'S FILLED WITH...

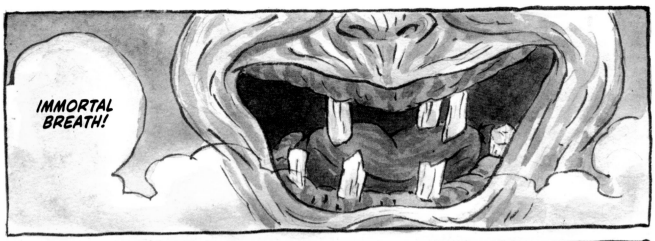

IMMORTAL BREATH!

THE SECRET TO MAKING IT IS KNOWING HOW TO INFLATE IT!

IT'S KINDA FUN...

AS IF YOU'RE BLOWING UP A BALLOON...

FIRST, YOU KNEAD THE DOUGH, WITH PRECISE PROPORTIONS OF NORMAL RICE FLOUR AND STICKY RICE FLOUR...

THEN YOU BLOW IT UP, WHICH ISN'T THAT EASY...

WHFF...

WHFF...

MUSTN'T BLOW TOO SOFT. OR TOO HARD, 'CAUSE YOUR SALIVA GETS IN, AND...

BOOM!

...THE DOUGH EXPLODES!

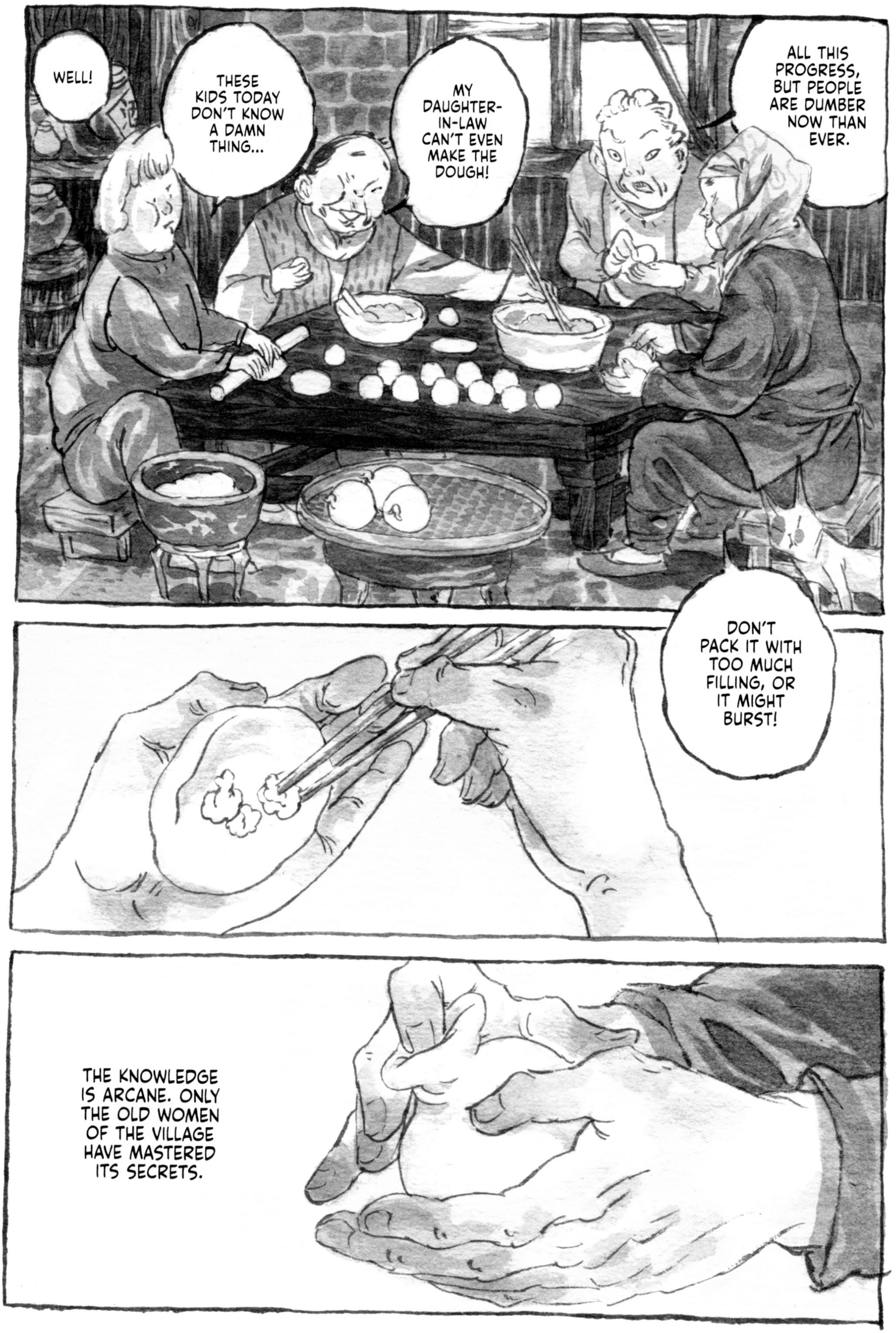
WELL!
THESE KIDS TODAY DON'T KNOW A DAMN THING...
MY DAUGHTER-IN-LAW CAN'T EVEN MAKE THE DOUGH!
ALL THIS PROGRESS, BUT PEOPLE ARE DUMBER NOW THAN EVER.
DON'T PACK IT WITH TOO MUCH FILLING, OR IT MIGHT BURST!
THE KNOWLEDGE IS ARCANE. ONLY THE OLD WOMEN OF THE VILLAGE HAVE MASTERED ITS SECRETS.

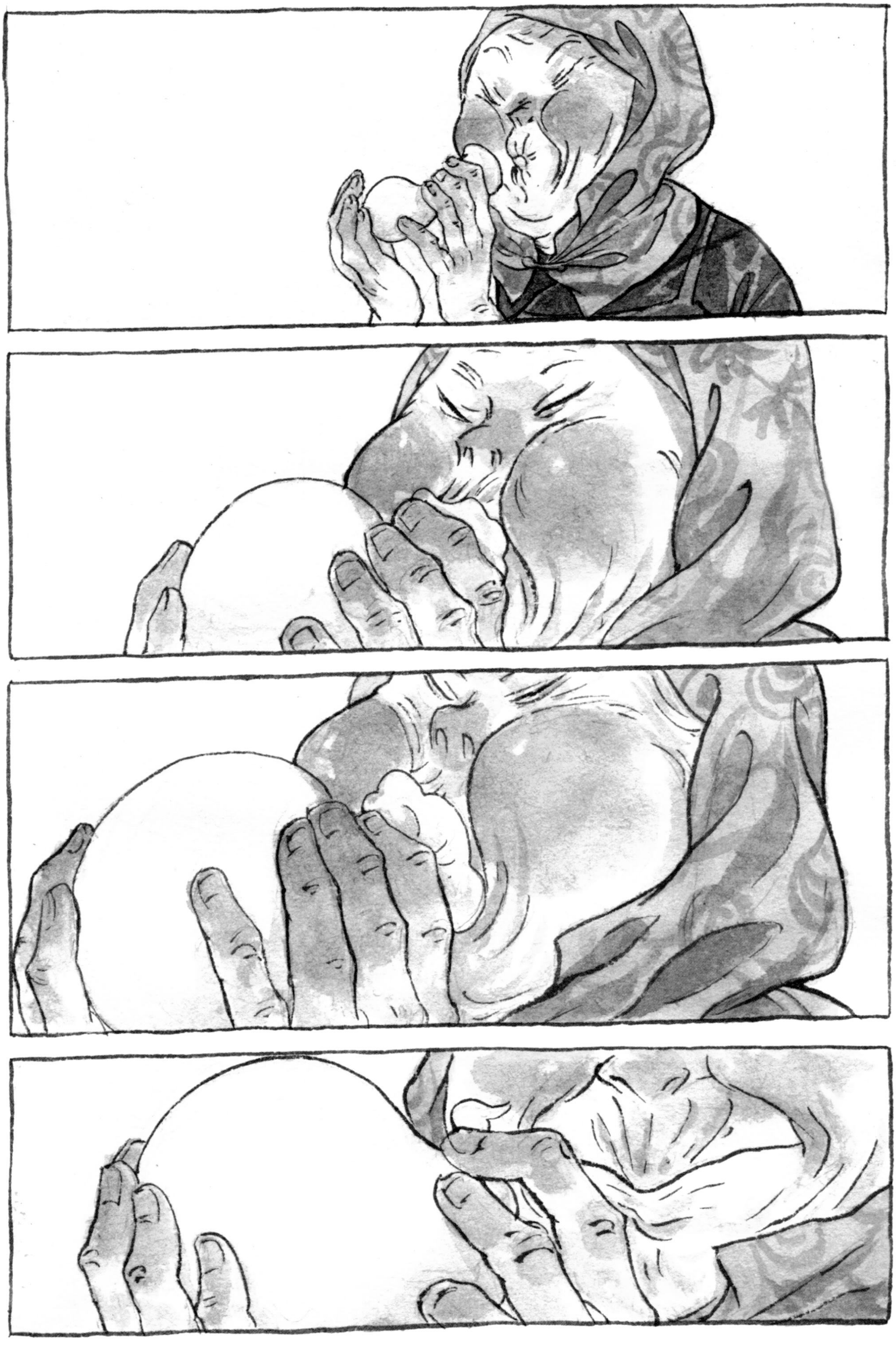

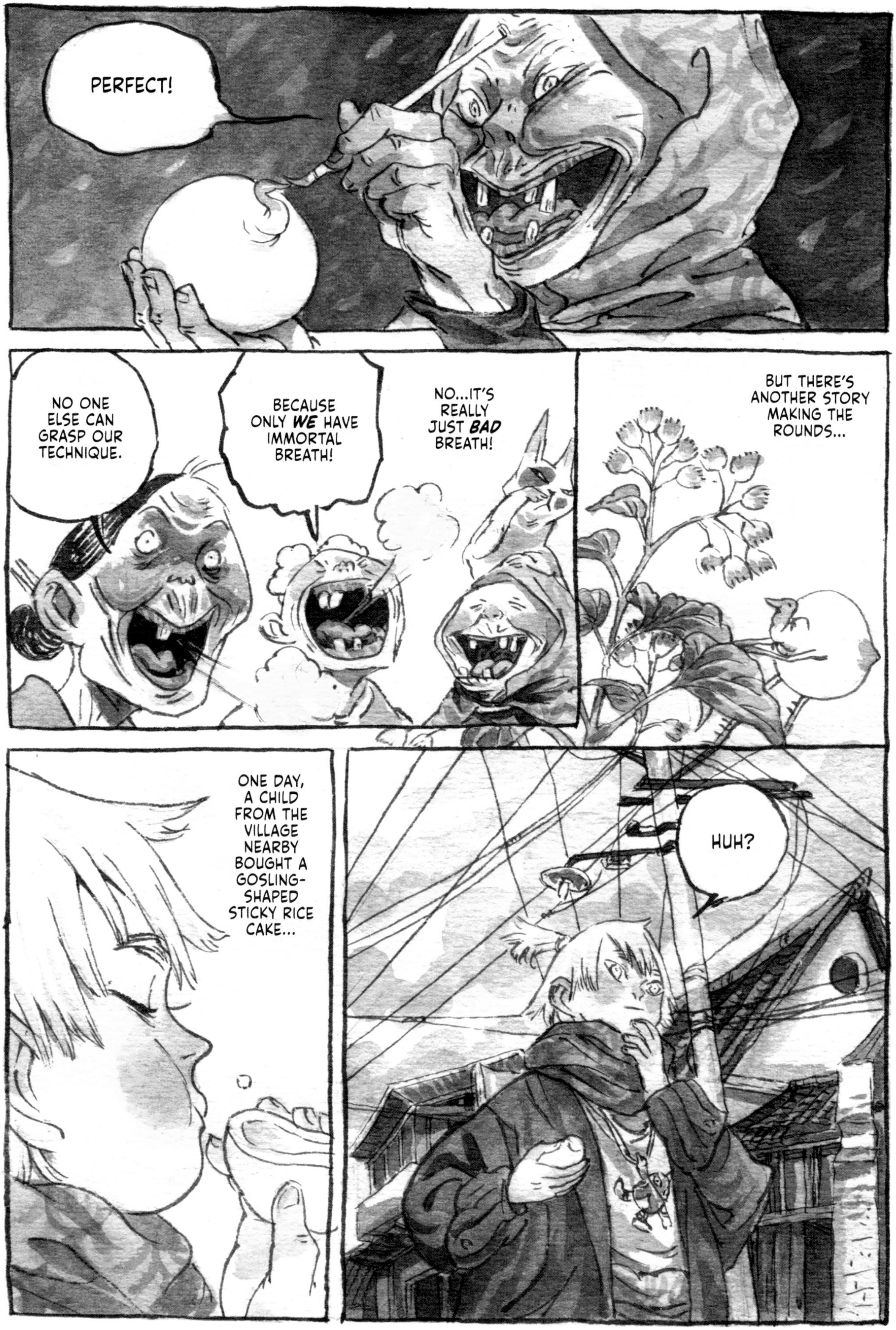
PERFECT!
NO ONE ELSE CAN GRASP OUR TECHNIQUE.
BECAUSE ONLY WE HAVE IMMORTAL BREATH!
NO...IT'S REALLY JUST BAD BREATH!
BUT THERE'S ANOTHER STORY MAKING THE ROUNDS...
ONE DAY, A CHILD FROM THE VILLAGE NEARBY BOUGHT A GOSLING-SHAPED STICKY RICE CAKE...
HUH?

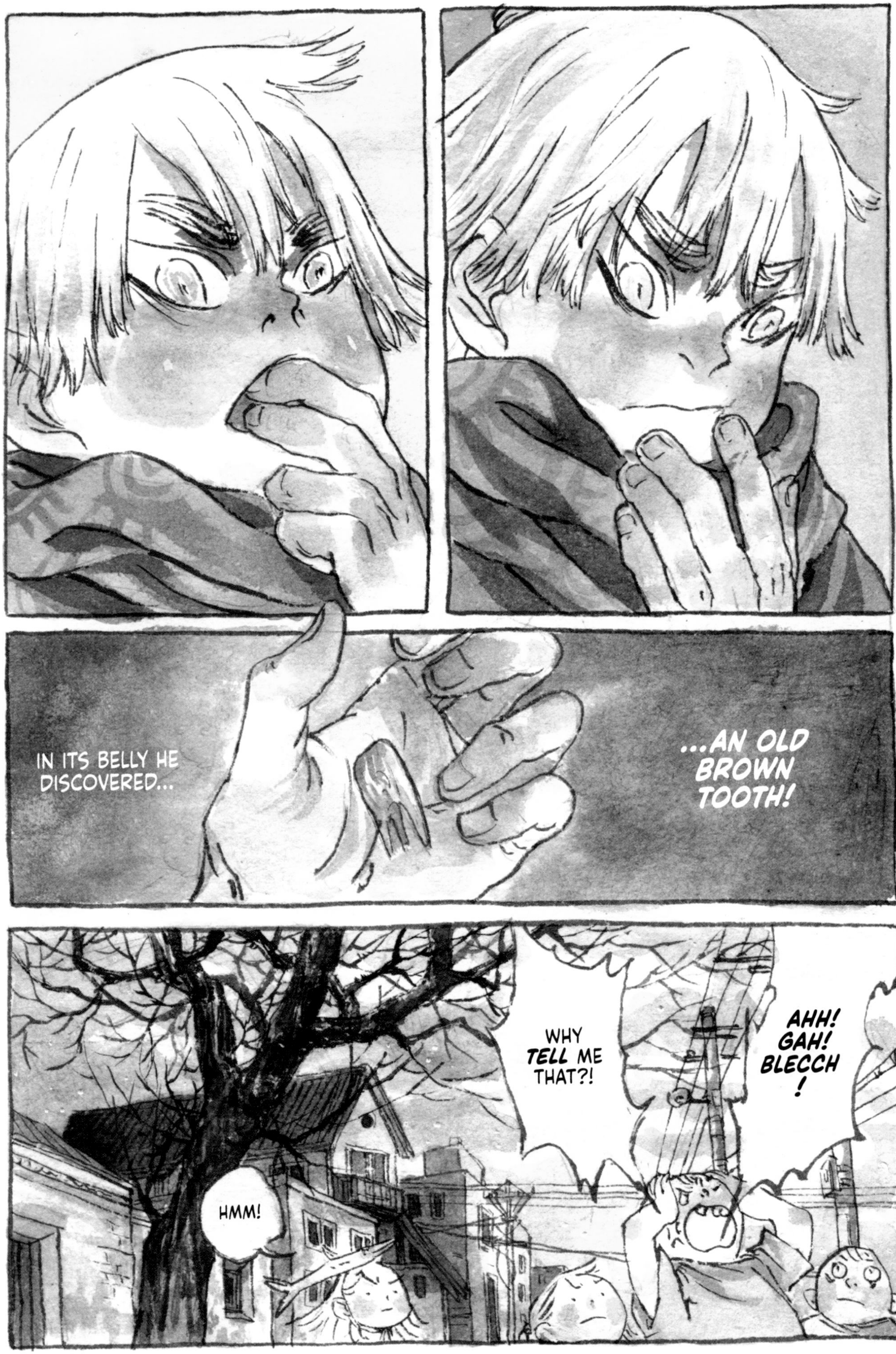
IN ITS BELLY HE DISCOVERED...
...AN OLD BROWN TOOTH!
WHY TELL ME THAT?!
AHH! GAH! BLECCH!
HMM!

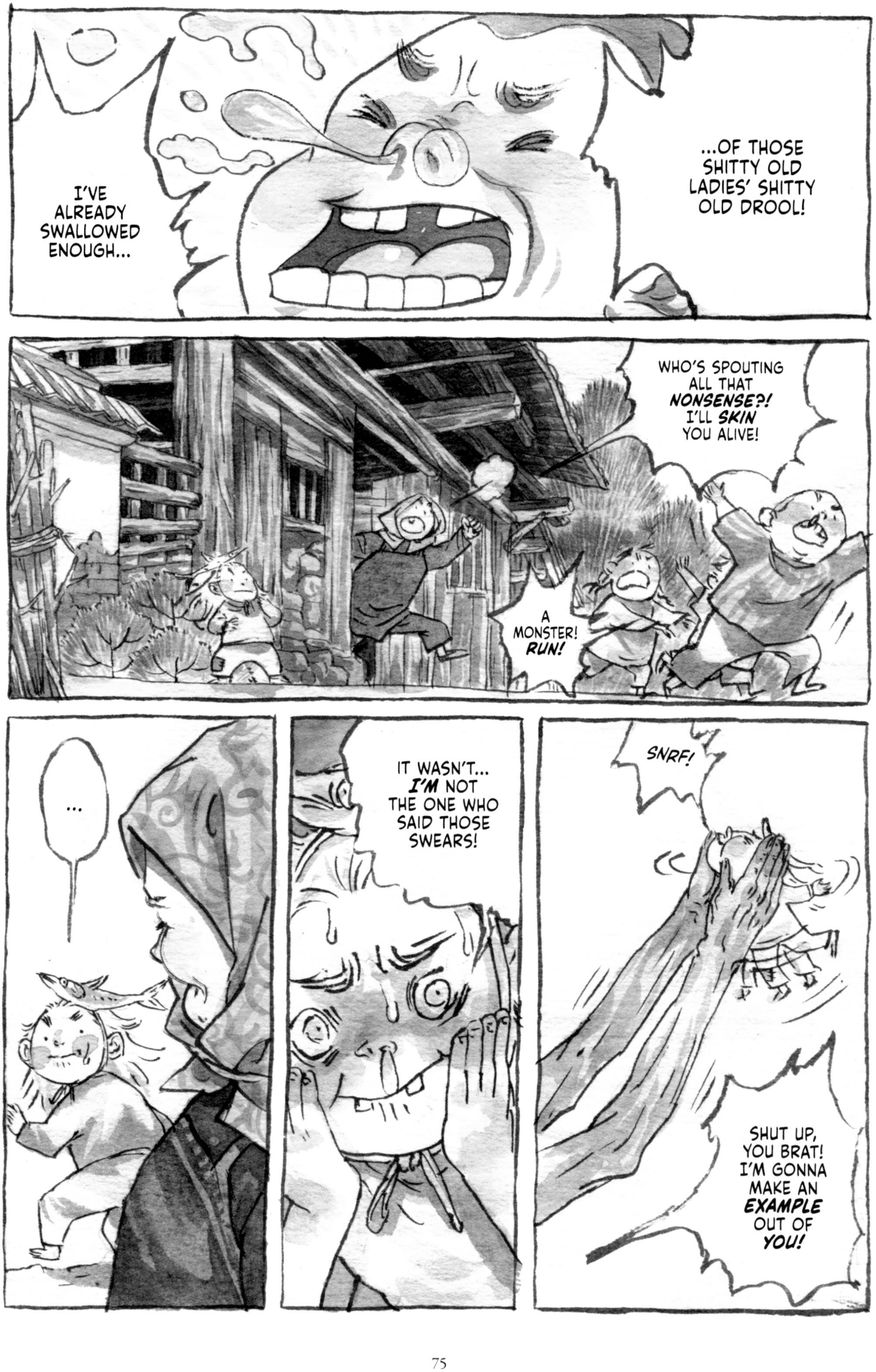
I'VE ALREADY SWALLOWED ENOUGH...
...OF THOSE SHITTY OLD LADIES' SHITTY OLD DROOL!
WHO'S SPOUTING ALL THAT NONSENSE?! I'LL SKIN YOU ALIVE!
A MONSTER! RUN!
...
IT WASN'T... I'M NOT THE ONE WHO SAID THOSE SWEARS!
SNRF!
SHUT UP, YOU BRAT! I'M GONNA MAKE AN EXAMPLE OUT OF YOU!

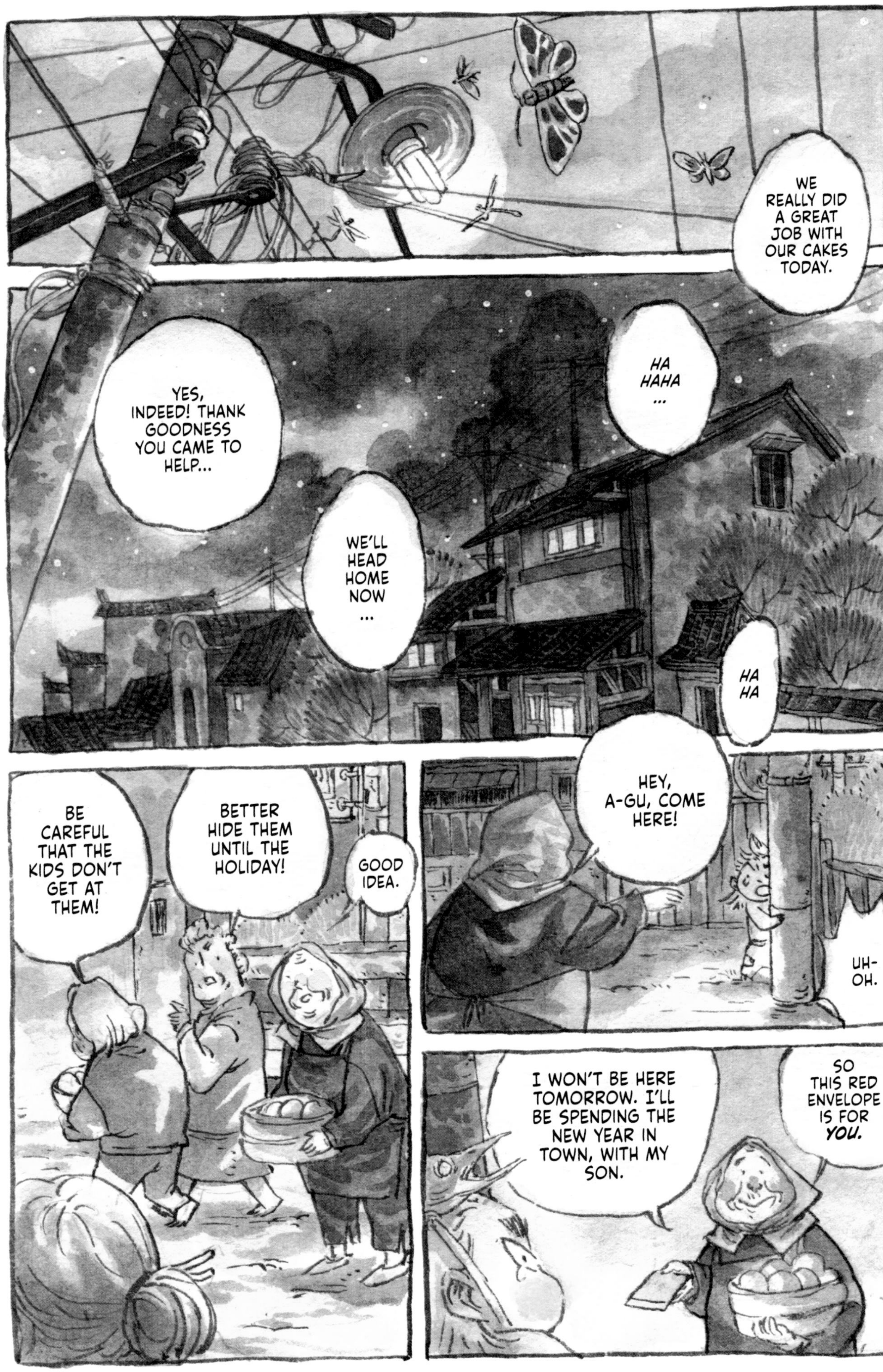
WE REALLY DID A GREAT JOB WITH OUR CAKES TODAY.
HA HAHA ...
YES, INDEED! THANK GOODNESS YOU CAME TO HELP...
WE'LL HEAD HOME NOW ...
HA HA
BE CAREFUL THAT THE KIDS DON'T GET AT THEM!
BETTER HIDE THEM UNTIL THE HOLIDAY!
GOOD IDEA.
HEY, A-GU, COME HERE!
UH-OH.
I WON'T BE HERE TOMORROW. I'LL BE SPENDING THE NEW YEAR IN TOWN, WITH MY SON.
SO THIS RED ENVELOPE IS FOR *YOU.*

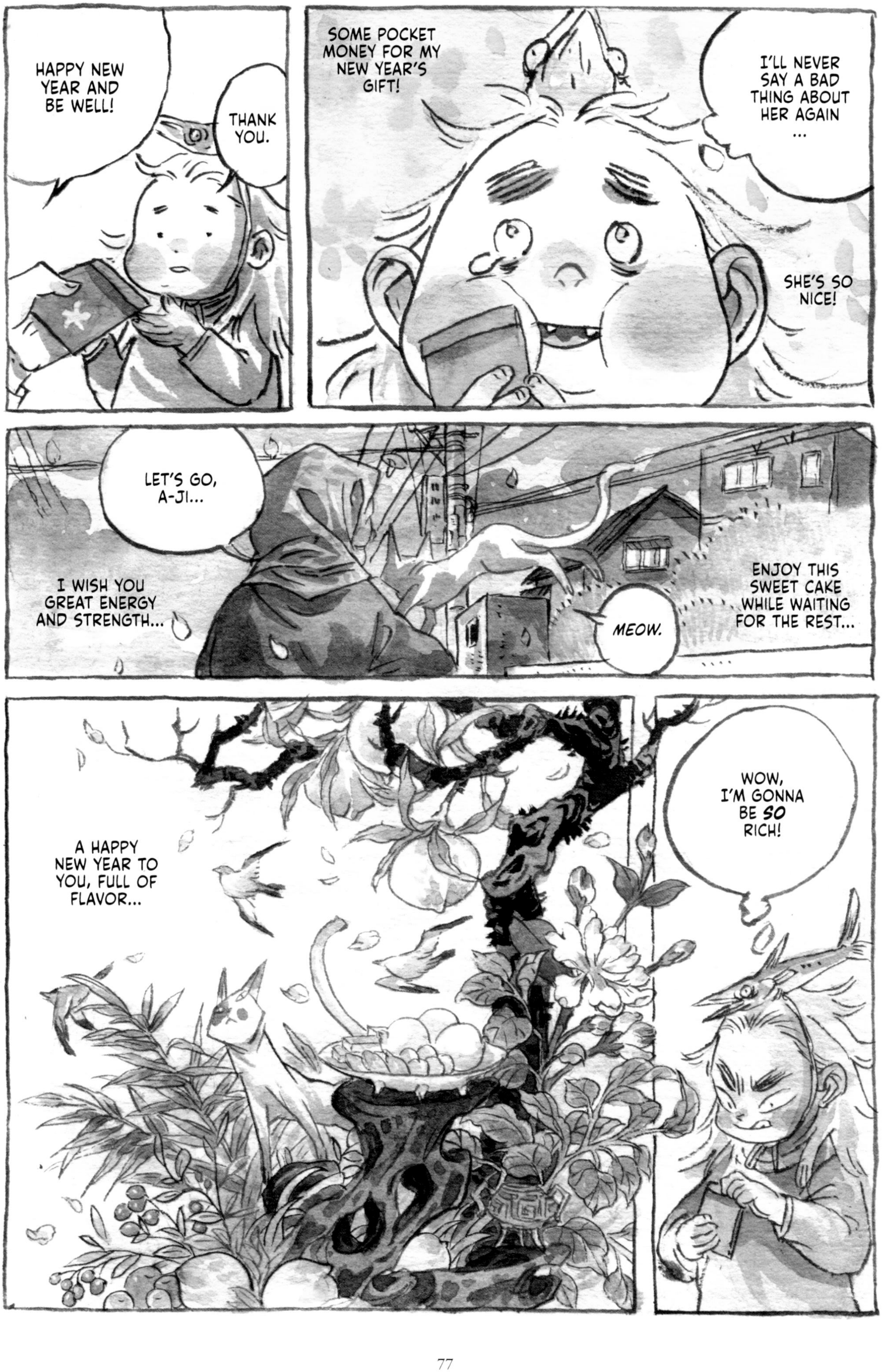

HAPPY NEW YEAR AND BE WELL!
THANK YOU.
SOME POCKET MONEY FOR MY NEW YEAR'S GIFT!
I'LL NEVER SAY A BAD THING ABOUT HER AGAIN ...
SHE'S SO NICE!
LET'S GO, A-JI...
I WISH YOU GREAT ENERGY AND STRENGTH...
MEOW.
ENJOY THIS SWEET CAKE WHILE WAITING FOR THE REST...
A HAPPY NEW YEAR TO YOU, FULL OF FLAVOR...
WOW, I'M GONNA BE *SO* RICH!

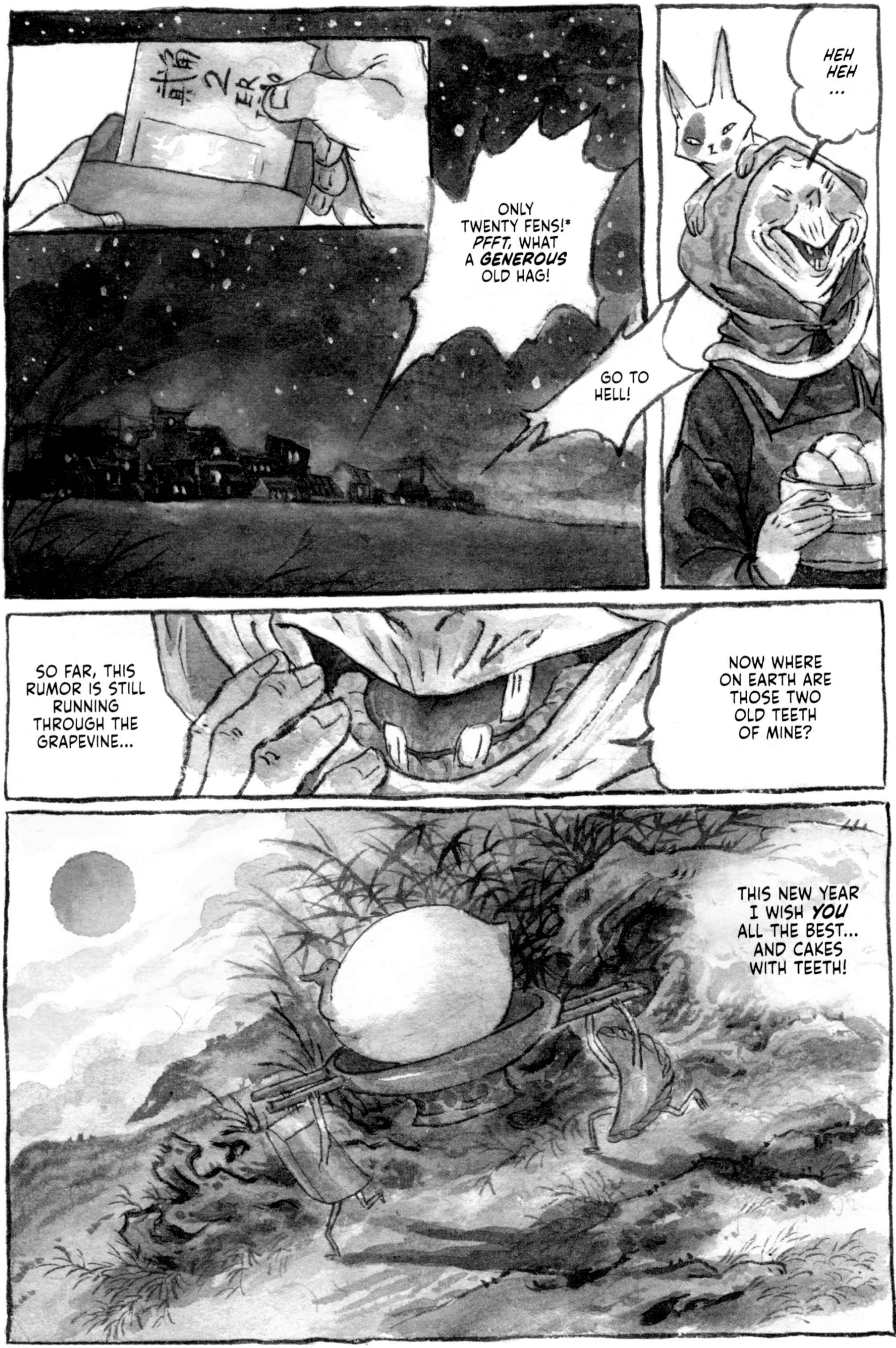
ONLY TWENTY FENS!* PFFT, WHAT A GENEROUS OLD HAG!
GO TO HELL!
HEH HEH ...
SO FAR, THIS RUMOR IS STILL RUNNING THROUGH THE GRAPEVINE...
NOW WHERE ON EARTH ARE THOSE TWO OLD TEETH OF MINE?
THIS NEW YEAR I WISH YOU ALL THE BEST... AND CAKES WITH TEETH!

*ONE FEN IS A CHINESE UNIT OF CURRENCY WHOSE VALUE IS VERY SMALL, LIKE ONE AMERICAN PENNY.

丑乙 二

早稲

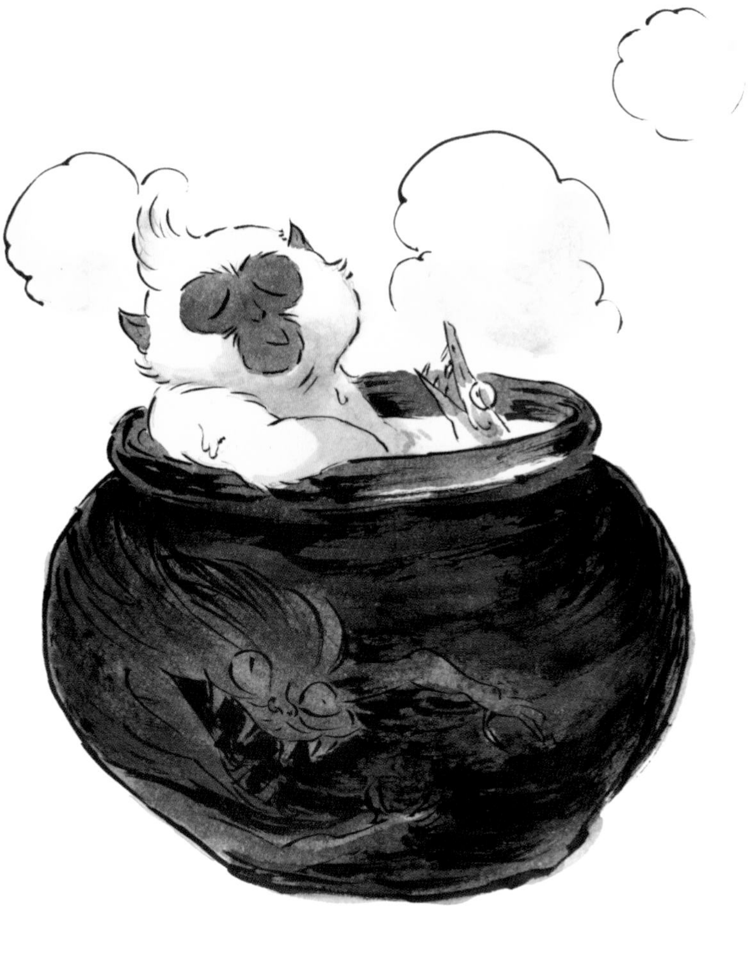

A-Tchoo and A-Yi

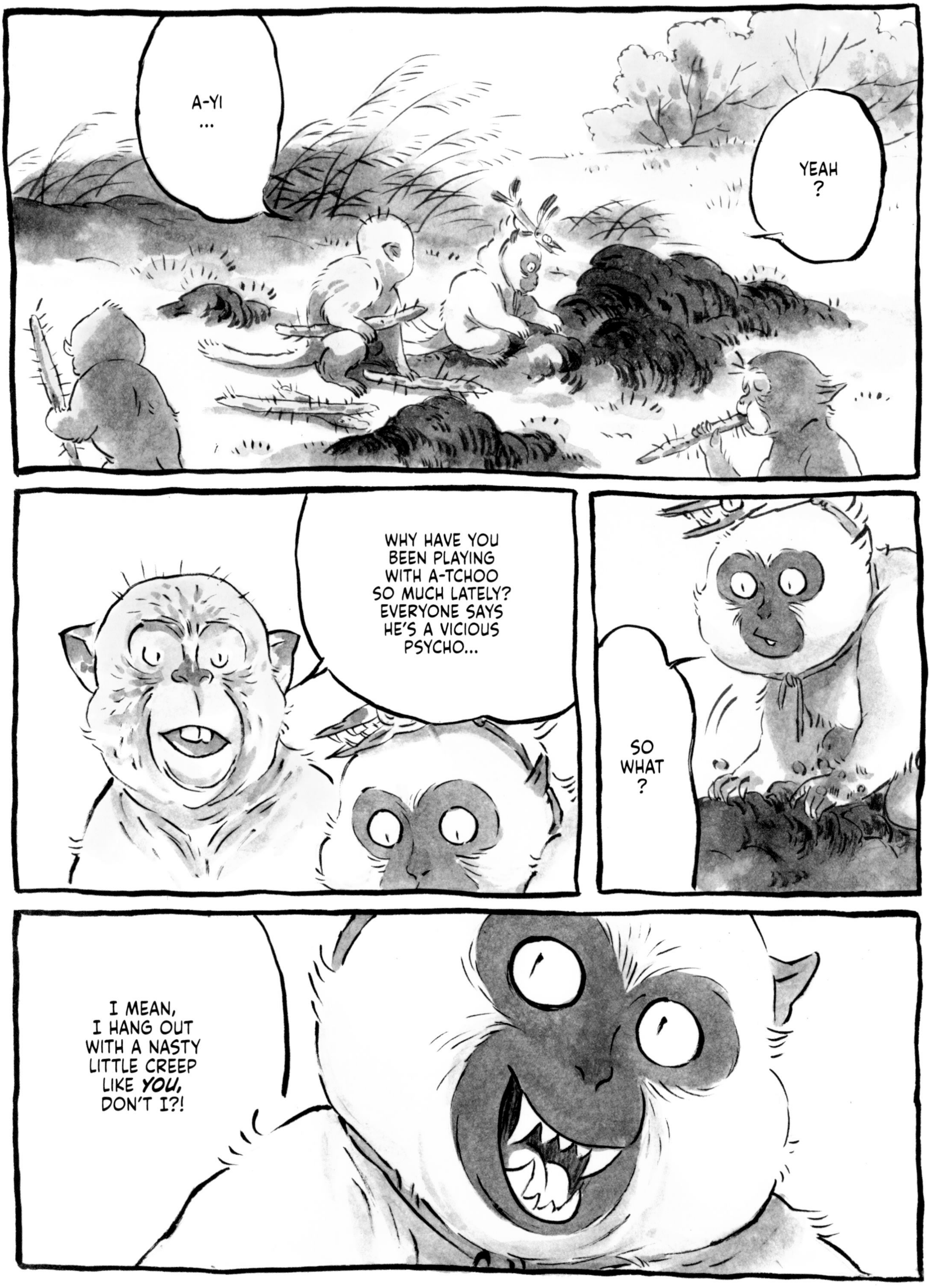
A-YI ...
YEAH ?
WHY HAVE YOU BEEN PLAYING WITH A-TCHOO SO MUCH LATELY? EVERYONE SAYS HE'S A VICIOUS PSYCHO...
SO WHAT ?
I MEAN, I HANG OUT WITH A NASTY LITTLE CREEP LIKE *YOU*, DON'T I?!

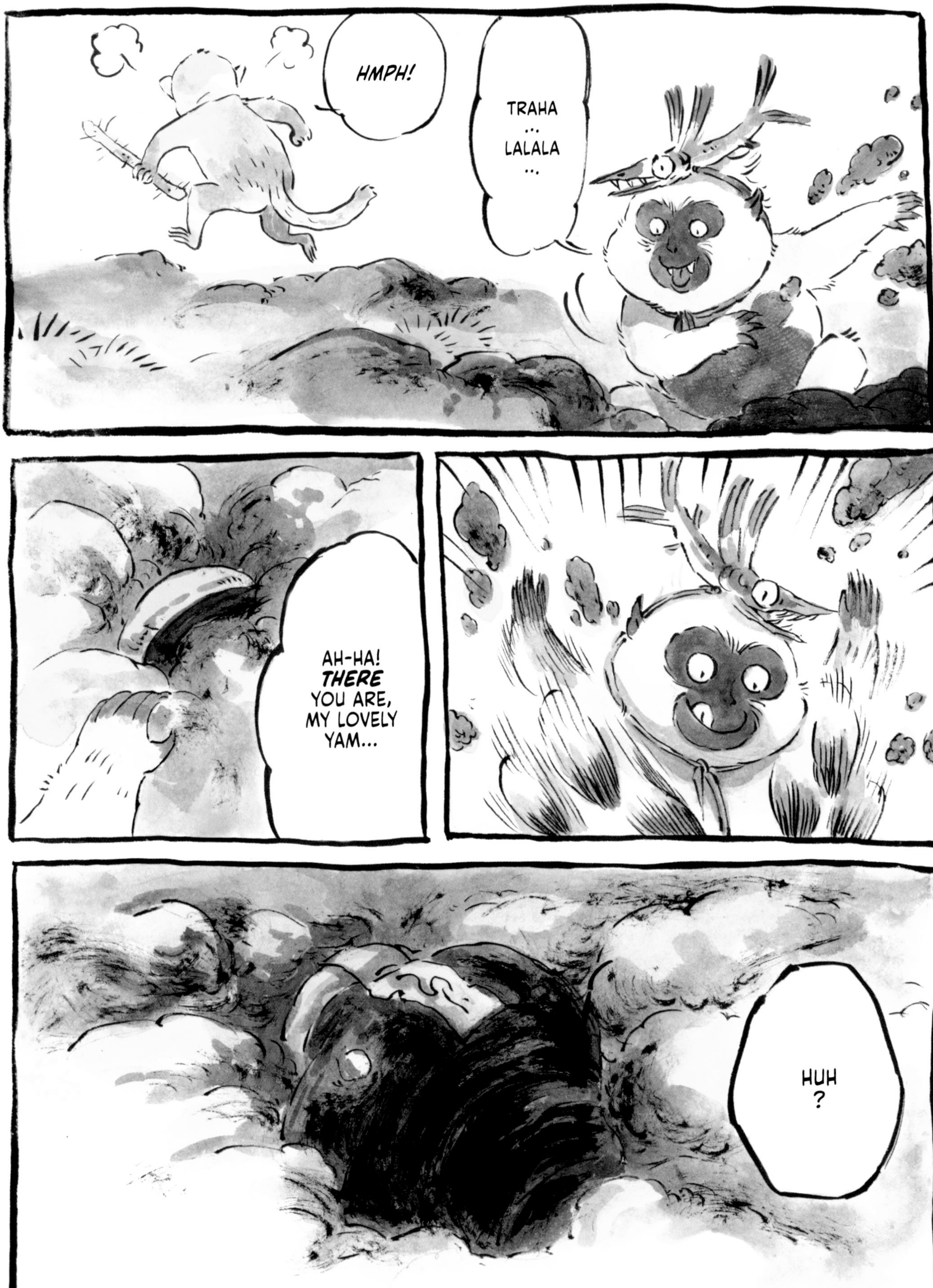
HMPH!
TRAHA ... LALALA ...
AH-HA! ***THERE*** YOU ARE, MY LOVELY YAM...
HUH ?

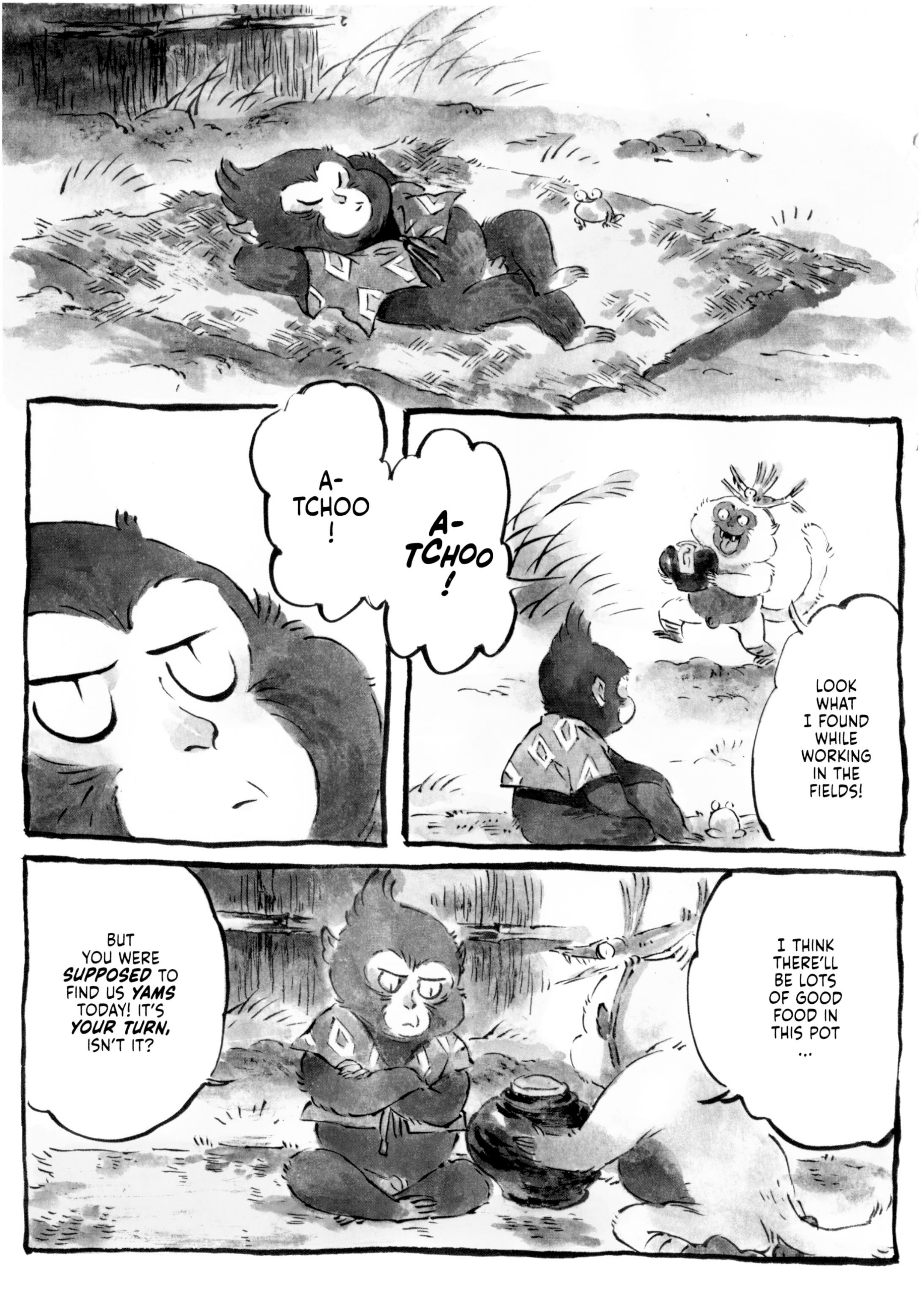
A-TCHOO!
A-TCHOO!
LOOK WHAT I FOUND WHILE WORKING IN THE FIELDS!
BUT YOU WERE SUPPOSED TO FIND US YAMS TODAY! IT'S YOUR TURN, ISN'T IT?
I THINK THERE'LL BE LOTS OF GOOD FOOD IN THIS POT ...

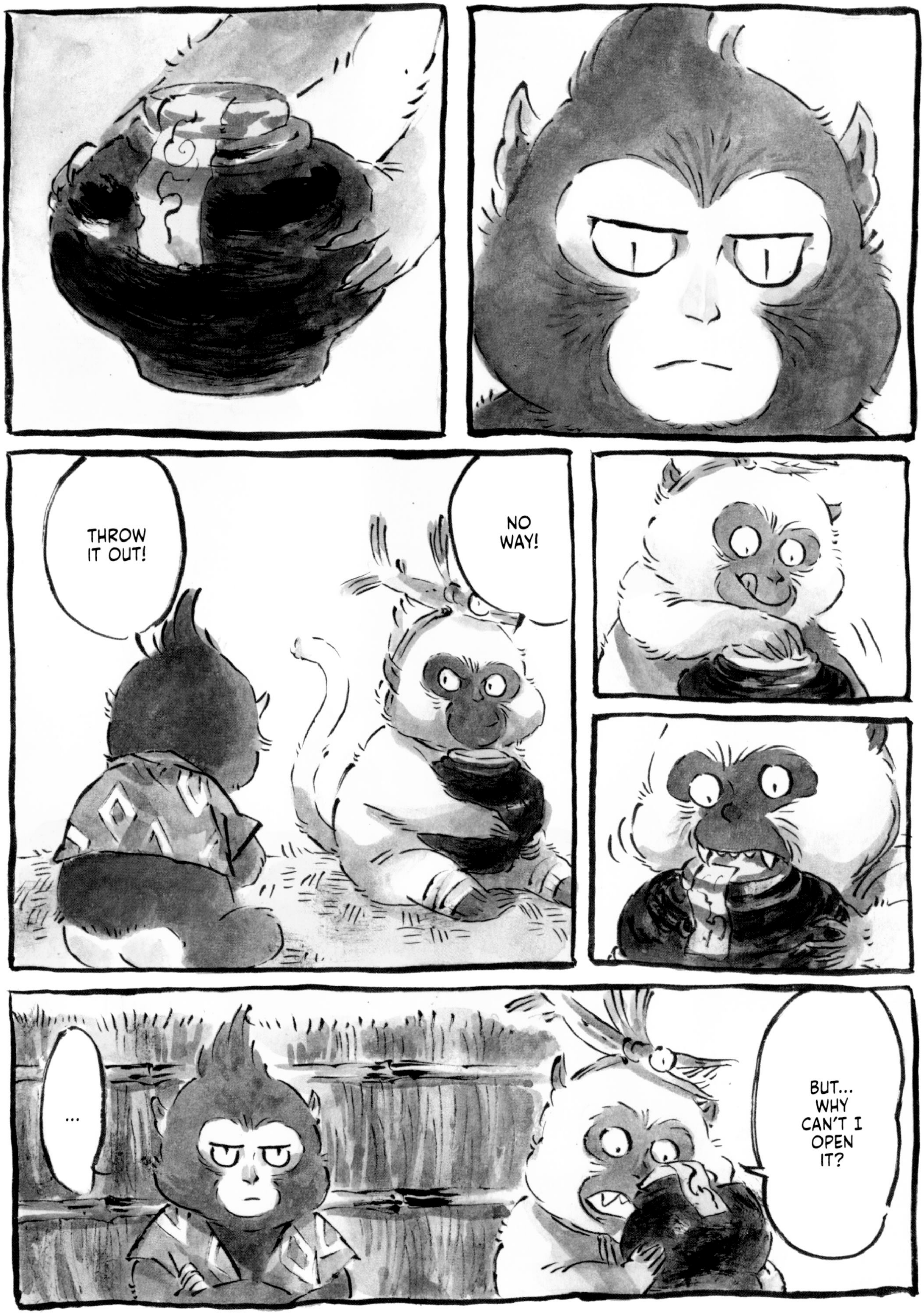
THROW IT OUT!
NO WAY!
...
BUT... WHY CAN'T I OPEN IT?

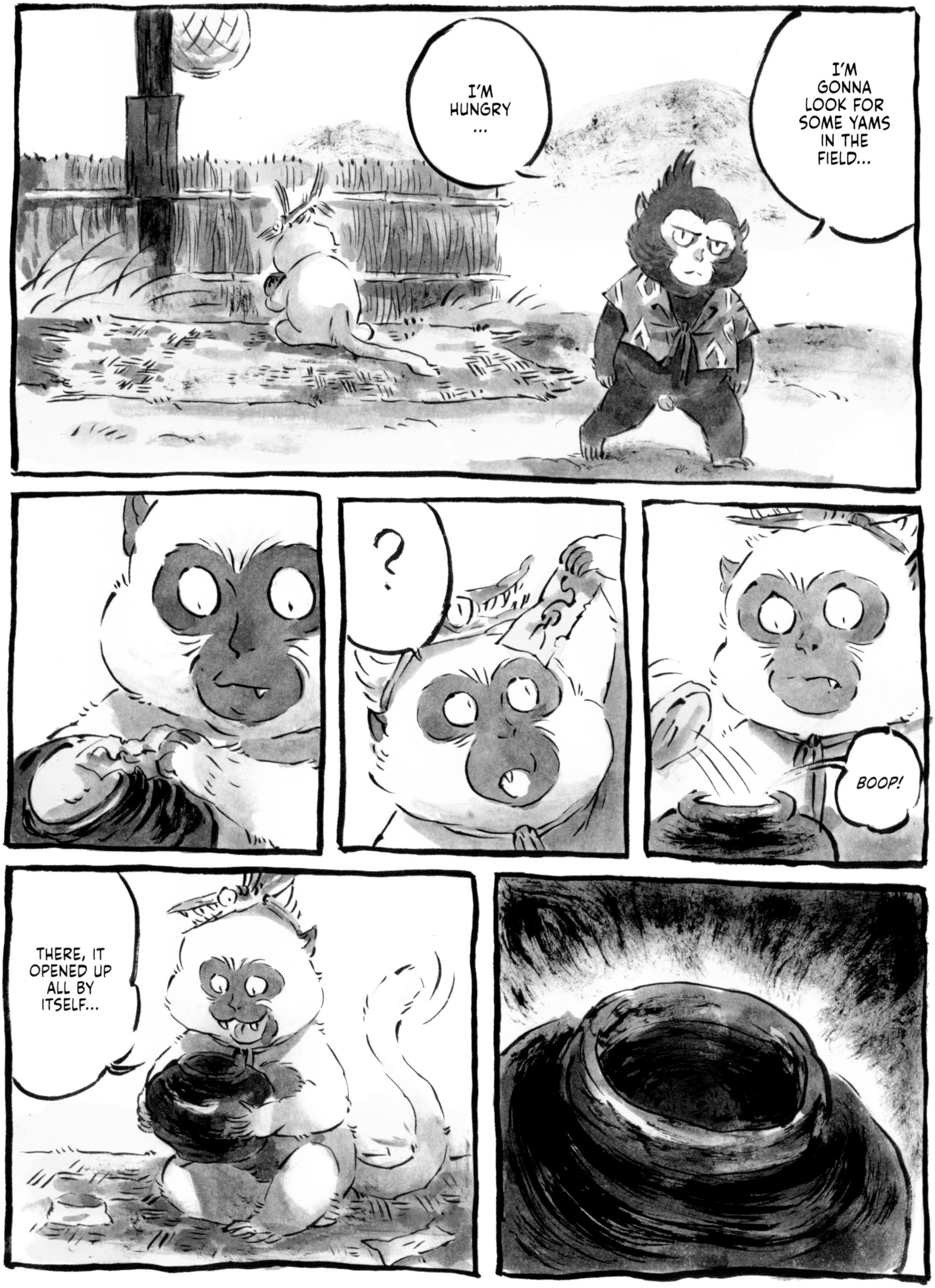
I'M HUNGRY ...
I'M GONNA LOOK FOR SOME YAMS IN THE FIELD...
?
BOOP!
THERE, IT OPENED UP ALL BY ITSELF...

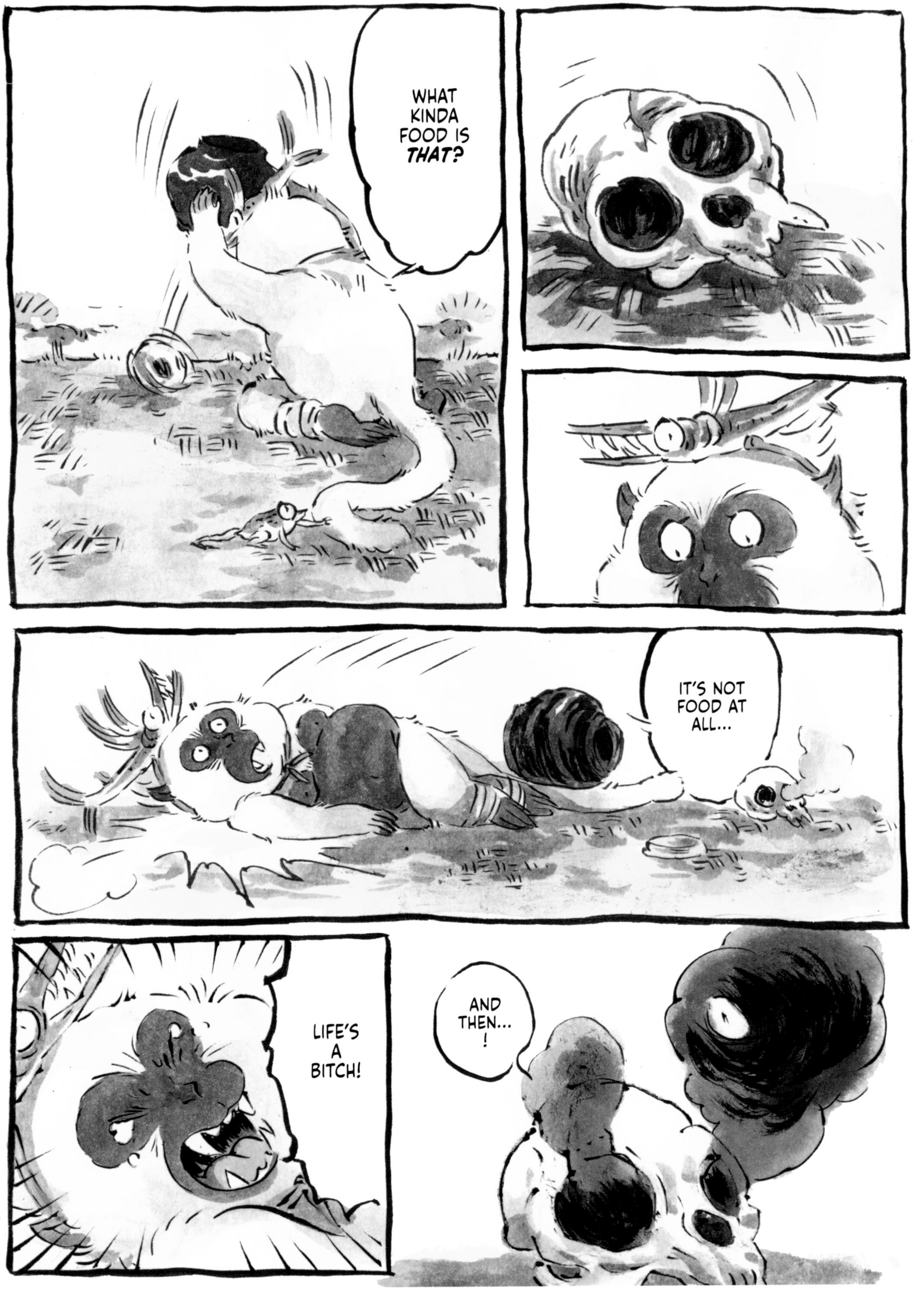
WHAT KINDA FOOD IS ***THAT?***
IT'S NOT FOOD AT ALL...
LIFE'S A BITCH!
AND THEN... !

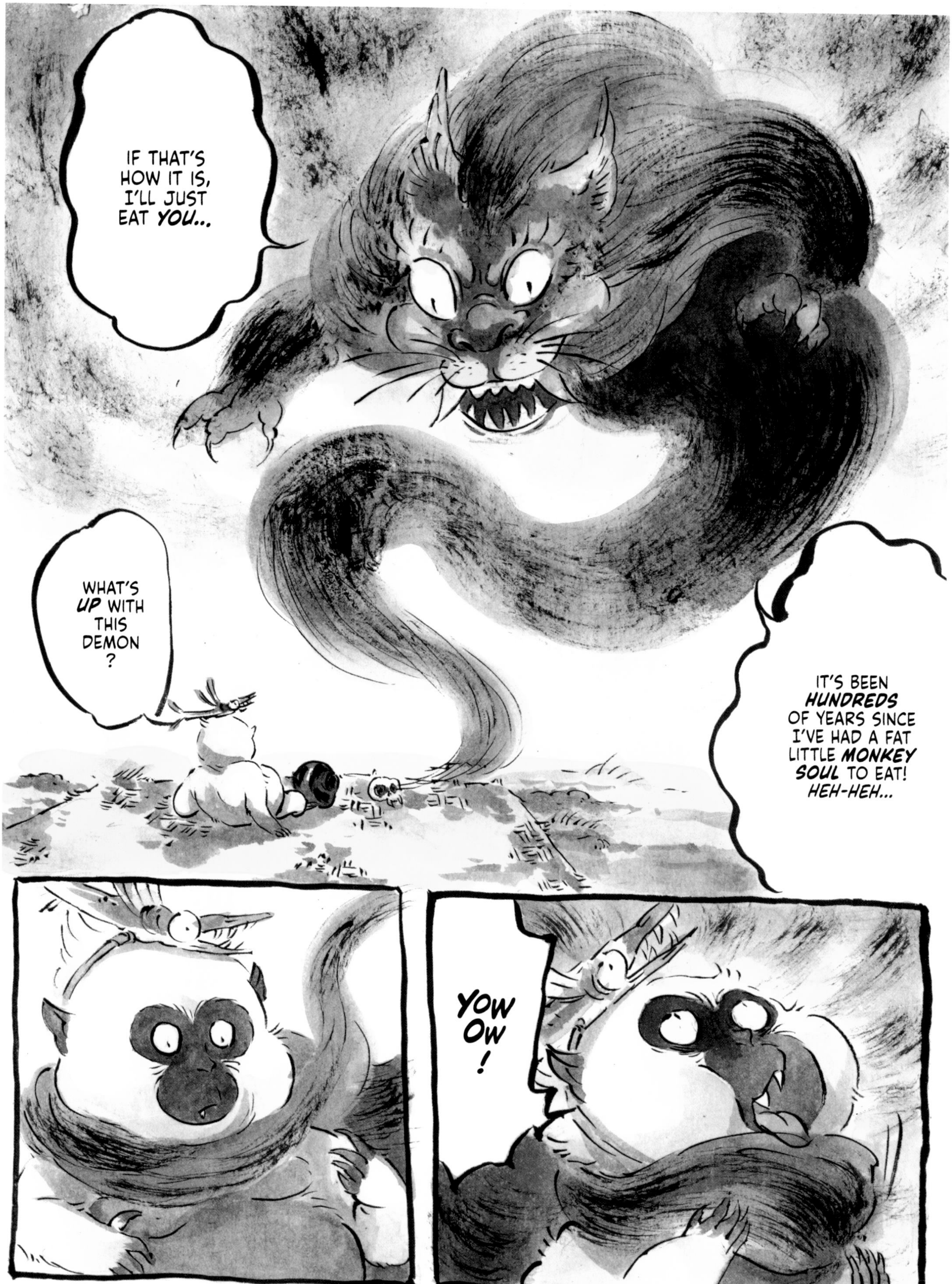
IF THAT'S HOW IT IS, I'LL JUST EAT *YOU*...
WHAT'S *UP* WITH THIS DEMON ?
IT'S BEEN ***HUNDREDS*** OF YEARS SINCE I'VE HAD A FAT LITTLE ***MONKEY SOUL*** TO EAT! *HEH-HEH...*
YOW OW !

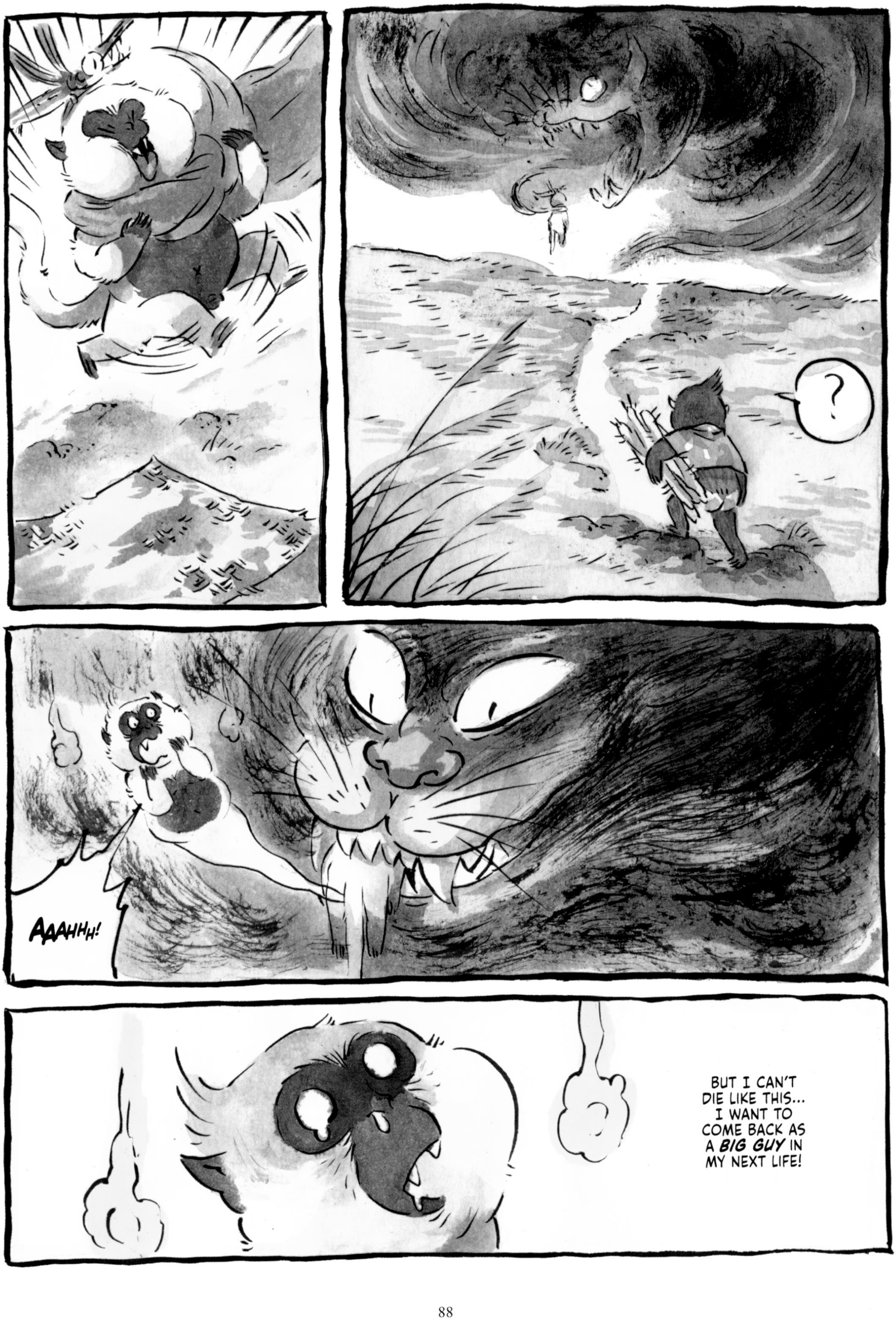
?
AAAHHH!
BUT I CAN'T DIE LIKE THIS... I WANT TO COME BACK AS A ***BIG GUY*** IN MY NEXT LIFE!

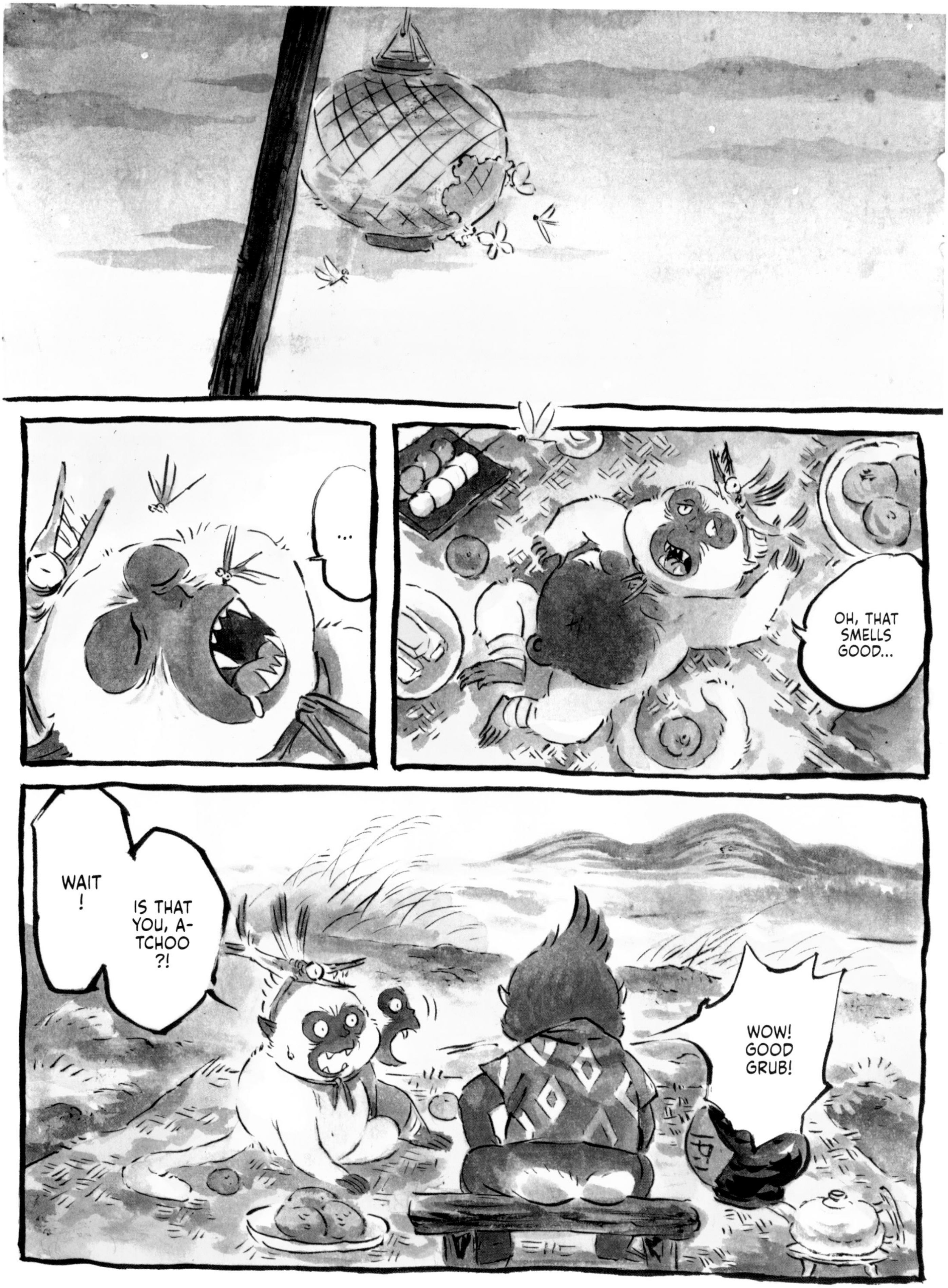
...
OH, THAT SMELLS GOOD...
WAIT!
IS THAT YOU, A-TCHOO?!
WOW! GOOD GRUB!

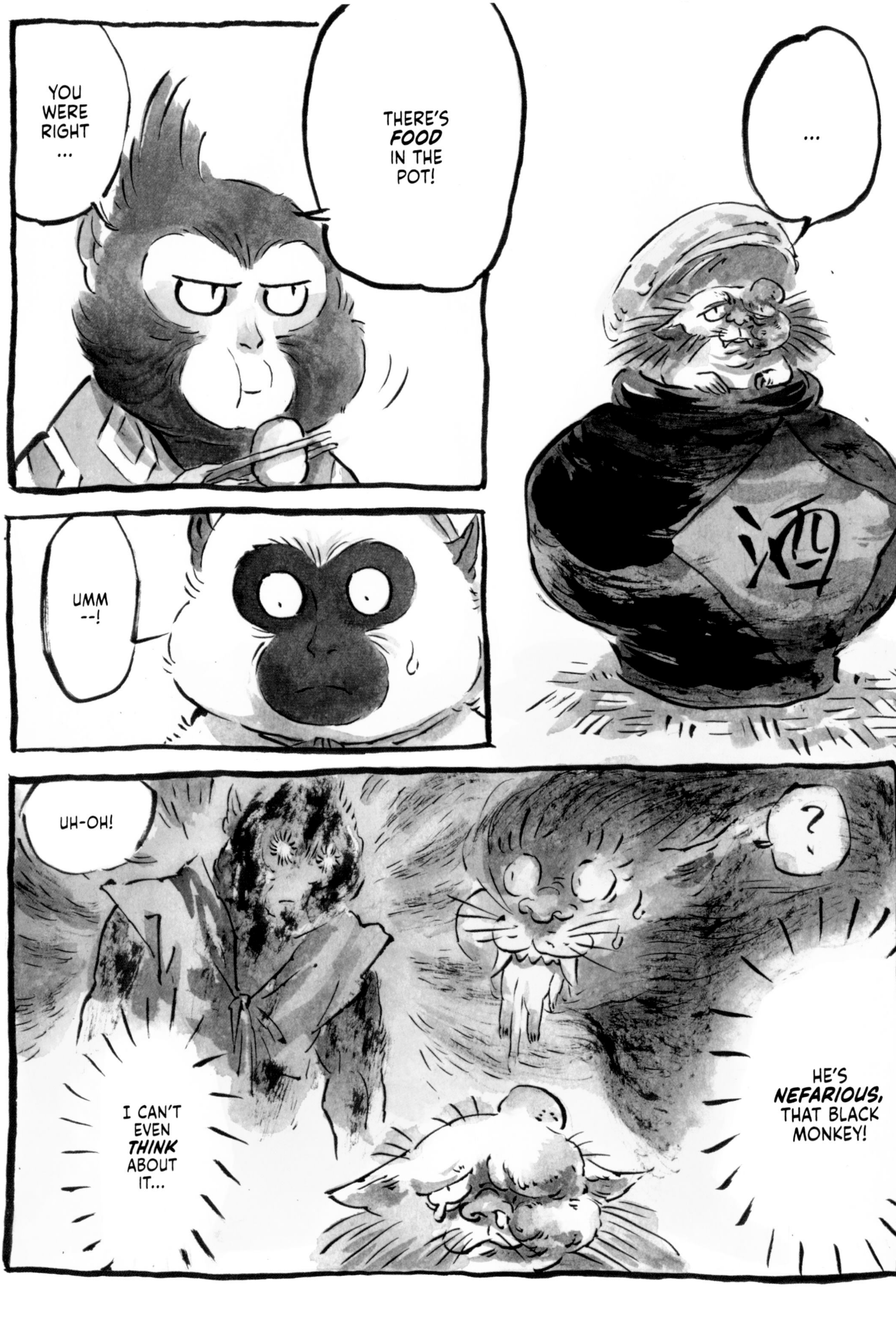
YOU WERE RIGHT ...
THERE'S FOOD IN THE POT!
...
UMM --!
UH-OH!
?
I CAN'T EVEN THINK ABOUT IT...
HE'S NEFARIOUS, THAT BLACK MONKEY!
酒

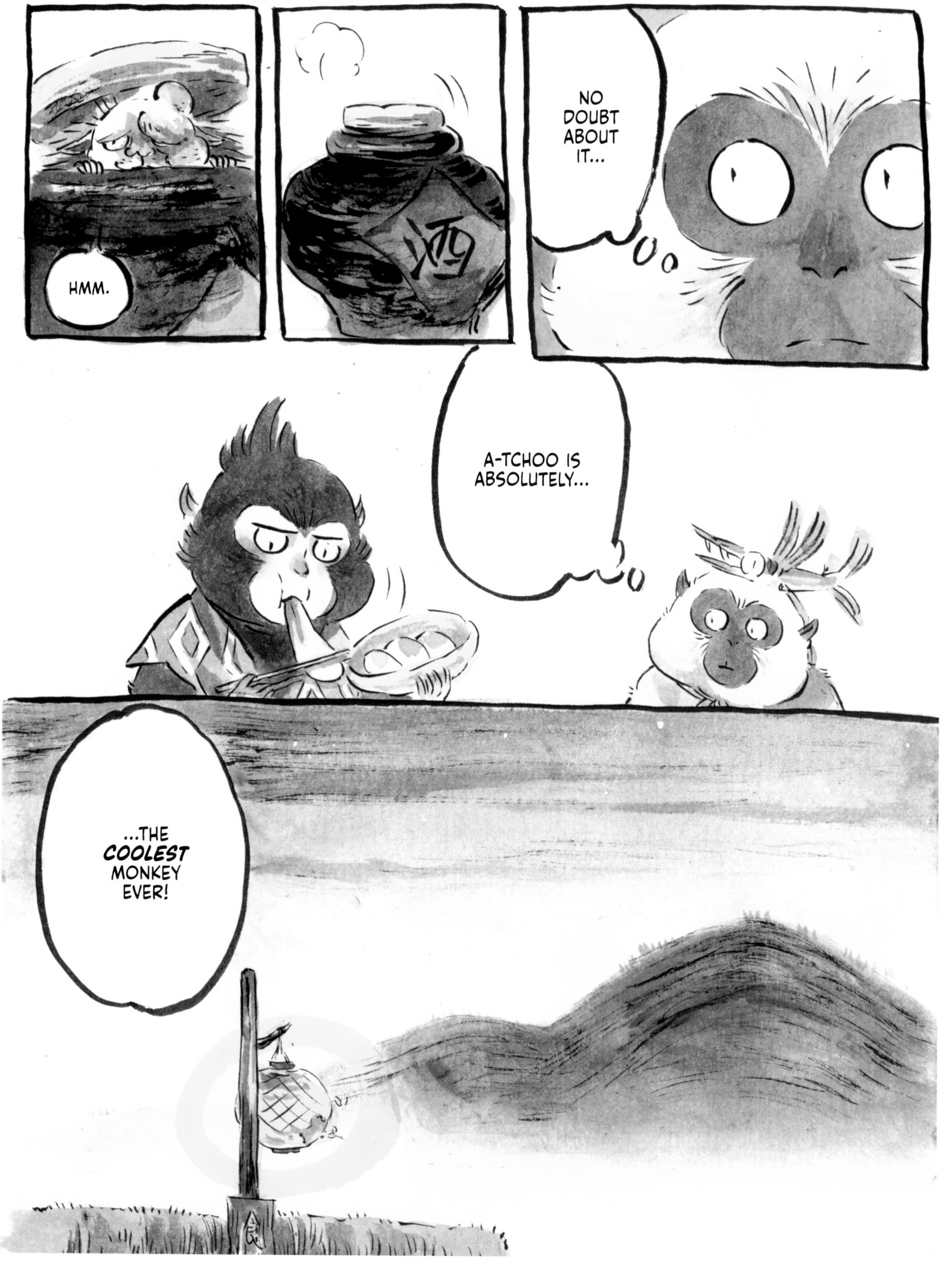
HMM.
NO DOUBT ABOUT IT...
A-TCHOO IS ABSOLUTELY...
...THE *COOLEST* MONKEY EVER!

NOTES ON THE TRANSLATION

Cuisine Chinoise *has been an unusual project, for a variety of reasons. First, this collection of stories introduces the wildly talented Zao Dao and her extraordinary work to American readers! This young artist's evocative painting is charged with atmosphere and emotion, while the tales she tells are profoundly informed by the Chinese cultural traditions from which they spring. Chinese cuisine, in particular, is imbued with layers of meaning: for instance, specific dishes can represent good luck, longevity, or even glad tidings for a family's young children. The fortune cookies served in every Chinese restaurant in America are just one indication of this rich heritage. Of course, these deeply embedded meanings—which can also differ from place to place—fail to carry over into English. Zao Dao's own* nom de plume *signifies "early rice," and refers to her July birthdate, a time of year when the first rice crops are harvested.*

Typically, when translating any text—literary or otherwise—it is always best to work from the original. Translating from another translation can leave the translator at a remove; like playing broken telephone, it risks similar pitfalls of interpretation. In this case, however, Brandon Kander and I were commissioned to work from a French translation. All of the six stories herein were created independently of each other in their original Chinese incarnation but assembled for print publication by Éditions Mosquito in France. Mosquito then licensed the English-language rights to Dark Horse under the aegis of editor Brett Israel. It was this particular French collection of Zao Dao's food-themed stories that then became the translation text. In an effort both to avoid any misconceptions of nuance and to remain as true as possible to the original work and its culture, we were helped on several occasions by curator and author Paul Gravett, by podcaster and martial artist Mimi Chan, and especially by Zao Dao's own representative, Wangning—all of whom gave generously of their time and expertise and to whom we are greatly indebted.

—DIANA SCHUTZ

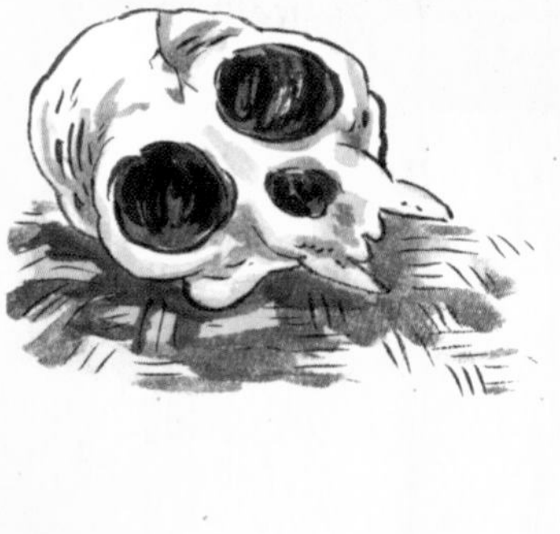

Insect Spirits

6.3

According to Zao Dao's representative, Wangning, Li San and his unnamed friend "are like ghosts of human beings." Although these two spirits have been surviving on dried insects, their taste preferences run towards the *freshly* dead. Perhaps through his own supernatural powers, Li San knows that many will die within the Zhu household that day, so the two set off to catch those insects' spirits.

7.6

A *longevity peach* is a type of lotus seed bun, a traditional Chinese dessert often served at birthday celebrations, especially for the elderly, as a blessing for long life. Longevity peaches are meant to suggest the fabled Peaches of Immortality, which derive from Chinese mythology and traditionally confer a long life on all who eat them. The one on this page is shaped like the dessert, which is itself shaped like a peach—but this one, as we learn here, is made of diamonds.

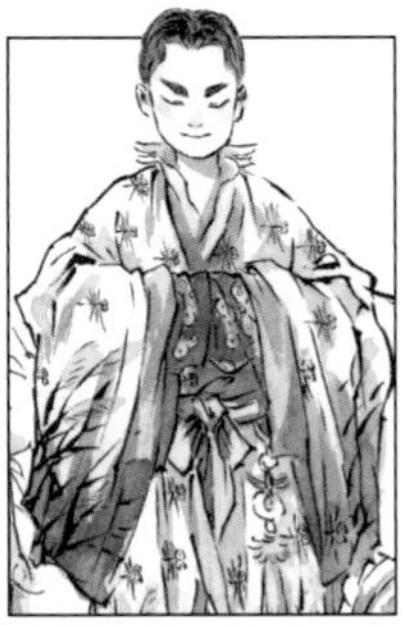

8.5

Young Master Li Ting's name is a reference to his insect nature—a dragonfly. *Ting* is the last half of the Chinese word *qingting*, which means *dragonfly*. The French edition gives the character the surname of *Bellule*, hinting at *libellule*, the French word for *dragonfly*. To do the same in English—using *Dragon* or *Fly* for this character's name—seemed too obvious. *Ting* not only has the advantage of being a real Chinese surname, but in fact, Zao Dao confirms that *Ting* is the name she used in the original version of this story.

Entomology

28.4

The two balloons in this panel are the voice of the child, and reflect his troubled, divided soul. The French edition alludes to this inner split by using a sort of editorial "we" in the first line: "What are we doing . . ." Fearing that this could too easily mislead the reader in what is already an enigmatic story, we changed the line to: "What am I doing . . ."

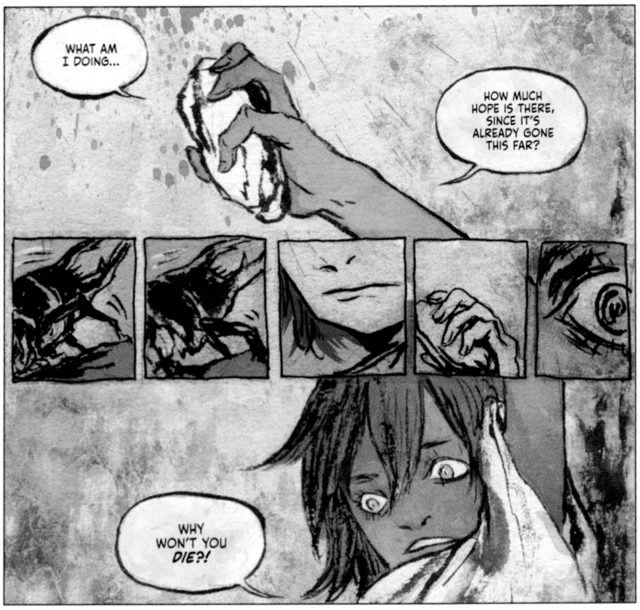
WHAT AM I DOING...
HOW MUCH HOPE IS THERE, SINCE IT'S ALREADY GONE THIS FAR?
WHY WON'T YOU DIE?!

Hai Zi

33.1
While the French edition uses the same term—*Papé*, meaning *Pops*—for both Yuzi's grandfather and his father (introduced in 39.3), we thought it best to distinguish between the two with *Grandpa* and *Daddy*.

41.1
Through Wangning, Zao Dao points out that the three portraits drawn in this panel are, from left to right: Yuzi's grandfather Xiazi, whom we meet at the start of the story; his great-grandfather Daizi; and great-great-grandfather Haizi. *Haizi*—used as the story title and the name of the dish served in 50.1—means the *sea*. *Daizi* and *Xiazi* mean *scallop* and *shrimp*, respectively. So, Yuzi's great-great-grandfather represents the sea, whose progeny are fish and shellfish. While this isn't revealed in the story itself, Zao Dao's use of these specific names is intended to reflect their deeper connotations.

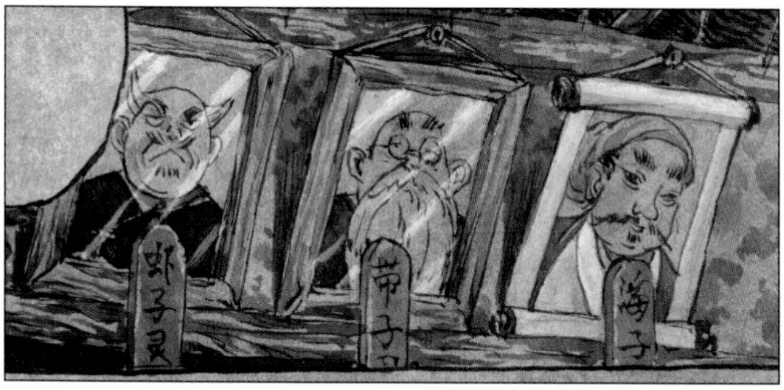
虾子灵
带子
海子

42.4
Comics translation is constrained by the drawn space of the existing balloon or caption, and traditional hand-letterers have long considered hyphenation as a very inelegant solution. Here, the French line spoken by Yuzi's mother is: "This money will not be enough to pay for the next prescription . . ." We rewrote the sentence to make it fit the space of the panel's conjoined balloons.

44.3
The *dough* pun is intentional and is made in the previous panel of the French edition.

52.7
The job of these two death dealers is to "take out" or "take away" Yuzi's sick father. However, the French edition mistakenly has them claim that their target is the grandfather, who, readers learn (in 42.6), has already died. Our translation corrects the error.

54.3
In the French edition, the first balloon in this panel ends with: "We will be scolded when we return." But given the potential provenance of these two dealers of death, we couldn't resist the English idiom *hell to pay*.

Untitled Story

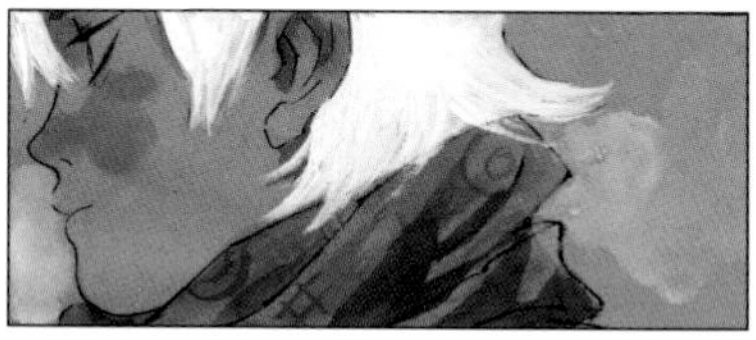

58.1
Although the older of the two characters here looks just like Yuzi from the previous story, Wangning explains that the two stories have "no intrinsic connection," and while Zao Dao may reuse certain characters from time to time, some of her comics are simply the result of "a mood or the feeling of drawing."

Immortal Breath

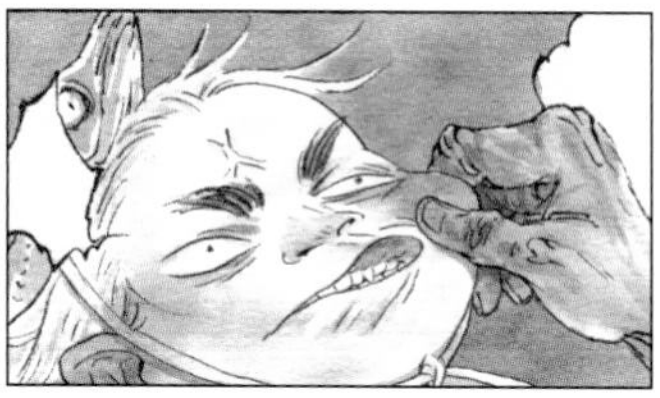

64.1
In the Mosquito edition, the elderly woman describes the baby's face using an untranslatable French idiom. We substituted *monkey face* for the idiom *tête à claques*—literally, *head for slapping* or *smacking*.

64.2
The Lunar New Year celebrates the start of the new year according to the traditional Chinese calendar: between January 21 and February 20.

67.1
Names, like idioms, don't really translate from language to language. This can be particularly true of certain prepared foods, whose designations are often culturally based. We're grateful to Mimi Chan for supplying the English names of the four signature dishes pictured here.

68.4
The cat (A-Ji)'s comment in this panel is our riff on a famous line from the Declaration of Independence: "All men are created equal." The actual line in French reads: "Not all the cakes are equally appetizing."

75.5
The French idiom used in this panel translates literally as: "I will kill one in order to calm the others down." But the idiom simply means that the woman will make an example out of the child by punishing him.

A-Tchoo and A-Yi

83.3
The two main characters in this story, pictured together in this panel, have simple nonsense names meant to replicate the sound of a sneeze (*atchoo*) and the sound of a scream (*aiiee*).

88.4
A belief in reincarnation has deep roots in Chinese culture, dating back at least to the third century BC and the *Zhuangzi*, one of the two foundational texts of Taoism. At this point in the story, when A-Yi is menaced by the cat-demon, he's less upset about dying than he is about his ability to reincarnate. In Chinese lore, demons are said to eat the soul, but the soul must carry through from one bodily incarnation to another. If A-Yi's soul is eaten, he won't be able to reincarnate at all—let alone as the big shot he hopes to be in his next life.

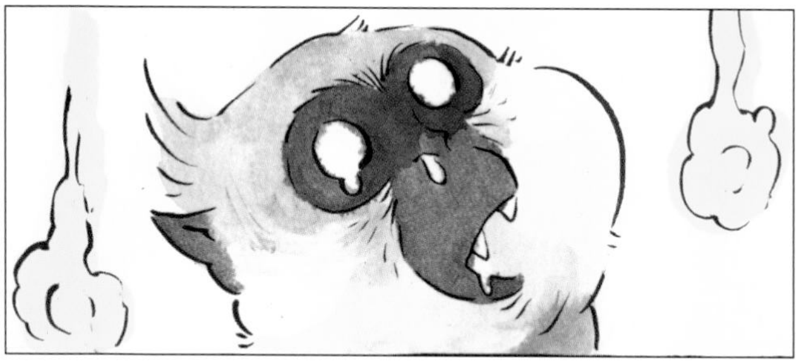

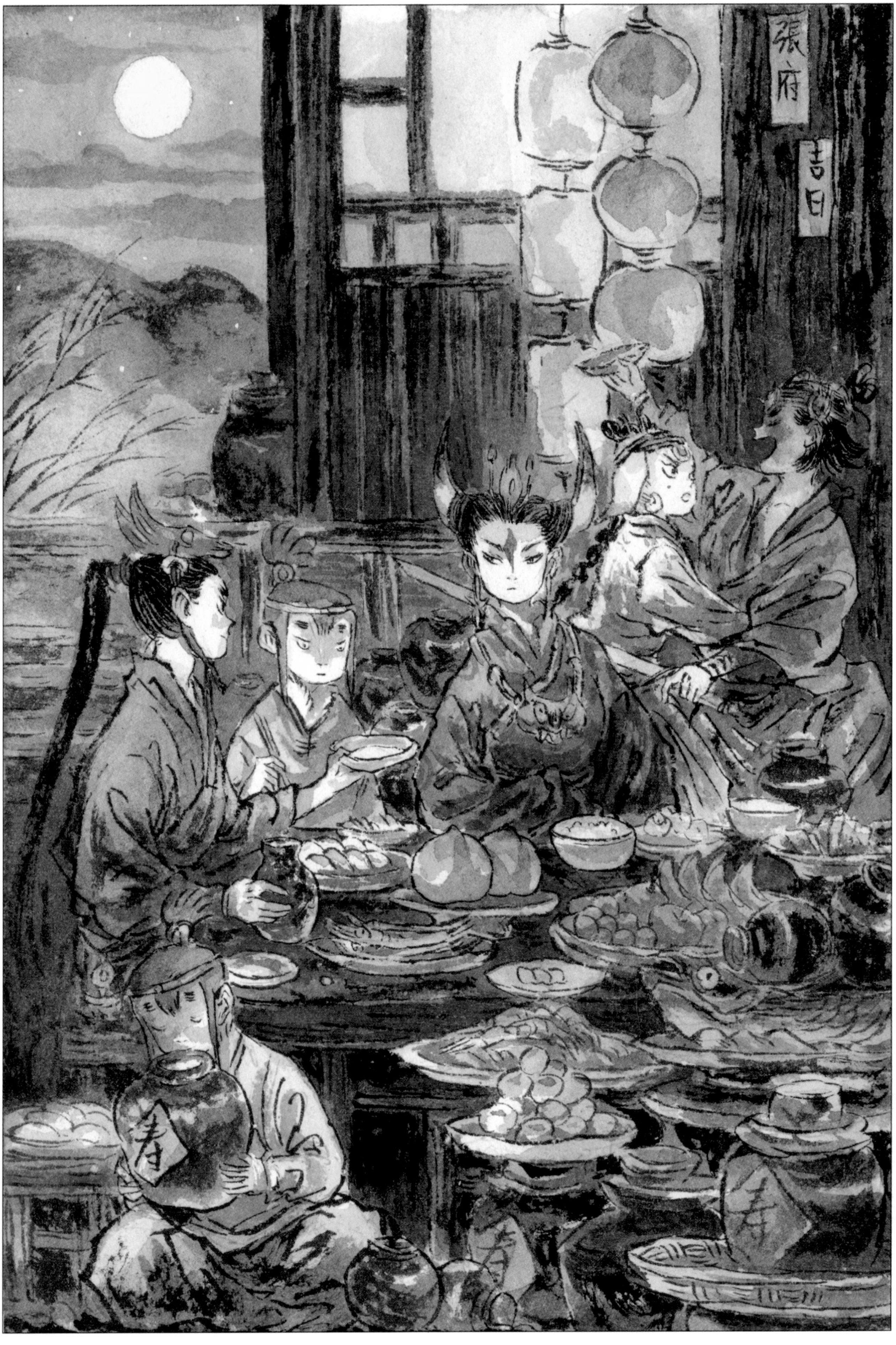
張府
吉日

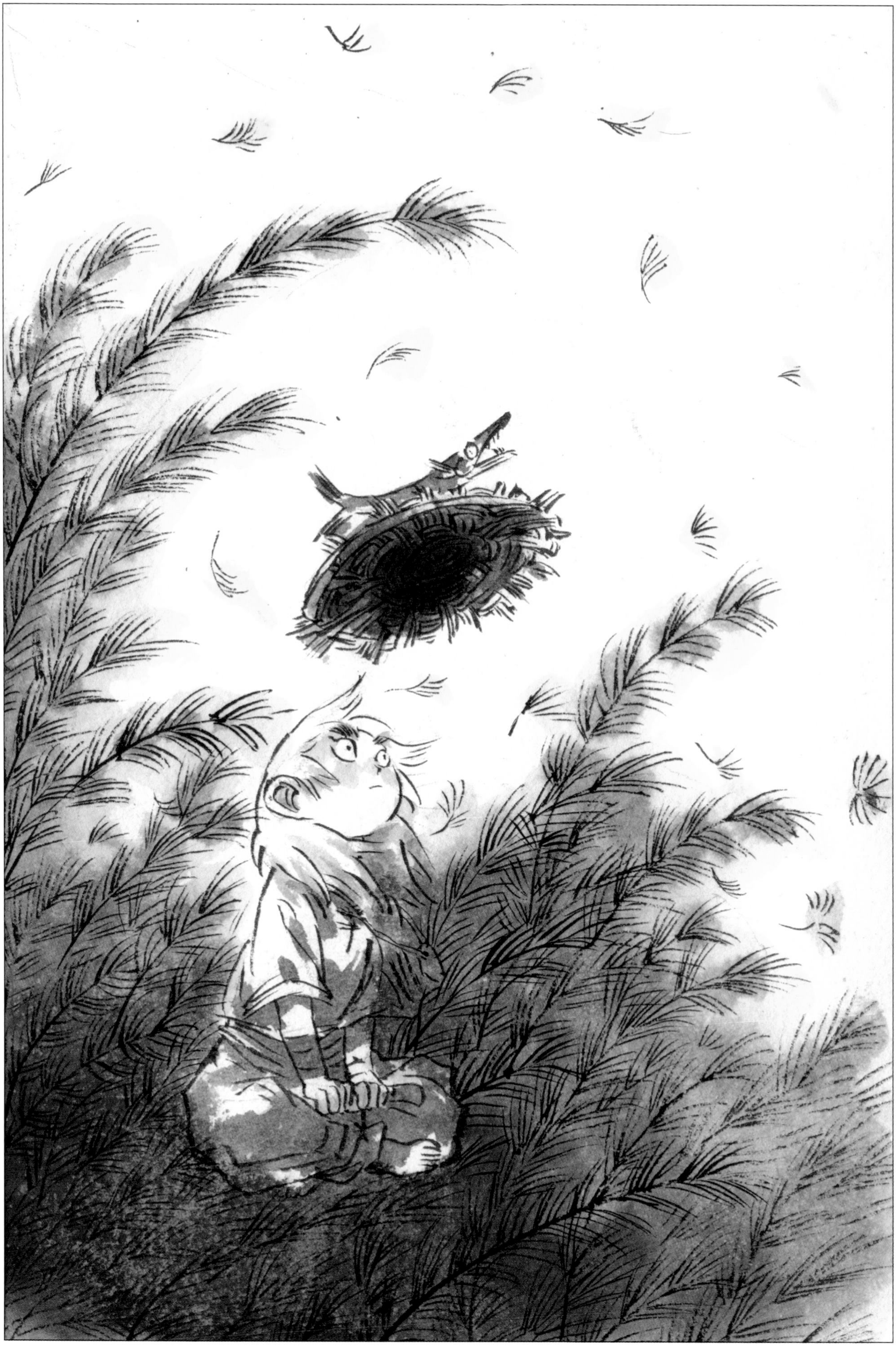

A VIRTUOSO CARTOONIST AND ILLUSTRATOR, Zao Dao is one of the youngest artists of the Chinese avant-garde. Born July 1990 in southern China's Guangdong Province, she began publishing her work on the Internet in 2011. Already universally recognized throughout her own country for her talent as a watercolor artist, Zao Dao evinces a highly original drawing style, blending traditional elements of Chinese painting with a modern graphic sensibility, adding textural effects through her choice of paper surface. While the characters formed at the tip of her brush might at times cast their author as an eccentric young rebel, the ageless pursuit of freedom remains her principal pledge of creativity.

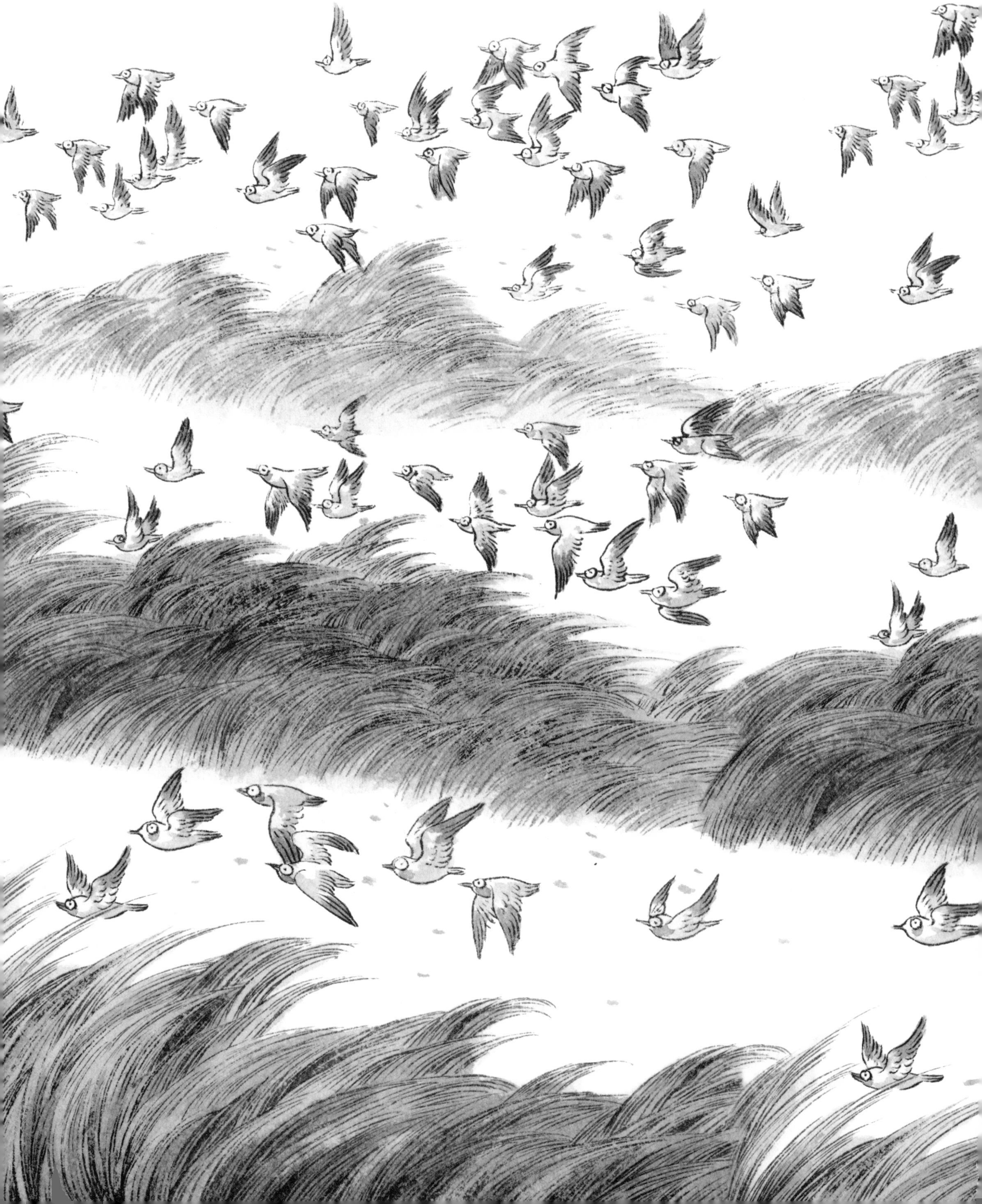